Contents

I	The Spiral	
II	Star t...	
III	How ...	
IV	Sex is ...	
V	A Nest ...	37
VI	California...	41
VII	Anyguy at ...	50
VIII	Tattoo Me!	54
IX	Lightning, Meet Thunder	57
X	To Hell and Back	68
XI	Evangelical Evening News	81
XII	Healing and Dealing	87
XIII	Buddy on the Loose	98
XIV	Buddy has a Vision	104
XV	Asmodeus Rising	107
XVI	The Blood in Buddy's Eye	111
XVII	Blood Ritual	118
XVIII	The Castro Street Fair	134
XIX	Baring Her Bosom	140
XX	The Hot Spring	144
XXI	Running into the Future	154
XXII	Pagan Goddess	161
XXIII	Buddy in the Lion's Den	167
XXIV	"If Thy Right Eye Offend Thee..."	174
XXV	"...And Cast it From Thee..."	180
XXVI	Bad Little Girl	185
XXVII	The Prodigal Daughter	190
XXVIII	Night of the Living Dread	196
XXIX	Play Party	203
XXX	Blood Wedding	220
XXXI	End Times	229
XXXII	Exorcism	245

TO CHARLES GATEWOOD

Dark Matter

Michael Perkins

Series editor: Maxim Jakubowski

DARK MATTER

ISBN 1 85286 636 5

Series editor: Maxim Jakubowski

Published by Eros Plus
An imprint of Titan Books
42-44 Dolben Street
London SE1 0UP

First UK edition January 1996
1 3 5 7 9 10 8 6 4 2

Dark Matter copyright © 1996 Michael Perkins. All rights reserved.

British Library Cataloguing-in-Publication Data. A catalogue record for this book is available from the British Library.

This book is sold subject to the condition that it shall not by way of trade or otherwise, be lent, re-sold, hired out or otherwise circulated without the publisher's prior consent in any form of binding or cover other than that in which it is published and without a similar condition including this condition being imposed upon the subsequent purchaser.

Printed and bound in Great Britain by Cox and Wyman Ltd, Reading, Berkshire.

I

The Spiral Dance

Gods, from your rocky home in the highest snow-capped Sierras of the imagination, swoop down now on San Francisco, the City of Perpetual Indulgence. Blot out all other sounds from your hearing and attend to the dark passage of one in your indifferent keeping — one touched by you, and like you, possessed....

Yet another turn of the wheel, another rotation of the earth: darkness is cast like a spell. A night without fog.

Straddling her snorting, fire-breathing Harley, Robin Flood roars up the steep undulating streets that slant to the sky and then down them to the Bay. She cuts a loud eructative path through the Marina and rumbles into stern Fort Mason, a former military facility converted into a cultural centre with shops, museums and a famous restaurant.

A bleached full moon leers down at her, one roguish lunar

eyebrow cocked; clouds of galaxies extend from it into forever. The dark matter that makes up the unseen universe holds the stars apart. The Gods pay casual attention.

It is the beginning of November, final year of the century, on the night of the Spiral Dance — a Saturday night that falls on Samhain, when the dead pierce the veil that hangs between breathing and not, children who will never die (at least not in the twentieth, accursed century) eat sugar skulls, and a thousand boisterous pagans gather to celebrate the disappeared.

Robin joins the crowd cloaked in the exclusionary circle she draws around herself with strangers. She does not know anyone in the laughing, gesticulating, high-spirited gathering of animals with horns, birds of prey, devils of all designs, medieval *jongleurs*, Green Men, maenads and vampires. Here, New Agers rub shoulders with Dark Agers. Here, imagination expresses the divine with profligate abandon.

Robin regrets momentarily that she has not worn a costume, but her eyes attract more attention than a mask would: they are an unfathomable cerulean, like the sea. Her glance when unguarded can be frightening in what it reveals of the cold wildness inside. Her features are small and finely chiselled, her mouth wide and lush. Her hair is cropped like glossy black feathers. One seashell ear is studded with five expensive earrings, the kind ear-nibblers cut their lips on. She's prettier than the Queen of Heaven tonight, but there is something indistinct, unformed, indefinable but dangerous about her, as if she might be willing to do anything.

Hidden behind their masks, people stare at her. Aware of the impression she makes, she tucks her ambient rage in a pocket of her black motorcycle jacket and grins like an ingenue on crack. She waits patiently in the line, examining everyone for signs of the roles they might play in the drama of her life. She has a hunger to find out who she is, and she can only learn this from others; she is unknown to herself. Tonight her whim is that she is a temple prostitute come to worship the Goddess, weep for her dead, and party down with the pagans. Her fantasies are usually realised.

The motley line snakes around the pier to Herbst Pavilion, a giant former troop embarkation shed surrounded by choppy Bay waters. The huge space is sombre and magnificent, a maritime cathedral filled with the anxious ghosts of the hundreds of thousands of apprehensive young men who passed through the building on their way to war, and the unhappy spirits of those who never sailed home. It is an appropriate place to celebrate Halloween.

After surrendering her ticket, Robin enters the Pavilion through a maze of long white curtains and is greeted by two beaming wood sprites in mossy green, and a motherly crone in a black *bustier* who speaks the traditional greeting, "Welcome home", to her. Inside, Robin's boot heels make dull clicking sounds on the concrete floor. She feels herself opening inside and decides to lift herself higher. Because pagans don't drink or do drugs at public gatherings, she sneaks a few guilty hits from a roach and quickly waves the smoke away.

She is new to San Francisco, having lived in Paris for over a year, and before that in various university towns; now she is seeking out her own kind. She walks in the direction of the stage, looking frankly and openly at everyone she passes, wondering if the women she sees are turned on as she is. She imagines herself swimming alone in a great ocean of space more vast than whales could comprehend. Schools of fish move past her....

Because she stands alone, each pagan who enters sees in her a reflection of the goddess, dorsal view. She is small and slender, and her tight black vinyl pants offer the viewer who looks closely an unforgettable image of desire. She is posing, but lost in the pose so that she is unaware of the many who stream in, an endless cavalcade. They surround her, spreading blankets and placing cushions to sit on. A vulpine woman in a derby hat wearing a fake handlebar moustache nurses a baby from her fat hard breast, and Robin imagines squeezing that breast and making the milk stream into her own mouth.

A musician tuning up on stage breaks a guitar string, snapping her out of her wicked fantasy. A choir of witches is being assembled on the other end of the stage. Awkwardly, Robin folds herself in with her fellow beings, plugging into the building energy, feeling a charge of anticipation. The music gets better and louder. A few people dance half-heartedly and then sit back down. Robin moves to the apron of the stage and watches the people in charge. They prepare calmly and efficiently the myriad details of a Samhain ceremony for one thousand. They laugh easily with each other.

For a moment she fades into a memory of other ceremonies — Christian and far from joyous ones: pursed mouths, hellfire and damnation voices, burning eyes, pinched souls. Blind faith in a book and man: her father, Thomas Flood.

A heavy touch on her shoulder startles her from this reverie. She recoils, about to snarl, but checks the impulse. Shivers.

"I'm sorry. I didn't mean to scare you."

The voice is obnoxiously self-confident. She turns and looks up at a well-browned, prime California hunk. She can tell he is a dedicated New Ager by his optimistic, sincere gaze and the t-shirt he is wearing, which boasts 'A Higher Power Within'. Even his eyebrows are earnest strokes in his bland face. He wears loose pants, so she can't see if he has genitals. She sneers, half-closing her eyes. If he came closer, she thinks she would bite his throat. Her hidden dark wings would unfold and envelop him, and she would soon have his blood on her tongue, running sweeter than semen down her throat.

But he keeps his distance and continues to talk. She sees that he will not be useful to her, that he is neither food nor fuck. He hears the echo of his own music, believes his own affirmations, and drops his shallow lines. She listens to him with the difficulty that even the hungry feel swallowing flies.

"Yes, my name's Tom, you sweet goblin, but I won't linger if you don't want me to...." he finishes, aware she is not with him. His name is not the least of his offensiveness.

"I don't want you to," she says softly. He's so dumb he still breathes through his mouth. Little gasps, as he tries to understand her.

He can't decide how to respond. The turmoil on his face makes her smile at how easy it is to fuck men up. She sticks out her small hand as if in surrender. He takes it and she presses down on a judo point and he nearly faints.

She releases him. It is unsatisfying to inflict pain on someone she doesn't know. He retreats with muttered imprecations indicating a lack of schooling and a deprived background.

The music from the stage insinuates its rhythms into her consciousness. The sound system is inadequate for the cavernous space, but the beat warms her. The band is playing, and a choir is singing an old pagan anthem. A bass drum booms as the divine array of mummers enters the hall and the magic show begins. First comes Cernunnos, the Celtic horned male god — she recognises him from her reading, and his identity is confirmed by the comments of people around her — striding with graceful giant steps on stilts taller than a tall man. He seems all-powerful and complete, his muscular acrobat's body worthy of a god's. The old god of the Underworld, the opener of the Gates of Life and Death.

His mask, Robin thinks, is terrifying. The stag's antlers, the snake coiled around his neck are symbols she can read. He moves with grace and speed like a giraffe, accompanied by

Apollo and Mercury, who move on their stilts with equal skill and assurance.

Robin is stirred to an emotion something like worship by this manifestation of the old gods. *It is my birthright to worship*, she thinks heretically. *Perhaps it is my aesthetic, too. As a temple prostitute, perhaps it will be the Horned God himself to whom I will offer my tribute.*

The fantasy pleases her. She is getting wet.

The lights dim and the crowd's attention is focused on the pagan parade. Spotlights hit a troupe of beautiful naked dancers with painted bodies, their breasts bouncing, long hair whipping back and forth. Their movements are sexual and serpentine and joyful, drawing on the energy building in the great hall. They perform a ballet of orgasm; its explosive movements convey the sacredness of lust.

Robin looks away from the dancers for a moment, distracted by the dizzy argument of two greying lesbians, and when she looks again magic is happening, magic greater than her father's Christian god has shown her in the twenty-six years since she was baptised.

Acrobats are descending on spidery ropes from the girders above and they seem to fall forever in slow motion while the excited crowd sets up a chant:

"*Climb down, climb up!*
Up to the bottom,
Down to the sky!"

Or so she hears. The words might have been different but she is transfixed by the acrobats, and cannot be certain of what she hears. She is in heat, glorious feline heat. She wonders, but only fleetingly, if her arousal is not simply keyed to the familiar pageantry of the circus, or to ceremonies she has attended in Catholic churches. But no: for the first time religion is part of her sexuality, not smothering it. The stilt walkers, dancers and acrobats are the gods who turn her on. The experience of conversion makes her tremble.

The music stops and the lights are lowered so that the crowd sits in darkness. There is a brief salutation to the four directions and the four elements, and then announcements are made from the stage. The purpose of the evening is to honour and mourn the dead who wait, in the minds of those who have gathered, just beyond the veil.

Candles are lit. A light show begins. Huge, breathtaking images of the beauty and brevity of life are projected on the walls and ceiling. Gaia, the blue planet, her jungles, forests, mountains and rivers of home; and then the faces of the beloved dead. The names of the dead, hundreds of them, are read by a woman with the voice of a doleful gatekeeper between the worlds. Most of the departed are unknown to Robin, but there are a few she recognises:

"Former President Jimmy Carter; Pinky Lee; Roy Rogers; the man known as Mr. Marvellous; Pat Robertson...." The list is endless, Robin thinks, like St. Peter reading the roll call at the Gates of Heaven. But the conjunction of famous names with one's own dead creates the sense of a community of grief.

After twenty minutes of sitting cross-legged or standing with bowed head, Robin no longer hears the names. She is restless, perhaps because she finds it so difficult to honour her own dead. Her anger prevents her tears from falling. Half aloud, she calls out to her mother. In her mind is stamped the image of the crematory flames that reduced her mother to bone fragments and white dust. Her mother who had been so alive eaten by the flames.

"Gods rest the soul of Rebecca Flood!" — loudly, to no one, and then the rest came, the bitter memories spilling forth.

"You left. You left me to him. You thought I would be kept safe, but *you* were never safe from him. The Devil!"

The author of her being, Robin's father, the Reverend Thomas Flood, said that her mother was not good, but bad; not a real mother or wife, but a slut, a whore of Babylon — a thing from the black pit flown up to liquefy his soul and drink it like blood. And Robin, eight years old at the time of her mother's death, was afraid he was right.

Wasn't he her flesh and blood, who seemed to sit at the right hand of God? Who actually *talked* with God?

Her mother's spirit whispers in her ear:

"He killed me. He entered my body in the night not like a man but a devil. He went all the way inside and I couldn't get him out, so I had to run...but by then he was always right there inside me, choking me. You are not safe while he is alive."

Hot tears form. Robin lets them roll down her face and jacket and onto her hands, which she lifts in helpless offering to her mother and to the careless cruel gods.

The crowd quiets its wailing and grieving when a tall woman with a midwestern accent begins speaking, in a mellifluous storyteller's voice, of the pagan legends. She guides them in a meditation, taking them with her across the River Styx, showing them Atlantis and Avalon, the Isle of Apples.

"You have come a long way, and it has been a difficult journey. Life has been a search through many lands, and now you have come home."

Her words entrance the crowd. They are beautiful words, but Robin — burned out forever on sermons — tunes her out. It is not for her, this mass prayer, this journey with a thousand others.

Sex and sex alone is her salvation. When she falls on her knees, she worships Priapus.

Since childhood, during sermons she has masturbated without touching herself. Simply by contracting her pubococcygeus muscle she can pleasure herself without anyone knowing. Between her vagina and her anus she bears down and squeezes. The erotic intensity of the sensation between her legs can bring her to orgasm. This private act of subversion has kept her sane through years of Sunday School, sermons and crusades.

So sex has become entwined with religious ceremony for her. But what in the past had been a method of avoiding a religion of pain is transformed tonight into a way of accepting a spiritual movement that respects the earth and its gifts. The Christianity her father preached sanctioned the rape of the earth because his flock would all ascend to heaven.

So Robin wriggles her pelvis imperceptibly as she sits cross-legged, paying no attention to the meditation that so absorbs her fellow pagans. She wonders if they are listening or if they too are masturbating. She wonders if this isn't how most people — women at least — endured church: each secretly playing with herself, pressing the pleasure button. Perhaps masturbation was the true secret of worship.

After all, it would be the most wonderful hypocrisy — and she had become a connoisseur of hypocrisy by watching her father tend his flock. The simulation of virtue is the tribute Eros pays normality, but Robin's motto since college has been *'kill normality before it kills you'*.

The long meditation ends. People stand and stretch, feeling at one with each other. They have raised some magic together while peering through the veil. Robin feels it moving around the people near her. Then the music starts up and the communicant pagans are told to form a giant circle around the outer perimeter of the great space and join hands with people on each side.

This is not to be done lightly, Robin knows. She looks for a man and a woman who interest her. By her secret use of it, she has made her vagina the centre of her being: they must be sexy.

Most of them look too nice. *Nice* is a look Robin fears because it's the look of the self-deluded. Her father's mask when he wasn't being stern. The women are earth mothers, even the leather dykes; the men for the most part wear compassionate, caring looks. They bore her. Their sincerity scares her.

Her eye is caught by a tall middle-aged blonde woman with a knowing smile and something — Defiance? Mischief? — in her green eyes that Robin responds to. She is wearing a denim shirt open to display her brown breasts, and a short black leather skirt with black stockings on strong, youthful legs. A necklace of claws circles her throat. When she smiles, which she does often, Robin sees that her fangs have been filed into points. A diamond glistens on one of them.

Yes, this one can teach me something, Robin thinks to herself. Standing next to her is an equally tall man with a fringe of black beard, no moustache, who balances precariously on his only leg. He seems amused by his problems with balance. He is striking in the way young men can be who have survived something more trying than college.

Robin slips between them and takes their hands. They accept her easily, as an unanticipated gift.

"I'm Robin. Can I dance with you?"

The tall blonde smiles. "Join us, Robin. I'm Laura. And this is Stump."

"Captain Stump," the tall man corrects. "If I start to fall, I'll have to rely on your strength. Are you strong?"

"Strong enough," Robin replies.

The line starts to move, the pressure of linked hands pulling and stretching it.

"It's my first celebration," Robin confides to Laura. "What kind of dance is this?"

"I think of it as the dance of the DNA. We move around in a double helix. You'll see."

The line surges, and Robin feels the electricity of the crowd passing through her hands, from Laura's slender ringed feminine hands with long nails like talons, and the strong smooth hands of the man with one leg. She feels supported, part of the strand of rhythmic, celebratory life.

The beauty of the Spiral Dance is that everyone in the line passes before Robin's eyes. She sees every single smiling face. Some are in tears at the experience. The varieties of people and their sexualities as they flow around the room is like watching the past, present and future at the same moment.

Stump's grip tightens and loosens as he deftly balances himself, but his dependency is not demanding.

"My leg was stolen by some evil trickster," he explains to her during a pause in the dance. "I left it standing against a chair in the movie last night."

Was he crazy? He laughs at her puzzlement.

"I took off my prosthesis because my stump ached. I usually take it off at the movies, and then if I have to go to the bathroom I just hop there with my cane. I've gotten good at that. Well, last night I got back to my seat — right on the aisle — and it was gone. My leg! Who would steal a leg but some coyote? An artificial leg!" He chuckles, as if losing a prosthetic limb was to be expected in a life where you could lose a leg so easily.

As the pagans dance, they sing a pagan anthem:

"We are a circle, with no beginning and never ending...."

Their faces are open, and the clean sexual light shines through them — unlike the church faces Robin had grown up with, sombre and closed. Despite her reserve, she is seduced into imagining that she is one of them. The faster the line moves — until it is like playing crack-the-whip — the more Robin feels her resistance leaving her. Her face is flushed and she is singing. There was nothing like the freedom of this whirling connection with the life force.

Laura yells to her to be heard over the crowd: "It's high energy, isn't it? Like sex with angels."

She nods and smiles back at Laura, whose fangs seem improbably sharp to Robin. She imagines them in her neck and feels a rush of desire. The *frisson* of fear that follows adds to the sensation, as do her memories of old movies in which vampires bend exaggeratedly over their pale victims, mouths buried in virginal necks.

The music stops and so do the dancers, although the dance goes on echoing in their minds. Robin braces herself against Stump's strong tug as he lowers himself to the floor — he sprawls, leg akimbo, head thrown back, ecstatic. Laura hugs Robin and they stand together belly to belly, breathing hard. They are sisters in that moment. Laura's breath in Robin's nostrils dizzies her, but she does not pull away as she normally would.

Then Laura grinds her pubic bone against Robin's hip and gasps with pleasure. Around them the crowd of pagans is separating into individuals who see that it's getting late. They make preparations to leave, many exchanging phone numbers and hugging like Laura and Robin.

"I want you," Laura murmurs in Robin's ear. Robin feels the older woman's warm breath on her neck and anticipates what doesn't come.

"You want my blood, Laura? Or is it my soul you want?"

"I want to see blood trickling over your nipples. You're too young to have a soul."

"Where can we go?" The heat is spreading from Robin's centre and creating an urgency of need.

"Not here, not tonight. But come to see me." She slips a card into Robin's pocket. They cling together until Laura kisses Robin on the lips and they step apart. No tongue; not yet.

Robin feels a hand on her leg. It is Stump asking to be helped up. The two of them pull him to a standing position and he puts his arm around Laura's neck and smiles sweetly.

"I'd do anything if you'd touch me like that," he says to both of them. Laura reaches into his shirt and pinches his nipples.

He smiles impishly at first but then she uses her long nails and he screws up his face in pleasure-pain and groans happily.

"I'd do anything," he says pleadingly to Robin, who feels generous and slaps him hard. "I worship you," he says self-mockingly, hand to his cheek.

"Tomorrow?" Robin says to Laura, then remembers, "No, I can't come tomorrow. I'm going to have a tattoo done on my back. Star is finishing a design."

"I can't wait to see it."

"You'll be the first," Robin promises, feeling flirtatious and frustrated at the same time. They kiss again, like sisters, but wicked sisters: the points of their tongues touch.

"Merry meet, and merry part, and merry meet again," Stump says to Robin as he and Laura move away from her towards the exit. Robin remains where she is while around her the stilt walkers, the dancers and the acrobats, their bodies glistening, don street clothes and straggle towards the exit. Acrobats descend down ropes from the girders high above and land near her.

They are like angels visiting earth, Robin thinks. One

bounces to the concrete floor before Robin. He is a muscular Chinese man with a long thin black moustache and glossy black hair worn back in a pony tail. His chest is flat and there is a bird unlike any Robin has seen tattooed between his nipples.

"Hello," he says to Robin, who stares back at him, hypnotised. He is handsome, this angel with the watchful eyes of an animal.

"I watched you," he tells her, "from up there."

"I don't think I like that."

"I was getting into you, that's all. When I'm swinging up there I pick one person to look at so I don't get dizzy when I look down."

"What's it like to be up there?"

"What's it like to be in heaven? It's wonderful. I want to stay up there all the time. Want to come up with me?"

"I can't climb like you."

"Don't worry. I have a friend. Come."

He leads her by the hand to the thick rope he descended on.

"Just hold onto my waist." At his signal they are in the air.

His muscular arms enfold her and they are lifted from the shed floor to the girders, high, high over the heads of the departing crowd. The rope swings with their combined weight.

Looking down sends a tingle through every cell in her body. She is helpless. Her body is in the keeping of a god, who has manifested himself in the form of a Chinese acrobat. There is nothing she can do but realise the fantasy she brought to the Spiral Dance. His hard body pressed against hers has caused her every nerve ending to throb, her nipples to harden, the muscles in her thighs to flutter. She wants him, to suck and bite and fuck.

"I want you," he said, as Laura had. But there is a hard male urgency in his voice that will not wait for another day. The temple prostitute has been chosen. His strong hands touch her everywhere, squeezing her breasts, cupping her buttocks and pulling her into him as he thrusts against her.

He lowers her carefully onto the steel girder, which is just wide enough for her to lie back on as he tugs off her vinyl pants and then plunges his head between her slender thighs.

He licks her bare pubic mound, running his tongue in little circles around her wet slit before pulling it open with delicate fingers so he can take her clitoris in his lips and gently suck it, while one finger explores her contracting vagina. She feels his little finger in her anus, pressing up against the finger stabbing now into her vagina, while his other hand moves up her body to caress first her breasts and then stroke her mouth, demanding that she suck on his fingers, that she surrender to his power.

She cannot move for fear of falling from the girder. She is a helpless sacrifice to his lust, and she wouldn't have it any other way; but she wants to see his penis. She needs him to move up on her so she can feel its hardness on her body, but he won't stop sucking her and teasing her, making her lick his hard fingers. He won't give his maleness until he has torn an orgasm from her throat, until he hears her cry out, *"Fuck me! Fuck me!"* and he rises on his knees to show her the gift he brings her. His liquid black eyes bulge with the strength of his desire. His penis is not long but it is thick and purple with engorged blood. His face is shiny with her juices and on his mouth is the stamp of the satyr.

It is a slick spear he holds and brings to the hunger between her thighs, slowly so she must beg for it, beg to be sacrificed to Cernunnos. When she is pricked by his spear she thrusts herself up so he can impale her up to the hilt of his pubic bone.

She is filled with the god, and he is moving inside her with the divine sexual energy of a god, his hands clasping now her waist, now her buttocks, so that there is no escape from the satisfying savagery of his attack.

Her need matches his and then surpasses it. She feels herself losing touch with any last remnant of reality. Above her, girders buttress the black roof, while far below mere mortals clear the floor of sound equipment and decorations. She is suspended in space and time while the god Cernunnos gives her the divine gift of the strongest orgasm she's ever experienced. She's coming and crying out "Hail, Cernunnos!" again and again until nothing comes from her throat but sighs, and she floats back into her consciousness, thinking:

I am such a slut.

II
Star the Skin Artist

"To find the right tattoo you have to know who you are."

"I don't know who I am, Star. Maybe the tattoo will tell me."

"Sometimes it works that way. Mostly not."

"I just feel like I don't know anything — that I'm empty, like a cup. Just waiting to be filled up. It's like when I look out at the stars at night I'm weightless, and I could be sucked right up to them. But maybe they're empty, too. Do you ever think about that, Star?"

"Yeah, sure," Star said, Brooklyn still in his voice like marbles rumbling. "You know, astronomers and physicists wonder the same thing. Now they think that maybe ninety percent of the universe we look up at is missing."

"Who took it?"

"God knows. They call it dark matter. It's these strange, invisible particles that haven't ever been observed before, but now, because of the Hubble Telescope, they can. It's obvious. Nobody really knows shit. The universe is incomprehensible — and empty."

"It's like it says in the beginning of *Genesis*: it's chaos. 'Tohubohu' is the Hebrew word for it: the formless chaos of the primordial universe."

"How'd you know that?"

"My father talked about it. He says the end is coming, when it all returns to tohubohu...."

L'heure bleue. They have been working all afternoon, with breaks for herbal tea and cigarettes. The studio is warm and the musk of her body hangs in the air.

Star the skin artist bends to his work with the fine concentration of a painter in love with his work and his canvas. His lips press together and he frowns. There is a faint sheen of perspiration on his forehead. He massages Robin's back with sharp steel and sometimes she hums low in her throat because of the pleasure this pain gives her. It is utterly sexual but diffuse, without object, so that the tension slowly tightens as Star works.

Robin sits upright on a wooden chair, turned so she can straddle it, her arms resting on its back. She stares out at the street before Star's storefront studio through a window that is a one-way mirror. She can look out, but no one can see her watching. When someone stops to admire himself in the mirror, to adjust his tie or comb his hair, he seems to be staring straight at her. Then she reflexively hides the puffy dark tips of her breasts, pressing them against the wooden chair back. Her nipple piercings make a soft sound against the wood.

This afternoon with Star is the fourth and final sitting before the canvas of her back is completely filled in. From her shoulder blades to her waist, the image is taking its final shape with each tiny stab of the outline needle, fifty stabs per minute. It is a vibrant, luxuriant garden with elaborate vine work in which danger lurks: serpents and dragons rise from the base of her spine and curve over the tops of her buttocks.

When it is finished her lovers can watch her sleep and study the intricate painting on her slender back, looking in it for clues to their fates with her. The great scar would be covered and her disfigurement transformed into art.

Star's warm left hand holds his epidermal canvas stretched as he makes the next line, and the next. Each line flows from the gods into his hand, she hopes. The painting must be perfect. Star's voice is reassuring, insinuatingly intimate. His rumbled words assume a lover's intimacy, in fact. While he works Robin stares out the window at the street scene. It is 16th Street, in the Mission, not far from her apartment. The sign outside reads:

ASTERION STUDIO
FINE TATTOOING
By Appointment Only

"I'm sliding a little now, baby. Let me wipe you."

Robin shivers when he stops, turns off the needle, and reaches for a sponge. He washes her back tenderly, his touch a caress magnified by the heightened sensitivity of her punctured skin.

"You comfortable?" he asks. She turns to smile at him.

His over-large dark eyes are intensified by shaggy eyebrows and there is a five-pointed star low on his forehead over his third eye. His body is bull-like, heavy, and covered with tattoos from his neck to his toes. He has been tattooed by the world's masters.

She is open to him as she would not be with a lover, as if in creating the jungle on her back he has gained access to her insides beneath the skin. As if he could reach in and touch her heart if he chose to.

The needle whirs as he starts up again.

"This tigress will be your secret totem animal — I mean, it's a lady tiger, a tigress — and where it is you'll never know, but it will be there to protect you from the dragons and serpents. I believe in balance."

Robin watches the street as if watching a movie. A homeless woman pushes a shopping cart full of precious bundles, stopping to pick up a cigarette tossed by a black man in a leather jacket. Two Mexican labourers in straw hats cross her viewpoint. An Indian waiter in a white jacket comes next, and after him an old man walking a little dog. A sleek police car rolls by, the evening officers inside blinking in the glare of the evening sun hitting their windshield. Three pigeons land on the sidewalk and begin pecking at a plastic bag with a few potato chips in it.

This parade of life recalls her vision of the variety of people in the Spiral Dance the night before.

"Star, what about witchcraft? Paganism? Where does that fit in your scheme of things?"

Star has a theory, often expounded and elaborated upon in long sessions, that everything fits into patterns very much like his tattoos. His own version of chaos theory. All you had to do was to find the key that unlocks perception and the world would show itself to you as the painting it was. Tattoos help you to see it.

"It's just people with their need to make sense of things. And from what I know and the people I've seen, witchcraft makes more sense than a lot of things do. It seems to me that anything that increases the amount of awe in the world is good."

"Awe? What do you mean? Like in awful?" She knows the word, of course, but seeks to draw him out.

"Like in a recognition of the sacredness of things. Pagans respect nature. Witches know that underlying all the bullshit of a consumerised world there is magic. I like that."

"What about Christians?"

"What about them?"

"Did I ever tell you about my father?"

"No. But I'm afraid you're going to tell me."

"He's a Christian."

"So's my old man. Doesn't make him a bad dad. He let me do a cross on his arm...."

"No, I mean he's big time. A professional Christian."

"Like one of those crazy evangelists?"

"Did you ever hear of Thomas Flood?"

"You're kidding. That guy on television who asks people to send in donations? He must rake it in."

"Half a million dollars on a good day."

"Good Lord, what a racket. What's a good day?"

"When there's trouble. The stock market drops, there's a war starting, hurricanes... people send more on those days."

"Well, there's always disasters. Just look at the past six months: Nevada declared off-limits because it glows in the dark with toxic radiation. Earthquakes everywhere. Floods. Two major riots. I'd say your old man has a guaranteed cash flow for the foreseeable future. Is he a good guy?"

There is no hesitation in her voice. It is flat and hard when she answers: "He burned me, Star. I'll kill him someday."

Star whistled long and low. He shut off his needle and ran his fingertips over the ridges of scar tissue he had covered with his inks. "All this?"

"All of it."

Robin feels the familiar rage in her throat and swallows hard, willing herself to choke it down, like a snake forced back into its hole. When would she be rid of this terrible anger? She was afraid that she would never be free until she could breathe the fire or rage out of her, like the dragon on her back.

Anger now distorts her vision. Star resumes work without further comment. Now when she looks out the window the people who hurry past are guilty of every crime. The slightest imperfection is distorted. A man with a limp seems like the most grotesque of cripples, maimed by flaws in his character, not the traffic or the world. The buildings across the street are shabby ruins, covered with dried black blood. The sunlight now fading from the street is somehow ominous as shadows fall.

It is in this state of mind that she first sees Buddy Tate. He stands before the mirror, tall and pale, with red hair tied in a pony tail. It looks like he is searching for something in the mirror, perhaps some speck of self that he's lost, but to Robin it is as if he is looking straight into her eyes, drilling into her unconscious where the monsters lurk.

He is not ordinary looking, but he is not handsome except in the way some outlaws are when defiance moulds their features into masks that don't come off. His nostrils are large, like great holes in the lower half or his face. His mouth is a slash. He is probably a few years younger than she is, but he might have been much older. There is something primitive about him, something she cannot name.

Why does he stand there, staring at himself? Could he see through the special glass?

"Do you see him, Star? What is he looking at?"

"Not us, baby."

Then the strange young man does an extraordinary thing: he takes a lipstick from his pocket and as they watch, he draws a large red 'X' across the window with it.

It is only when he moves that he reveals himself. He is an alien. Star could probably find a place for him to fit in the scheme of things, but most people wouldn't — not ever. It is as if she recognises herself in him, and she is sad when he goes.

Then the buzzer rings.

III
How I Began

I was really depressed yesterday, and maybe I'll be depressed tomorrow, but I'm strong today and nothing's going to stop me. Fuck everybody who gets in my way. I'll run them down. I'll smash them flat, I mean like road kill. I swear, nobody better mess with me today, because they just don't know who they're dealing with. They'll never know what hit them.

Now hear this, world. Believe this. Buddy Tate is comin' at you. Diss me again and I'll seek you out and cut off your toy hands so you can't beat off....

When I turned eighteen and was just beginning to wonder what I was going to do with my life outside of riding the sweaty bed, my old man gave me a shot of straight advice I've always kept in mind.

He said, "Be extravagant, boy, whatever you do. People don't even see you unless you give them something to look at."

It was just about the only advice he ever offered sober

except to tell me when I started running around to keep my zipper up unless I wore a raincoat. AIDS was a nasty disease. I waited for him to say something more educational, but he just winked and asked me to fix him another drink and turned back to the TV. For a minute I was the focus of his attention, and then, you know, I wasn't there. I always felt invisible around him, which I guess proved his point. He never gave a fuck about anything.

I decided then that I wasn't going to be invisible the rest of my life, no matter what I had to do to get people's attention.

He was the one who sent me out into the world to find my place. I almost never think of the hard time I served as a kid, but I remember him teaching me how to shoot. Daddy liked guns, so it didn't surprise me when he joined the Militia and went up in the mountains with a bunch of other guys dressed in camouflage. I took to guns the way I took to pussy.

The other thing I remember is us watching television together. He used to say in that quality time period that even an asshole can be a somebody in America, shaking his head at the nobody of the moment on the tube. Fame is everything, he said. I'd be invisible until my face was on that screen, even if I was an asshole. Television was the goal, and there were many paths to it.

I know the way we lived was not normal. I guess I was lucky that way. My old man was not what anyone would call normal. Because they were afraid of him, most people just called him crazy. He didn't give a shit and you never knew what he was going to do next. Could be anything, so I got used to surprises early.

We always lived on the edges of things. When Daddy got a new job we'd hit the road and end up on the slummiest street of some subdivision from hell. We'd be smack up against a sewage treatment plant or a gas station. Or we'd land in some trailer park next to a closed fast food place where you couldn't bring a girl. Some bump in the asphalt on a road in the Ozarks. We covered a lot of territory but the landscape didn't change much.

This kind of life kept me out of school a lot, but that was all right with me. I didn't see any difference between a jail and a school until I discovered girls. Some times we'd come to a new place and the Old Block (the same one I'm a chip off, he reminded me) would drive me to the school and tell me to get in there and register.

I hated every minute of it until my fourteenth birthday. To celebrate, Daddy bought some doughnuts and gave me ten bucks. Then he went out and got tanked and brought a whore home. Not for me. They came in while I was watching a talk show and they were pretty happy with each other. She was leaning on him and he was doing a good imitation of a sleazeball. He took her right into the bedroom and the trailer started rocking. Daddy liked to enjoy himself in the bedroom, and he didn't care if the whole world knew when he was getting his rocks off.

I knew what they were doing because I'd made a hole I could peep through. They'd be on his messed up bed and he'd have her pronged, I knew that, from the noises.

Christ, it was enough to take your breath away. She wasn't built badly for a slag who'd been around the block a few dozen times. Face like a pony, but titties to drool over. Pointed and firm and fully suckable. She was on her knees on the bed with her ass in the air and Daddy was pumping it to her from behind. He'd push it all the way in and pull it all the way out. Daddy's dick was a real poker and it shone in what light there was from the bed lamp. Once he pulled it all the way out of her and whacked her ass with it as hard as he could — just beat her ass with his dick. I got hard just watching that, thinking that what he had in his hands I came out of once, in a manner of speaking.

His other hand was playing with her boobs. Wouldn't let them alone — squeezing them, pulling the nipples way out, bouncing them, pulling her long hair up so he could kiss her. She was going crazy with all this good treatment and gasping like she couldn't breathe. My bone was stone.

"Give it to me, give it to me, give it to me you fucker, you son-of-a-bitch fucker!" she kept begging. Boy, he'd give it to her. Energy like a rabbit fucking a wall socket. He drove her flat on her face on the bed he was riding her so hard and then he collapsed on top of her. I couldn't even see her, just heard her whimpering, and then he rolled off her and stood up beside the bed. She turned over and spread her legs wide, holding them up with her hands under her knees, inviting him, begging him, but he wanted some head. His big long john looked like an animal he was restraining with both hands.

"Suck me off, you cheap whore."

"No, come and fuck me with that baloney. Come on baby, just fuck me some more. Just a little bit more."

"I might, but first come and get it. Do me."

Reluctantly she got up on her knees and moved close to him. I held my breath: it was my first sight of sucking, and it made a sweet impression on me.

She didn't take her eyes off his cock. They got big and round like she was watching a snake approach her. She shook her head and tightened her lips like she wasn't going to do it, but I could see that's all she wanted to do in the whole world. She was happy thinking about what came next.

He grabbed her long dark hair and pulled her face to his dick. When she wouldn't open up, he banged her cheek with it.

I saw it was a game they were playing.

"Come on, baby, open your mouth and later I'll fuck you in

the ass, I know you like that."

Everything was magnified by lust, the dirty talk and the pleasure and the game of it. In a world full of bullshit, this was the real thing.

She laughed like she was growling and opened up, her wet red lipsticked lips stretching over his meat as she took him all the way down. She was a sword-swallower, her face pressed into his belly, his hands covering her ears as he fucked her throat, his ass muscles tightening and clenching as she took it all and then released, with this look in her eyes like she owned him.

When he pulled out to let her get some air she gasped and grabbed for it like Daddy might just walk out at that moment. There was a big hungry smile on her face and her lipstick was smeared and she growled again. Daddy had his dick in his hand but he was bent over and he was cursing her but not like he was angry: "You fuckin' cunt, you sweet pussy, oh you goddamned fuckin' whore you made me come, I'm coming now, just suck it, suck it...."

When he came it looped and spurted on her titties and chin until she got him back in her red mouth and sucked the rest out of him while he held onto her shoulders.

He grunted. She giggled like she was proud of herself.

Then Daddy did something that put paid to it. He slid down so he was kneeling in front of her and she kissed him and gave it all back to him.

I came in a pair of clean pants I had to wash out. Nothing was the same after that.

IV
Sex is Everything

After that I knew sex was everything, at least for me, and I set about getting my share. But I had to learn the rules of the game. The very first one I learned was about supply and demand. Vagina owners controlled the supply of sex, and the demand from men is always greater than the supply. The second was about access to the supply.

I went back to school with a different attitude because that's where the girls were. I stalked them: I watched for the door to open to their bathroom for a quick peek. I watched them bending over to pick something up. One way you might get to look down their blouses, the other you might be able to make out the lines of their panties. In class, sometimes they were restless and they shifted their legs so you could see up their skirts. Cheap thrills, but what else was there to do in school?

My dick drove me. My hormones were running down the road screaming. Ask a girl for a date and she'd look at me like I was a werewolf.

Pornography saved my ass. My right hand became my best friend. I got my high school education looking at dirty books that didn't lie about sex.

Everybody lied about it. Sometimes I used to think that everybody who wore clothes lied about it. People all wanted to dress the wild thing in fancy clothes. They talked shit like love, romance, wedding, family, commitment, values, and I thought, *in and out, in and out, pole and hole, pole and hole.* Sex was sex. I didn't think it needed dressing up.

I mean, I wanted to wallow in it. Maybe sex was my calling, like they say preachers have a calling, because I've never felt bad about any dirty thought I had — they were just like other thoughts. Pictures on my own private screen.

I'd mope around the town where we were living or I'd mope around school. Dark nights would find me outside windows, looking for what I'd seen Daddy and the happy whore doing.

I saw things I can't write down. People are really fucked up when it comes to this activity. Everybody did it a little bit differently. Sometimes I took my binoculars along for a closer inspection of the plumber with his wife, the postman and his girlfriend, the doctor and his daughter.

I knew other guys felt the same way I did, but they didn't have the balls to admit it. Or a Daddy like mine.

But if it doesn't come out one way it'll come out another. I used to go shooting with a kid named Jeffrey. We'd go off to the dump and shoot rats with our .22s. I'd try to get Jeff to talk about girls, but it was hopeless. He was a very quiet, shy kind of guy, just the opposite of me. He was a swimmer, too. Maybe all that time by himself in the water was like sex for him, or maybe he'd got water on the brain.

"Jeffrey," I'd say to him after he'd shot enough rats, "why don't we go over to Miranda's house and see if we can catch her with the shades up? There's a tree that's easy to climb, and you can see right into her bedroom. She's got melons, man."

But not Jeffrey. He'd go, "You're a disgusting pervert, Tate. Miranda is on my swim team."

A few weeks after that trip to the dump, Jeffrey was big news. Instead of shooting rats, he waited after school for his parents to arrive home and ambushed them as they walked through the front door. He used the .22 he shot rats with to put nine .22 LR slugs into his father, then another four into his mother. Then he took off in their car and the cops didn't find him for two days. But he'd left a note that sounded like his father had given him the same advice Daddy gave me about making people notice me. He said he wanted to go on national television to tell people why he killed them. I just wanted to get laid, but I took the lesson to heart about shooting people and getting famous.

Most of the time I felt like an animal in the zoo. I was in a cage looking out at people who were looking in on me. When I walked down the street I looked at people around me and they just seemed like pod people, or zombies. I wasn't like them, despite the resemblance. I was something else. I could shoot one of them. Not a girl, but there were lots of pricks out there.

I couldn't get laid even if I paid. There was an older girl in the trailer park who'd dropped out. She wore tight white shorts even in the winter time, and there was a steady traffic of cars most nights at her house. I watched her especially. I liked her face. Pouty. Big lips, usually wet. Boobs on her like spikes, they were so hard and pointed. I watched her from behind a little fence where I could stretch out on the grass and make myself comfortable for the evening.

LaDonna put on quite a show. She was an exhibitionist. She must have known I was watching her, and she got her kicks showing me her power over men. I was the watcher and she was the watched — a fair deal, I thought.

She had a screen porch she sat out on most nights when it was warm. Sometimes she would turn on a little lamp, and other times the only light came from inside the trailer. Most of the time I could only see her shadow. She had a chair and a cot on the porch, and she sat there like a spider in a web, waiting for the flies to come to her. They were mostly older men and LaDonna still looked young despite her work.

While I watched her with the dirty old men my bone was usually buried in a hole I dug in the ground with my knife. I remember thinking that the wet dirt wrapped around it was probably the closest I'd ever come to the real thing. I didn't have the nerve to go up and knock on LaDonna's door.

But night after night that summer when I was fifteen, I went to see LaDonna's show. An old guy in a rich car would pull up in front of her trailer and kind of sidle up to her door, looking around like hypocrites do to see if anything is watching them. She'd usually open it before he started to knock. Inside it was hard to see much — except clothes were taken off and she'd disappear — like she was kneeling. Or she'd sit on their fat old laps and dance, making shadows move with her. She must have given a lot of hand jobs because she got them in and out so fast.

The night it happened, she'd just finished doing a guy and saying good-bye when she walked over to the screen and pressed those points of hers against it. The tease that pleased — I decided it was now or never. I had to ask.

I stood up but didn't zip up and walked right towards her following the only part of me that counted. I stopped not far from her. She hadn't moved.

"How much?" was all I could say. It was not easy even to say that. Her nipples were so big they were like rubber nails.

She laughed.

"What do you want, anyway? You're gonna trip on that

thing."

What did I want? I wanted it *all*...! A dozen of my favourite fantasies came to mind. Which one to choose?

I wanted my cherry popped so I told her, "Your pussy."

She laughed again and stuck her tongue out at me. It was fat.

"You're not old enough, boy." She looked down at my pecker. "You just might be big enough, but you're not old enough. Now go away." Her eyes got big, like here comes trouble....

Maybe she was saying that because she could see what was happening behind me.

Spotlights. It was the cops.

"You're a sick boy," one of them said to me. "Did you know your genitals are exposed?"

They'd caught me at it. Then they took me home and found all my porno magazines, and that was that. I was a pervert. A peeping Tom. Wrong. Bad. Immoral. Sinful. Going to Hell. Disrespectful of women. Dirty. Sick. Irresponsible. One-track-minded. My mind was in the gutter.

I listened to what people said and I thought, *in and out, in and out*. They couldn't stop me from thinking that.

Daddy was reassuring when I asked him if I'd done wrong.

"Hell, no. Nothing wrong with fucking except the people who try to fuck you because of it. It's how we all got here. Any way you look at it, it's a superior way of spending your time."

V
A Nest of Perverts

The Court didn't agree with Daddy. I was shipped to a clinic for perverts in Salt Lake City. It was called the Greater Salt Lake Sexual Misbehaviour Clinic and it was filled with sadists, *frotteurs,* exhibitionists, peeping Toms, pornographers — the list of fancy words for what's-your-pleasure? What I learned there could fill a book — just guys like me who thought sex was everything. A nest of perverts.

The clinic was run by scientists. That's what they called themselves. They wore white coats with badges and I.D. tags on the front so they wouldn't be mistaken for patients. Their faces said they didn't get laid, but maybe they tortured white mice for fun.

The first day I was on the ward — a big room with lots of chairs and tables — an older guy came up to me.

"You're too young to be in here, kid."

I'd never seen a Jew before in my life, much less a Jewish pervert, but that's what he was. Dark and sleazy looking, just like I'd hoped. Dark pockets under his eyes. Beard stubble. Curly black hair. And a weird look on his face like he wanted something I wouldn't want to give him.

"Who are you?"

"What'd you do?"

"I exposed myself to the neighbourhood whore."

"That's it?"

"They say I'm a peeping Tom. They found porn in my closet. Wham bam, here I am. Just wanted to get laid."

"I'll bet you did. You look like you could use some relief."

He looked like he might know who could give me some.

I shook my head. "Sorry, I like girls." My throat was dry.

"What's your name?"

"Buddy Tate."

"Well, Buddy, I'm Markus Bloom. You know how they treat people here? I mean do you know how they try to cure us all of being horny?"

"How?" I was sure they wouldn't cure me.

"Masturbatory satiation is what they call it."

"What's that mean?"

"You make guys masturbate to death."

I like a sense of humour. Markus Bloom made me smile. "Shit."

"You like to look at girls? Well, they'll give you porno tapes and magazines to drive you crazy, and you'll jerk off sixteen hours a day."

"Well, that's a relief. Sixteen hours a day in a place like this, what else is there to do?"

"They're betting you'll get bored."

"You mean I get my choice of the porn that turns me on? Anything I want? I don't think I'll be bored. Not me."

It was like I became invisible. He was disappointed. He turned to go.

"You're too much, Buddy. See you around."

"Wait a minute. Why are you in here?"

"I make the porn you jerk off to." Big smile. He was proud of it.

"Pleased to meet you." This was someone I could look up to. He had something to teach me, in this nest of perverts.

"You are a wicked boy, aren't you?" We sat down in a corner in chairs like we were talking and I let him do me, what the hell. It felt strange to feel my prick in someone else's hand, but it was exciting because he knew what he was doing.

When the deed was done he wiped his sticky hand on a handkerchief and sniffed it. So I'd popped with a guy, not a girl the first time. I knew I wasn't a fruit from what turned me on — and it wasn't men. But what's a hand job between friends?

A lot of pervs in the Clinic were sick, I couldn't argue with that. Child molesters and rapists that nobody liked, and they were kept in a special locked section where they were forced to look at pictures of helpless women and kids until they couldn't stand it anymore. Most of them became impotent.

I spent a lot of time with Markus Bloom, seeing the world through his eyes. He told me about San Francisco so that I wanted to go there. I guess I'd always thought it was full of faggots, but Markus told me about the parties he went to there and they sounded like something out of movies. Women who pierced their tongues and went naked all the time, witches, strippers, stuff like that. He talked it up so I could imagine it to the point of jerking off to the fantasy of being in bed with two witches or strippers and doing anything I wanted with them.

Markus got out when he convinced the white coats that pornography made him panic. Just the thought of the stuff made him get the dry heaves. I thought he was overacting, but that's what it took.

Spanking the monkey does get a little boring when white

coats are forcing you to do it. I rubbed off five times a day, then ten times a day. Calluses formed, but I kept whacking away until one day I decided it was time to play along with modern science if I wanted out. It wasn't as hard as I thought it might be. People whose own sex lives are boring can't imagine someone like me or Markus Bloom. They want to believe we might get bored and "cured" because they're bored.

They let me out on condition that I stayed at home until I was eighteeen and kept my nose clean and my dick in my pants.

Soon as I got off the bus from Salt Lake I went straight to LaDonna's trailer like a homing pigeon and popped my cherry properly up her heavenly snatch. I rooted like a pig in her body — it was like all that jerking off I'd done had just turned me on. She didn't think I was too young anymore, and I think I stretched my penis in my six months at the Clinic.

After that I knew how to get girls to lay down and like it. It was something they could smell. I knew the secret now. I spent all the time I could in bed, but I had to sneak around. I had to pretend. I went to church, I even had a job after school. I learned how to be one of them on the outside, and inside still be myself. The price of freedom was hypocrisy.

VI

California Here I Come!

It took me a few years, but I grew up to see Daddy had it right. I was a nobody. Much as I liked my sleaze, I had to get out of bed and go out to be part of the world's business. So I left Daddy in his trailer in East Asshole, Colorado and got on board a plane for San Francisco. I had some money I'd saved doing foolish, invisible things and I carried everything I cared to own in a duffel bag. I felt pretty good, I looked pretty good, I was ready for anything and light on my feet.

I took a taxi from the airport to North Beach, because that's where Markus had said the strip joints were. He told me about one in particular that was so big and had so many ways of turning you on that it would put lead in a dead man's pencil. It was called something like the 'Erotic Exotic Exploratorium' but Markus said everybody just called it the Pussy Palace. I had to see that. A local landmark.

It was a Saturday afternoon in November and there were

more people on one block than in whole towns where Daddy dragged us. I cranked my neck until it was stiff. San Francisco was a mess because of the earthquakes, but the neighbourhood of the Pussy Palace hadn't been hit. We rolled up in front of it.

The driver obviously thought I was some kind of hick. His I.D. on the dash said his name was K. Farouk, and he tried to rob me with a smirk and a nod at his meter, where the numbers were way too high. I'd been too busy eyeballing the town to notice how he cheated with the machine, but I told him he had to be a dickhead to think I'd pay that.

He turned to look at me through the scratched plastic partition. His eyes were hot and slitty and he was chewing on a toothpick.

"C'mon, kid. Give me."

"Fuck you, thief." I heard the locks in the back seat click. "Let me out of here."

He opened the sliding door in the partition that separated front seat from back and pointed a pistol at me. His temper was up.

"No tip necessary. Just the fare." He looked like a crazed rat.

That barrel was looking at me without seeing me. It wasn't very big, but I knew what it could do. Still my teeth didn't start chattering, my knees didn't knock. I was cool.

I faked the fucker out by pretending to reach for my wallet while I brought my knee up fast and jammed the pistol hard up against the plastic. He tried to pull it back but I took a big chance and grabbed it, so it fell on the floor in the back seat without firing. His hand was stuck through the window and I grabbed it and twisted. I could see his yellow rat face scrunching up while his other hand flailed about behind the Plexiglas. If I let go there'd be hell to pay, so I went to work bending back his trigger finger until I felt it snap.

The cool sound of a breaking bone.

I scooped up the pistol, a little .38 Special, lightweight, no hammer sticking up to snag on your pocket, and pointed it at his hand. Tickled his palm with the barrel.

"Pop the lock or I pull the trigger."

He was screaming. I let go and he did it quickly. Guess I had him psyched. I pushed open the door and jumped out, getting in the front seat with him. His money was in a metal box under the seat, waiting to fly into my pocket to join my savings. K. Farouk had quite a wad.

"Now take off your shoes and pants." He was hissing and his face was worked up. But the pistol hypnotised him. While he divested himself of his dignity I looked around at the street. No one was paying attention to us. Japanese tourists were checking into the Pussy Palace.

San Francisco. I liked it. I threw the asshole's pants and shoes in a trash can and just stood there on the sidewalk for a minute watching the passing parade of queens and hookers, trying to take it all in: the people, the lights, the hustles. I picked up my duffel and K. Farouk blasted off with my warning that I'd kill him if he called the cops. Probably an illegal immigrant. He wouldn't tell. The laws were hard on immigrants.

The Pussy Palace wasn't shy about its advertising. Your fantasies were their business. The signs outside under the marquee promised everything, hot and triple X. 'Live girls' one sign promised. I thought I'd have one of them.

I paid admission and opened the door. I could smell them: no dead girls here. There were mooks and geeks of all kinds milling around the shop section, looking at porno mags and videotape boxes and getting up their courage. A woman's voice was saying over the loudspeaker system, *"Pussy, pussy pussy, guys don't be shy...."* calling you upstairs to the booths, where it was you with a girl, one on one.

I wasted no time gliding up those sticky steps to paradise. A harem was waiting for me. Ten nearly naked women, white, black, Chinese, big, medium and little, gave me the eye. I chose one after some serious looking. She asked me if I was old enough to see what she had to show me.

"I'm big for my age." I said, palming my crotch. My power.

She stuck out of a pink push-up bra and a short leather skirt in the right proportions. But it was the look in her eye and her large pink lips that got my attention. She was small, but I like tiny packages. Yeah, she was a chocolate bunny, but black happens to turn me on.

I'd made up my mind when a shoulder bumped me on purpose and a large African-American gentleman with a mop and a pail and a bad attitude asked me how come I wanted black pussy?

"I didn't notice her colour," I told him. He wouldn't want to hear that I preferred chocolate to vanilla.

I walked off to buy twenty bucks worth of tokens for some time with my choice.

She was waiting for me at her booth, and she stepped into her side of it with a wink at me. I opened the door on my side and squeezed inside with my duffel bag. I was faced with a Plexiglas window with spuzz streaks on it. Dropped a heavy token in the slot, and the curtains opened.

My eyes bugged out, she was so fucking gorgeous. She still had her skirt on, but she'd taken off her top. Bodacious ta-tas and a hurry-up, come-on look.

There was a phone. I picked it up and talked to her.

"Hello, sugar," I blurted out like a kid.

"What's your name?" she asked.

"Buddy Tate is my name. What's yours?"

"Pearl Dollar is my stage name."

I stared at her chest and grinned. She smiled back.

"Looks like you've been travelling," she said. I looked down at the duffel at my feet and back to her black nipples.

"I've come a ways, I guess."

"Well, where do you come from?"

I was staring hard at her lacquer-bright nipples, watching the points come up. I had trouble swallowing and it was getting hot in the booth. Then I looked at her eyes, soft brown shining marbles full of play, and I felt the sex magic working in my upper thighs and creeping into that little space between your stones and your butt where it feels great to be licked.

Markus Bloom was right about the Pussy Palace. I was getting hard just looking into her eyes. I dropped another five dollar token in the slot so the automatic curtain wouldn't close. I had to see all of her.

"Take off your skirt, why don't you?" I said through my teeth. But she was set on having her answer. She put her hands on her hips. Cocky.

"Where you from, I asked you."

"Why do you want to know where I'm from?"

"In my line, sugar, I've seen guys from just about every state in the country, and from Japan and England and all kinds of African countries — so I just play this little game with myself. I try to guess where they're from."

"By what their cocks look like?"

"You'd be surprised what you can tell about a man."

I told her. "Colorado, Kansas, East Texas, Idaho. You name it. Out on the range."

She was satisfied. Pouted, with those luscious pink lips turned out at me.

"You say you want to see my pussy?"

"I would like to see that part of you, yes. If you have no objections."

She pulled the short leather skirt up slow and easy until it was bunched around her waist. She was shaved except for a black strip of kinky pubic hair like a stripe above her naked wet slit. The lips puckered outward and her hole was oozing syrup. I just gawked. She giggled.

"You like that?" She smiled and sat on a stool to spread for me.

"Show me some more. Hold the lips open." She smiled again like she was as fascinated as I was about what she was showing me.

Delicately, with two fingers, she opened herself, and stuck one long red fingernail inside, then slid it up to play with her clitoris, then back to move in and out of her hole, like stabbing a wet rose.

My biology had so weakened my legs I had to lean back against the booth wall.

"Why don't you just take it out and show me how much you really like me?" She must have said it to a thousand guys, but I welcomed the invitation. I unzipped, tugged my suddenly tight underwear, unreeled the hose.

Her saucer eyes got wide. "My God," she whispered, as if half-strangled by the thought of having to put it in her mouth.

"That thing's a python. It could hurt a girl," she said, but her voice was hungry. So now we were even: she was looking as hard at me as I was looking at her. The experience was new for her.

"Show me your ass," I asked, as I'd ask any friend to do me a favour. We were equals now. She turned and bent over, her hands on the stool, showing me the firm brown globes of her perfect African-American butt. Her pussy glistened, so did her inky asshole. I wanted to put my nose there to snarf up the odour and taste, and then follow it with my big ten incher.

"Are you playing with it? Let me see."

What had started out as a simple business exchange was turning into something else between us. I took myself in hand, standing on rubbery ankles.

"You've got lots of energy, I can see that. You're a strong young man."

"Buddy. That's my name. I wonder..." I heard the curtain start to close and fumbled for my last token.

"What?"

"Can I see you outside here?"

"That's not allowed," she said, her eyes saying something else. *In and out, in and out,* was pounding in my head.

"I've got to fuck you."

"You'll kill me with that thing, you put that serpent up inside my little *chocha*."

I had her attention now. She wanted to feel it for herself.

Her hands were squeezing her tits hard, so the taut flesh bunched up, brown and satiny. She smiled sweetly.

I wanted to see how much of a slut she was. I wanted to give her a reason hotter than curiosity to want me like I wanted her. I reached into my pocket and pulled out the cabby's wad.

Her eyes nearly crossed. "Plenty of dollars for Pearl Dollar," she crooned approvingly.

"Is there anything you won't do?"

"Looks like you have got what it takes for a girl to have some real fun."

"Where can I find you?"

"Hotel Napa. It's in the Tenderloin on Eddy Street."

"When?"

"I don't get off for an hour."

"I'll walk around, see what San Francisco's like, I guess."

"Not with that, honey. Not unless it rolls back up."

She was right. It was a stone boner. I couldn't stuff it back in my pants.

"I hate to see that go to waste," she said slowly, licking those cock-cushion lips.

"Do me right here. Just a lick and a promise is all I need...."

"If Albert or George catch me, my ass is grass. This is not a house of prostitution they tell us all the time. Just sleaze and tease, that's what we do here."

She sank to her knees with the glass between us and opened her mouth, bringing it close to the glass, wiggling her tongue and pointing it like she wanted to stick it in the tip of my dick. I moved closer, and bumped into the glass.

"It won't take more than a second," I promised her. "Come on in here with me."

She just wanted to see if I'd beg.

"You want a free sample, you mean?"

"How's this?" I guess the sum I held up was enough to impress her. The curtains closed. She was gone, and I was left, but then the door was being pressed against, and she squeezed in, kneeling on my duffel bag. She knew what heat was: no sooner had I closed my hands over her ears, pulling her to me, then she had half my aching gristle down her slippery throat. She was hungry but she couldn't swallow it all.

There was a rapping on the door, but I didn't know if it was really knocking or the sexy slurping sounds Dollar was making as she sucked. I couldn't have stopped if you'd put a gun to my head. Then the train roared out of the tunnel and my entire being focused on the flash of coming: I shot spurt after spurt and her tongue just lapped like a kitten's until she'd swallowed it all. God bless her.

We were both panting. Maybe two minutes had gone by. The knocking continued, rattling the thin door.

"It's Albert. Just tell him I'll take care of him, too."

I zipped up, still gasping, heart like a damn hammer, and turned sideways to open the door, leaving her on her knees looking up at me with my come on her lips.

"After you, he'll be like nothing at all."

"I need my bag." She moved and I picked it up, left her

kneeling in prayer.

Albert stood glaring at me, fist half raised. He was the same African-American gentleman who'd inquired about my taste for black pussy.

I slipped him a twenty off the wad and pushed by.

"You're next, Albert. Treat her right."

I looked back when I'd crossed the dark room, and saw the door moving, like he was banging it with his ass as she sucked him off for dessert.

Or maybe he liked something a little kinkier.

VII
Anyguy at Home

Outside the Pussy Palace the neon lights were popping on. The strip clubs, topless bars and restaurants were drawing customers. I walked through North Beach asking directions to the Tenderloin. I thought I'd head straight to the Hotel Napa for the main course with Dollar.

Yahoo! I liked San Francisco, big time. I liked the way the people strutted down the street like they weren't afraid of being sexy. I liked the Chinese guys with their fruit stands. The barkers — all ugly little fucks — standing outside their own pussy palaces. It seemed to me that it was a wide-open town with its own rules. Civilised, like I'd never seen.

Then I ran across the homeless. You hear about them back where I grew up, in the trailer parks, but you can't believe such pathetic examples of human life can exist, like cockroaches. Old ladies with shopping carts. Young guys with one leg. Everybody begging. It was disgusting. Shit, with a .22 they could have done some damage. No guts.

I saw an old Indian sitting in the doorway of a closed theatre. I guess by then I'd walked down those slanting streets to the Tenderloin. I read his sign first, like you always do:

> PLEASE HELP
> Native American Elder needs a bus ticket
> to go home where he can RIP.

I couldn't help wondering whether RIP meant he wanted to go back to the reservation and Rest In Peace or go back to his favourite bar and Rip It Up. So I looked at the old guy, while he looked me over. Then he closed his eyes like a turtle.

He wore a black hat with a beaded band on it over his white braids, a red shirt with a big collar. Silver rings on his hands. He was missing a tooth. A real grandfather Indian, just like in the movies. There was a cigar box in front of him with some coins and a five dollar bill in it.

I would have gone on past him, but with that big-nosed face he could have been fucking Geronimo. Geronimo was cool. I dropped a token from the Pussy Palace into his box and he opened his eyes and looked up at me. He blinked, like he couldn't believe he was looking at me, Buddy Tate. Then he reached in and picked up the token.

"What the hell's this?" he croaked.

"A token for a booth in the Pussy Palace, if it's any use to you."

"I can get it up." His blanket came open and he showed me the big knife in his fist. I stepped back.

"Don't disrespect this old Indian. I'll cut your heart out and eat it for a snack, right here on Market Street."

"No offence intended, Geronimo."

"He was an Apache. I'm Ahlone, from right around here."

"So why does your sign say you want to so back to the reservation?"

"People think Indians belong on the rez. They're not going to put money in the box to keep me in my home town."

"I've never seen an Indian begging before."

"Other Indians got some land to call their own. They have a language. Ahlone got nothing."

"You don't speak your own language?"

"I speak only one: green dollars. Money. Give back what you took from us. Drop it right in my box."

He smiled, not a pretty sight. One tooth missing, the rest black. He must have said that line a thousand times, then smiled.

"You must know this neighbourhood pretty well. Maybe you can tell me how to get to the Napa Hotel."

"It's on Eddy Street. Lots of fine women hang out there."

"I'm on my way to meet one of them."

"Well, that's good. You look like a strong young man. You got energy, I can see that."

"That's what she said, too."

"Who's that?"

"A girl I met at the Pussy Palace named Dollar."

That big-assed smiled flashed again.

"You know her?"

"I know Dollar well. A credit to her sex." He even chuckled. Dirty old man, goddamn. *In and out, in and out.*

But I'm not the jealous type. As long as I can rent it, I don't have to own it.

"Well, I've got an appointment with her, and I don't want to be late."

"You're a lucky boy. Drop some money in the box, and I'll watch out for your luck for you."

It wasn't my money, why not spread it around? I dropped a twenty in his box.

"Now we're blood brothers," he told me, making the bill

disappear in his blanket. "Any time you want my services, just ask for Inigahi."

"That just went right by me," I told him.

'In-ee-gah-hee."

"Well, if you say so. I'm Buddy Tate."

"Everybody calls me Anyguy. You want a drink?" He pulled out a hip flask and took a swig before handing it to me. It wasn't some old bum's brown bottle, but a silver flask inlaid with turquoise. I tasted brandy and passed it back.

"See you around, Anyguy. Keep an eye on my luck, like you said."

"You watch out for that girl. She's real bad."

"That's what I'm counting on."

VIII
Tattoo Me!

The Hotel Napa had seen better days a long time ago. There was a metal grill over its big lobby window. Everything inside was shabby and tired. I thought for a minute about what I might be letting myself in for — what if Dollar had a badass boyfriend waiting for me? But there was nothing I wouldn't do to have her by myself on a bed. I would ride her like a pony, and she would know where to go.

I took an old elevator to the floor Dollar told me to go to and knocked on a door. Dollar opened it slowly, and there she was, stark naked. She had a big grin on her face and her eyes were on my zipper. I didn't flinch, just stepped forward and shut the door behind me. We stood about six inches from each other breathing in, breathing out. Then I grabbed her around the waist and put my tongue between those cock cushion lips. Just licked the inside of her mouth. It was sweet and musky with cigarettes, a taste that always turns me on.

Her hand was in my zipper in a flash. Out popped Old

Willie and she grabbed him at the throat and choked him. We hurried into the bedroom.

"Now it's my turn, honey. You know I like it *long* and slow."

I fell on the bed. "Well, let's get started."

"You got something for me, honey?"

Money was no object. She slipped a condom on me and licked it wet. She had a way of turning up my thermometer that made me forget everything. For a minute I held onto her head, digging my fingers into her kinky, oily hair, and fucked her face. But I wasn't going to let her off that easily. I wanted her pussy this time. I wanted all of her so bad it hurt.

I cooled off by spreading her legs and putting my tongue in her tiny slit. I settled in for a good long taste, and pretty soon she was thrashing around on the bed trying to get loose from my tongue fucking her. But I knew she was only pretending, the way whores do, so I just kept on. Sucked her little bud until it was hard as a marble.

When she came, when she really came, I had to get out of the way. I just sat on the edge of the bed, mouth dripping with her juices, watching her roll around on the sheets, pulling them in rucks around her, pillow stuffed in her mouth so she could scream. I noticed she had a tattoo on her back of a dragon, which was about to take a bite out of a big dick.

When she stopped, I turned her over on her belly and slid it in the back way, holding onto her titties as I moved in and out. I made it last the way I taught myself to do when I was just starting out. Then, when I was ready, I really let loose and by then she was begging for it. Size didn't seem to bother her now, she was just gasping and screaming into the pillow. Junior had stretched her out and the fit wasn't tight enough so I pulled out and plugged into her butt. Now that was *tight*. My head came off.

In and out, in and out.

We collapsed and shivered together, the electricity zipping through us.

She had a cigarette and teased me by dropping hot ashes on my belly. I looked at her firm caramel body and felt lucky. I guess the Indian was looking out for me.

San Francisco, here I came!

"You're naked," she said.

"You're telling me. So are you."

"I mean, you don't have any tattoos."

"You mean like the one on your back?"

"You like my dragon?"

"I like your dragon. I like your ass, I like your tits, I like your mouth, I like your eyes, I love your pussy...."

"I've never had a redhead before. Are they all as big as you?"

"No. This cock is custom made. Hand-stretched, you might say."

"I think you should have a tattoo. I'll send you to a friend of mine. Star's a real artist. He'll give you a good one."

I figured she probably got a commission from the guy for telling all her clients they should get tattooed. Little did I know.

"Why should I get a tattoo?"

"So other people like you can recognise you. Like a signal."

"Nobody's like me. I'm Buddy Tate. I'll be famous one day."

"I'll bet you will. But in the meantime, you're special, and you should have a tattoo to say what kind of special you are."

"Is he your boyfriend?" That got her mad.

"No, and he doesn't need your business either! Dollar's just giving you some good advice. Just call me the Welcome Wagon."

First the Indian, and now Dollar. Everyone was looking out for me. It was a good sign, because I thought I'd probably need every bit of help I could get.

I rode the Welcome Wagon until we both fell asleep.

IX

Lightning, Meet Thunder

I write in here so people will know who I am in the future. What I am right now I don't know, but maybe people in the next century will be able to put it all together. They'll read this little notebook and think about the late, great Buddy Tate... and maybe about how much fun he had in bed.

I woke up with a sore penis. This happens sometimes in a man's life if he's lucky. There was a note from sweet bad Dollar taped to the bathroom mirror. I didn't look in the mirror but I read the note.

"You are my kind of guy but a tattoo makes a boy a man. Go see Star at the Asterion Studio. 16th Street."

There was a white tissue on the sink that she'd blotted her lips on, like she'd left me one last red kiss. She'd forgotten her lipstick. When we were playing in bed she'd put some on her pussy and then let me lick it, so my face was smeared with her lipstick and her juices. I put the lipstick in my pocket.

I thought about it. If tattoos turned the lady on, I'd get a tattoo. I'm easy that way. I figured what the fuck, destiny knocked, you know?

I got dressed and left the Hotel Napa after sliding my duffel bag under the unmade bed. I carried K. Farouk's .38 and his roll in my jacket pocket.

I bought a map so I could find my way from the Tenderloin to the Mission and started towards 16th Street. It was a cool, sunny afternoon and as I walked along I looked into store windows, not noticed by the people in restaurants and bookstores, grocery stores and thrift stores. After a while I started to feel invisible again and depressed.

I saw a cab at a crosswalk and got in. It cost me $10.00 to get to 16th Street but the driver didn't try to cheat this time. He said he was from the Kingdom of Serbia, so I guess he didn't hang out with people named K. Farouk.

Asterion Studio was a storefront painted black. There was a metal door with a small sign:

> ASTERION STUDIO
> FINE TATTOOING
> By Appointment Only

Next to the door was a mirror where a window should have been. I stood there looking at it like I was hypnotised. I used to be afraid of mirrors. If I went into rest rooms or stores I avoided looking at them. I knew if I looked into them I'd see somebody who wasn't me. I was convinced that the person in the mirror was someone imitating me. That's what I thought for a long time. Then I decided that it didn't matter if it wasn't me. I'd pretend it was. If the Buddy Tate in the mirror was playing me, I was playing him.

Now I couldn't pass a mirror without looking, and saying to

myself, *hey, that's me*. I really do exist, after all. Sort of.

So I stood looking at myself in the mirror outside the Asterion Studio, wondering if I had the nerve to get a tattoo. Needles make me nervous. The idea or some *guy* working on my body wasn't so pleasant, either.

I put on my sunglasses, took them off. Combed my hair. Winked. The features worked just like those on a ventriloquist's dummy. I wasn't bad looking, just strange looking. My Adam's apple was too big, my nose had a bump in it, and when you have red hair and fair skin it looks like you don't have eyebrows. I don't think people like my eyes. Don't trust them. Well, they shouldn't.

I went to push the bell on the door, but the mirror held me so I couldn't move. Suddenly I was afraid it would show me my future. I was stuck.

There I was, Buddy Tate, and I was a big man. Ten feet tall in the camera eye. Everyone saw me. They couldn't miss me. Then I blinked, and I was getting smaller — tiny, tiny, tiny — with a little teensy tiny voice like a fly must have, and no one paying any attention at all around me.

I got a chill, believing for a minute that I was disappearing, that I would vanish, and nobody would be in the mirror. No Buddy Tate. I don't know why, but I took Dollar's lipstick out of my pocket in self defence, like it was a magic charm that I could use to show people my power. I struck at the mirror that was vanishing me and cut it twice, like this — 'X'.

When I was a kid, I would've run away after doing something like that. But I wasn't a kid, and I wasn't going to make myself invisible, into nothing. So I rang the doorbell and heard it buzz inside. I stepped back quickly when it opened.

A man filled the doorway, a muscular guy with a five pointed star on his forehead between his eyes.

"Halloween was last week. You missed a beat there."

He didn't sound pissed off, like I expected. I decided to tell him what I'd come for.

"I'm here for a tattoo people will notice."

"The sign says 'By Appointment Only'. I guess you read it."

"It was Dollar who sent me."

"Who?"

"She works in the Pussy Palace."

His eyebrows clenched around the star tattoo.

"Shit. Come on in," he said. He stood aside and I saw her for the first time.

Her. She was small, but I couldn't see past her.

She stood there just staring at me. She was topless, with sweet little buds like on your first girlfriend and a look on her face that I'll never forget. Like somebody struck by lightning.

She *saw* me. She saw that I was somebody special. I heard the door close behind me, but I didn't take my eyes off her.

"Why did you do that?" she asked. I knew she meant the mirror, so I turned to look at it from the inside. They could see out, but I couldn't see in. She had been watching me. Maybe she even knew what I'd just gone through.

"Do what?" I said so she would say something else, so I could draw it out. I couldn't believe the way she kept staring at me, like I was out of some comic book. I felt big again. It was like she knew me — like she recognised me, you know?

It was as if she could read my mind — knew what was happening inside me — and that made her nervous. She put her hands up to cover that breast beauty, but she made it like an offering. One nipple poked through her fingers.

"You were watching me," I said.

"You couldn't see me."

"No. But something happened when I looked...."

I could feel her closing up on me. She was shrinking down into the room like a genie going back into a bottle. I was losing contact with her. And there I was, gawking at her while Star watched me.

"Pull your thumb out of your ass and sit," he said.

He motioned towards a couch and I sat on it, about half a room and acres away from her. I looked around and the room seemed to flow over me in waves. One whole wall was covered with thousands of coloured pictures and designs. It was like the wall was alive — like a hundred little red tongues and fingers and flowers all wanting to be paid attention to, to be picked. In a corner of the room beneath a low lamp there was an island — a white metal sink and table with instruments on it. Jars of stuff.

She sat on a chair turned to face me and Star picked up something that looked like a dentist's drill and started working on her back.

"You messed up my window."

"I'll clean it off for you."

"No, I think I like it that way. It's like a warning curse. In this neighbourhood, that's not a bad thing."

"Mirrors do something to me."

"Why do you want a tattoo?"

"Dollar said it would help identify me to people like me."

He raised one bushy eyebrow, like Daddy does.

"Dollar has a vivid imagination. But with you, she might be right."

"Are those the tattoos you do?"

"Some of them," he said, moving on light feet to bring a chair so he could sit behind her and lean into his work. I went to look at the wall of images. I didn't even know what half of them meant. They were all symbols, like there was this secret society of people who recognised each other by them.

"What kind do you want?" he asked.

"Something small, but something that stands out.

Something with... stones, you know?"

Star chuckled, shaking his head. "A tat with 'stones'? A most macho request. You a motorcycle man?"

"I took a cab."

"How about a Japanese fire demon? The Grim Reaper? Nah, too ordinary for you. Am I right?"

"Something small to start with. So people will see it and know I'm Buddy Tate." I couldn't make myself more clear.

"How about a small Maltese Cross? King Edward the Seventh had one."

"I'm not a king, and I don't like crosses."

I was frustrating him. "Well, then. *Where* do you want one?"

I thought about that, watching his needle move on her back, wondering about the pain, wondering if I could stand as much. The painting on her back was so beautiful it was awesome. I knew if I got a tattoo, it would have to be one that impressed her.

Then it came to me. Where I wanted it.

"I want one on my dick," I told them both. Star turned off the needle and just stared at me like he was mentally measuring if I had the guts. No attitude. Just considering.

"Today is my lucky day, I guess. I'm finishing a beautiful back and now I've got a penis canvas to work on. How big?"

He was making fun of me in his own way, I guess, but I didn't care.

"I'm pretty good sized."

"No, I mean the tattoo."

"Small, like I already said."

"What do you think, Robin? What kind of brand do we put on Mr. X?" Her name was Robin.

She turned her head to look at me. It was a cool, long look. Something about her deep blue eyes said she knew exactly who I was and what I was placed on this green earth to do. I started to sweat with that look, trickles running down my ribs, and I couldn't make any spit.

"Teeth," she finally said, showing her own in a hungry smile that was first cousin to a crocodile's. Ouch.

I waited to see her breasts again, but she wasn't going to show them. Teeth she wanted tattooed on my johnson, teeth she would have.

"Why don't you take a break, Robin? I'll take a look and see what this guy's got to offer me. Maybe you could see about the coffee?"

She stood up from the chair, one arm covering the sweet things, and put a black leather jacket on. She was a little stick of dynamite. I could tell she had some mean tricks up her sleeve...

Star kept looking at me like he was sizing me up for a suit or a coffin as he sipped the coffee Robin handed him. She didn't offer me any.

"Tell me something about yourself. I like to know the people I'm working on. What's your name?"

"My name's Buddy Tate...."

"Well?" He cocked one eyebrow again, waiting for more. She was watching me with those piercing blue eyes.

"...and I've got a power in me that everyone can see."

"Calm down. Rap's dead. Just name, rank, and serial number. Where you from?"

"Just a trailer park somewhere between here and there. Someplace I left."

"A typical California immigrant. What brought you to San Francisco? The place is falling apart, in case you haven't noticed."

"I'm looking for a girl," I told him, looking straight at Robin. I realised I was telling him the truth.

He laughed. "I give up. Well, don't be shy, Buddy Tate. Take your pants off or take it out so I can inspect my canvas."

Robin came a little closer, and I could see a little scar like an old bite on her chin. It was like a tiny spider, hardly noticeable. We locked eyes again so there was something between us like a beam of light I didn't want to break. So I didn't take my eyes from hers while I pulled down my pants.

She didn't break contact and look down at my prick for the longest time, and when she did, her expression didn't change, but I could tell that she was interested. Something flickered in her eyes that I had seen before.

Something else came to me. She was embarrassed. Like a good little girl who went to church, she was just a little bit embarrassed. If I could find out why she was embarrassed, she might come to me.

And I wanted her to come to me.

"You are a specimen, Buddy Tate," Star said, taking a close look. Even when he touched me I didn't look at him. As far as I was concerned he could have been in the next room. It was just her looking at me, and me looking at her.

"You can put that log away now. We'll have to schedule an appointment for you. Sure you want just teeth? We could put the Eiffel Tower on this one. How about the Golden Gate Bridge?"

"Do it now, Star," I told him. "Or not at all."

I wanted to show off to her. It was as simple as that. Boy meets girl, boys shows off to girl, boy fucks girl.... No, maybe it wasn't that simple. There was something else going on here.

"I don't know. I'm just about finished with Robin...."

"I'd like to see, Star. Do him. You can finish me later."

"I don't know if I have the energy to concentrate...."

I pulled out the cab driver's wad and put five twenties in his hand. "Down payment."

He considered it. Nodded. "Well, why not? This whole thing is crazy. Stranger just walks in off the street and wants his cock tattooed after he messes up my window, it's got to be the fickle finger of fate. It's gotta be."

"It's a strange world," Robin agreed.

The three of us stood there looking down at the part of me under discussion, not saying anything. Strange how you make new friends and then everybody gets tongue-tied.

The doorbell buzzed before I could say anything. Star walked to it, stuffing K. Farouk's money in his back pocket. Robin turned to see who it was.

Star opened the door and a white bear stood in the doorway. But he didn't slam the door and run. He held out his arms to welcome the bear.

It was Dollar in a white fur coat and a blonde wig. Wild looking.

"That coat cost a whole family of little animals their lives, Dollar." Star said to her.

Dollar looked at me. "Well, don't just stand there with your dick out."

Saved by the bell.

"Are you following me, Dollar? What are you doing here? And why are you wearing that coat?" Robin's voice was hard and flat, like she was used to giving orders, at least to Dollar.

"I sent him to you, Robin. He's big for his age — but I guess you saw that for yourself. I just..."

This was getting interesting. A girl's mind is a wonder, like the inside of a refrigerator that hasn't been opened in a long time. You're likely to find anything in there.

Even girls who like girls. Mirrors kissing.

"I don't like people keeping tabs on me, Dollar." Before I heard the knife edge in her voice I would have put my money — or, at least, K. Farouk's money — on Dollar in an argument. But Dollar looked ready to cry.

"Where did that coat come from?" Robin demanded.

"Johnny gave it to me." She was whimpering.

"Johnny?"

"He was a special customer. Lots of money, just like Buddy."

"You're a whore!" She stepped into close range and brought her arm up to smack Dollar. Smack again. Dollar gurgled and her nose was running.

Star tried to cool Robin out, "Jealousy comes up to help you get through your paranoia, Robin. Don't forget the story I told you about Hippolytus. His name means 'horse-loosed' if I remember my Greek, and your horses are loose right now. Sometimes you have to let Aphrodite have her way…"

I didn't know what the hell he was talking about, and Robin wasn't listening.

A change had come over her. She stood differently, somehow. She was fierce. "Get down on the floor where you belong, you tramp!"

When Dollar didn't move fast enough, Robin hit her again. The white bear turned into a rug at Robin's feet.

"I'm sorry!" Dollar wailed. But Robin kicked her in the side, then kicked her again. It probably didn't hurt Dollar through the big coat she had on, but Dollar started blubbering and, shit, I felt a surprise. My zipper was getting tight on me. Cat fights are sexy, but this wasn't a fight. Robin was kicking the living shit out of Dollar, who hollered but seemed to be enjoying it.

"A little of this goes a long way with me, Robin," Star told her. "You'd better take this shit home."

"I'll teach this whore a lesson!" She sounded like some angry preacher yelling at the sinners. Wham! Bam! She let Dollar have some more kicks. I couldn't tell whether it was part of a game they played or if it was for real. This was something new to me, and I wanted a piece of it. I cut in.

"Robin," I said. "Why don't the three of us go some place and work this out?"

"Who invited you? This is a private party, cowboy."

"I'm not a cowboy. And you know there's something between us."

Her blue eyes were cold wild, but she listened to me.

"Just like there was something between you and Dollar?"

"That was just fucking."

"Why should we go anywhere with you?"

"Because I'm telling you to." It came out of me just like that, without planning it. Maybe it worked because it was so unexpected. Or because it had to happen.

She nodded. "All right, Buddy Tate, you're on."

Star smiled. Dollar got to her feet, still sniffling, pulling the white bear coat around her. She reached out for Robin's hand. They hugged.

"Do you know what you're getting into, Buddy Tate?" Star asked me. "These are two Valkyries from Hell."

"Hell's a place I know about," I told him. "Hell is where I'm headed anyway."

X
To Hell and Back

We took a taxi from the Mission to the Hotel Napa in the Tenderloin. The streets were full of people looking for a party, but I was bringing mine with me. I sat between them so they'd pay attention to me instead of each other, but Robin stared out the window and Dollar kept petting her coat like it was still alive.

I felt like a king with them one minute, and like a fly in their web the next. After seeing them together, even I could see they were twins inside. What one would say the other would echo, only an hour later, turned inside out but still recognisable.

In the room at the Hotel Napa, Dollar dropped the white coat that had been the bone they picked between them. She wasn't wearing anything underneath but white panties on her brown thighs, and a garter belt and stockings — she was a real tramp, thank God, no pretending with her. She had her priorities right, as far as I was concerned: sex and money. She walked across the shabby room like a tired hooker and took a cigarette from her bag, lighting it with her face bent to the flame so that smoke got in her eyes and they watered.

I could see the imprint of Robin's hand. Her blonde wig was crooked.

"You're a cheap slut, Miss Pearl," Robin said to her. "You'd lick a snake. Better learn how to crawl all over again."

Pearl Dollar smiled defiantly, looking to me like I might save her from Robin. But I wouldn't have. I wouldn't want to miss what Robin might do next. She was a magic show to me. The rest of the evening was whoopee, like sliding on ice.

Robin sat down on a fancy broken chair and told Pearl Dollar to pull her big black boots off. Then she sat up like a lady and took off her leather jacket. I noticed she winced, I guess because the tattooing had made her back sore. I saw her beautiful boobs, sitting right up there at attention, and was glad I'd come to hell with them.

She caught me looking, and didn't seem to mind.

"Buddy Tate, what do you do?"

Her eyes were level, looking straight into mine — maybe a little mischievous — and I didn't know what she was talking about. *Do?*

What did I *do*?

"I do what I'm doin'," I told her, not knowing what else to say.

"What are you doing by yourself in a sleazy hotel with two crazy women? Aren't you scared? A little bit?"

Scared? Not me. Her boots were off. Her skirt was high on her bare thighs, and I could see the dark furry outline of her pussy hiding up there, waiting for me to uncover it. She watched me look at her without saying anything. Her look back at me said she wasn't scared of what I might be thinking. She'd seen it all, the look said, and she was older than me. I might have been a mass murderer, a fucking vampire, and it wouldn't have mattered. Something had burned her and made her fearless. She knew she had the power.

When I didn't answer her because I couldn't, she asked me again:

"You know, boy, you could get in trouble playing with strange women."

"I guess that's what I'm looking for."

"Dollar, would you bring out our toys so we can play with this boy?"

Dollar went into a closet and brought out a shopping bag. She didn't look tired anymore, but like she was expecting some fun.

"That was expensive lipstick you used to make your mark. You deserve to be punished."

Her voice was stern, the way it was with Dollar, but it didn't push any buttons with me.

"So you fucked Dollar, right on this bed."

I surprised her by getting down on my knees in front of her like the horny hound I was and looking up her skirt for the furry animal I knew lived there.

"Let me kiss it a little bit," I said. "Then I'll play any games you want."

She looked down at me and smiled, letting her thighs fall open so I could see it. Without touching her I moved my head between her legs and she was opening them for me, spreading herself for my tongue — when suddenly she slapped me open-handed, making my ears ring.

But I had gotten close enough to smell the essence of life oozing at the centre of her being. It's a smell that makes slaves, because when she hit me my first reaction — a flash of blind rage — was to beat the shit out of her face with K. Farouk's .38. And then I didn't care, I was defenseless. All because of a whiff of pussy.

"Get your pants off and start praying," she ordered, and I did it willingly. I was beginning to feel very warm and happy. I didn't need prayers.

When I was naked I started to stand up. My penis already was. Both of them watched it grow.

"Stay down there and pray. Because I'm going to fuck you until you turn into a girl. I'm going to fuck you until your asshole screams, Buddy Tate."

No way. I stood up, my dick pointed at her like a spear. "You and what hundred Girl Scouts?"

"Get back down there on the floor. Put your butt up in the air and wave it at me."

But I wouldn't. Hell, I was no boy-butt. They should have seen that! But I'd forgotten about Miss Pearl Dollar. She had found the K. Farouk special in my jacket and was pressing its barrel against my neck.

"You'll like it," she whispered in my ear. "Just get down and do what you're told." There was a crazy power in her voice.

Now I felt fear. Since she put it that way, I got down like a dog. A live dog.

"Pray, baby, pray," Robin crooned above me in a husky voice choked up with lust thick as honey. "Pray I don't fuck you to death."

I looked up and saw that she had a big rubber dingus almost as big as mine sticking out from her crotch, attached to straps around her waist and thighs. Above, her tits were like dark spikes pointed at me. I thought of all the times girls had cried and made noises like I was hurting them when I drove John Henry deep inside them. I didn't know if I could take it the way they had. But then, I thought, they always came back for more, so I guess getting fucked just takes some getting used to. Besides, they're made for taking it, men aren't.

Miss Pearl Dollar was standing above my head, the pistol

loose in her hand. I could have taken it from her maybe, but they were both crazy. What if she fired?

"I think we require some lubrication, Dollar."

Dollar fell to her knees before Robin and began slurping on that black dingus like she had on me. I turned my head to watch. Just as I remembered, she had a wonderful talent for sword-swallowing. The rubber was wet when Robin pulled away from Dollar. Her face was stern and intent, those ice-blue eyes shooting sparks. She moved to mount me.

"You ready for a ride, cowboy?"

If girls could take it, then I should be able to, I told myself. The cold rubber of the dingus moved along my crack and poked at my virgin asshole. She smacked my ass and grabbed my waist to get some leverage. Her hand brushed my balls, but that was a tease. Then she forced it inside me. *Yow*!

I wasn't expecting how the pain would make me yell and growl, how it would take over. I didn't think I could stand it, but of course I did. It was like being split open to a new way of looking at things. The sweat popped out on my forehead and I bit my tongue not to give her any satisfaction, wanting to pass this test. Blood in my mouth.

I was filled up to my belly and my guts were being poked while she beat my ass and back with her little hands as hard as she could. She was saying something over and over:

"I'm fucking you Daddy, I'm fucking you so good...."

It sounded like that, but my ears by then were buzzing with the pleasure that was riding through my body in choppy waves, making me press my face into the carpet. The rough fibre's burned my cheek, but pain no longer mattered. I had gotten through pain to the other side. I was happy.

I was being initiated into a new world and I liked it.

I mark that as our anniversary: I'd met my match.

I was praying after that — maybe for the first time in my

life — that Robin wouldn't stop. She went on and on until she got tired moving her hips, and pulled out. The dingus was so big it seemed to take forever before it came out. My asshole wanted to keep it inside. Then I collapsed, drooling from my mouth and bleeding from my asshole, a delicious, luxurious feeling like my insides were letting go. I had a boner that ached, and — it took me by surprise — I felt myself coming, helpless as a baby, into the carpet.

I could hear Robin breathing hard above me.

"You liked it too much for a first time."

"Now he knows what it feels like to be a girl on the bottom," Dollar said.

"Get up, Buddy Tate. You've been baptised. Wipe your ass."

Dollar threw a towel at me and I got to my knees, sore from being ground into the carpet. It was obvious from Dollar's sour look that she was having a jealousy problem. She was pouting as she looked at Robin, who was sprawled in a chair still wearing the dingus. She lit a cigarette and blew smoke rings.

"That got you hot, didn't it?" she said to Robin.

"What if it did?"

"Well, I want some of it."

"Some of what?"

"Some of the same."

"Don't bother me now, Dollar. Let me get my breath."

"Fuck me, Robin, please fuck me like you fucked him."

"All right, but in bed this time."

"What about him?"

"What about him?"

"We're not through with him yet."

They went into the bedroom and I cleaned up, wondering what I should do — join them, or let them sort it out first. I looked out the dirty window onto the street. The night life people were standing in doorways and waiting on street corners for pigeons to come along for fucking and plucking. We were up four stories doing our weird shit and the people down on the street were going about *their* business, doing their equally weird shit. And none of us knew what we were doing.

No way to make sense of it, I told myself. *Just enjoy yourself.* My asshole hurt, but I felt calm, like I never had in my life before. I waited out there just looking at the sky getting dark until I heard noises in the bedroom and went to take a peek. I like to watch, and Robin was doing to Miss Pearl Dollar what she'd done to me, so it was like instant replay, only Miss Pearl was a lot noisier than I had been.

I didn't feel left out. I knew my turn was next.

Much later we were all in the bed, which was littered with the dirty dingus and plates of Chinese take-out, just getting acquainted. It was around midnight. We were all naked and at last feeling comfortable in our skins, and Robin was a woman again. She was turned on her side, and her tattooed back was bleeding a little bit, dark drops running down the jungle into the serpent's open mouth.

"It's dark out," she said, like she was surprised.

"It's late. Normal people are in bed."

"Nobody's normal."

"Well, I'm not, and you're not, and Dollar's not for sure. But there are normal people. I've met them, I'm sorry to say. Didn't you come from a normal family?"

She snorted like she was crying or laughing and pulled the covers up over our heads. The world disappeared and we were three kids under the blankets, telling stories and secrets. With my cherry popped I was one of the girls now.

"How'd you get to be so weird, Buddy Tate?" Dollar asked.

"Weird? I just do what I want, pretty much when I want to. And I don't believe bullshit. If that makes me weird, I guess I am."

I like to let girls do the talking. It saves my energy for more exciting things with them. But I was feeling pretty loose, I had to admit. My butt was sore and things were so wet between my legs it was like I had a pussy there, like my dick had disappeared... There were things I could talk about with them. We were relaxed, with Dollar turned to face me and Robin turned away, but touching, all touching. Their soft flesh was like what I imagined people meant when they talked about love.

And the smells under those covers!

Blood and shit from my ass. Great gobs of come drying. Sweat. Girl juices. Drool. Food. Perfume. Sweet aroma of fucking and sucking. It was intoxicating.

I took a deep whiff when it was my turn to tell them a few things about myself.

"I'm bound for glory. Everybody's going to know my story."

"What is your story, anyway?" Robin said, and we all laughed. But they wanted to know. They kept saying they'd tell me their stories if I told them, so I made something up that sounded true.

"Kansas. Oklahoma. East Texas. Up north again, Colorado, Idaho. That's where I grew up. Daddy liked to keep moving. He said if you didn't, they'd catch up with you. My mother liked to sit at home, so she got left behind. He had a trailer, and we'd go where he could find work. Or I'd get chased out of town."

"What'd you do to get chased out of town?" Dollar asked. Robin's back was moving like it was listening, like everything in that jungle was listening. Beneath the skin, her heart and lungs were listening. But she didn't turn.

"Well, I got in trouble over girls, mostly. I mean, the first time I saw a titty, I wanted to suck it. The first time I slid my finger into pussy, I knew I had to have that feeling every day, twice on Sunday. I got bigger, and bigger, and every girl I met was willing. I had a gift."

"You sure do, Buddy," Dollar giggled.

"But you can't just go around seducing every girl you see. They have parents, and boyfriends, and sooner or later I'd get in trouble with them. It got so bad they put me in a clinic for perverts...."

I stopped, I knew they were listening, but I didn't want to go on like we were on some stupid talk show. They were the first girls I really wanted to explain myself to. They should be the first to know about Buddy Tate.

Robin turned. "I've never heard of a father like yours."

"My Daddy taught me a lot just by leaving me alone. Other times he'd talk a little when he drinking. I guess the best thing he told me was about sex. Never to let anyone try to tell you it was bad, and to get as much as you can."

"Subversive big time. No wonder you're so weird."

"Everybody's weird about fucking, even the people who think they're normal."

"He's right, there," Dollar agreed. "All these guys I see at the Pussy Palace, they all think there's something shameful about having to come to the Pussy Palace, or they're ashamed of their dicks. Poor dumb assholes."

I thought I should shut up because I was talking too much, so I asked Dollar: "How come you don't feel embarrassed working in the Pussy Palace?"

"It turns me on, that's why. You saw what a wicked woman I am. And being a sex worker sure beats the alternative."

"What's the alternative?"

"Well, there's religion. My brother always be tryin' to save my ass. He's a preacher, and an uptight asshole. Or there's workin' on a job. What a joke. Booth girls have fun. We jerk guys around like they was on strings, honey. Makes Dollar feel *very* powerful."

"Oh, shut up, Miss Pearl," Robin said. "I want to go to sleep."

I wasn't going to let her get away with that. "You didn't say anything about yourself."

"Just say I had a depraved childhood. I'll tell you all about it one of these days. You'll be sorry you asked."

Eventually I drifted off, sandwiched in between them, their hot bodies like electric blankets, but in the middle of the night I crawled out of bed to take a piss and turned on the little television the hotel management had allowed the room. There was a dumb porno movie on cable I watched that gave me half a hard-on, but what the bodies on screen did to each other was pretty tame next to what had just happened. So I channel surfed until I hit a real con man, the Reverend Thomas Flood. He was in the centre of the screen and three female heads were bobbing up and down as they knelt before him like he was some kind of God instead of the con man I knew all these guys are. I turned up the sound so I could hear the bullshit from his lips.

"...followers of Christ, you will be anointed and rise into the heavens on that terrible final day, and it's coming soon," he was saying. "I pray that the Lord of Hosts will give these good church women relief from their symptoms. Friends, pray for them. These good women need your prayers."

I turned off the sound and watched the picture, feeling more turned on than I had with the porno film. You can see a porno film anytime, but to see a master hypocrite at work was a treat for me. I'd studied them for a long time.

I liked the way this one used his eyes. I studied them to see if I could do that little squint that spoke sincerity to the suckers. The wetness in the eyes, and the crinkles of caring concern around them. He probably wanted to be President.

I didn't hear Robin get out of bed. She came to me naked and caught me squeezing the weasel watching a television minister. Well, I'd warned her about me. It must have struck her as pretty strange, because she started to laugh hysterically when she saw what I was watching.

She laughed and I felt myself go soft, and she kept on laughing and pointing at the screen until she was peeing down her leg and rolling on the floor. I crawled over to her and licked the drops from her leg and waited for her to tell me the joke.

"That's my father. That is *my* Daddy," she said. I thought she was trying to tell me she was a Christian or something and he was the guy she prayed to, but it turned out she meant that his name was on her birth certificate. I shut off the tube and sat down on the floor again, pulling some cushions off the sofa for us to lean against.

"I'm Robin Flood. His baby, washed in the Blood of the Lamb."

I laughed. I looked deep into those blue eyes and laughed. She was hiding somewhere in there, and I hoped my laughing at her would flush her out.

"I guess you don't see much of him."

"I ran as soon as I could. But not before he got to me."

The way she said it was like throwing matches at the memory.

"What did he do?"

"Anything he could, any time he could."

"Do you ever see him?"

"Not in years. I get some of his money every month to stay away from him and keep my mouth shut."

"Tough."

"I didn't think you'd understand."

"I believe you, whatever you say."

Neither of us said anything after that for a while, and all the noise of the Tenderloin below the window came in to fill up the silence with 3am noise. Cars honked, bottles broke, a woman screamed, drunk. Sirens. When she opened her mouth again she was sitting erect with the cushions bunched up around her and her arms wrapped around her knees like she was trying to protect herself. She spoke in a voice so low I had to strain to catch it. Her head was down and knees aren't microphones.

"Buddy, have you ever killed anybody?"

"No." I was chilled. I thought about Daddy teaching me to shoot.

She let the question hang there and I waited for more. Finally, she raised her head and looked me up and down like I was applying for a job.

"Could you?" It was a whisper that pricked up the hairs on my wrists. I thought about it.

"I guess I could."

"What about my father? Could you kill him?"

"You're a Christian. Christians aren't supposed to think this way."

"It's not easy. Could you?"

"Maybe."

"I see it in you. I know you could. You're... special. I knew that when I first saw you standing on the street in front of Star's window."

"Why do you want to kill him? Just stay away from the bastard."

She turned over on her belly, knocking aside her nest of pillows. I could hear Dollar snoring in bed. There was Robin's fine ass and I wondered for a minute if she wanted me to flip her the big boy, but it wasn't that. It was the tattoo that covered her back. She moved her shoulders so that it moved.

"The tattoo is to cover the scars. He poured scalding water on me when I was thirteen because I refused to say my prayers on television. Said I was wicked, that he was going to cleanse me. They kept me in the Burn Unit for six months and it was the only time I felt safe as a kid."

"What about your mother? Didn't she protect you?"

"He killed my mother. Said she was evil, a slut, and that I would be just like her. So as soon as I could, I tried to be just like her. He wants to be bigger than God. He wants to run the country." She was shivering.

It made me sick. I got up and went to the bed for a blanket to cover her with. I thought she was crying, but she wasn't.

"Kill him for me, Buddy. You want to be famous? Kill Thomas Flood!"

XI
Evangelical Evening News

Thomas Flood's educated, well-modulated baritone rose in earnest supplication. Staring into the camera's tiny magnifying eye, he began to pray. When he prayed, people listened, and bowed their heads with him in millions of homes tuned to the Evangelical Evening News.

"My friends, recall *Isaiah* 5:14: 'Hell hath enlarged herself, and opened her mouth without measure; and their glory, and their multitude, and their pomp, and he that rejoiceth, shall descend into it....'"

He paused to let them imagine all that they hated and feared falling into the fiery stinking pit. They shuddered inside, feeling the triumph of righteousness spread into their cells. When Flood quoted scripture his voice illuminated a spiritual darkness so profound that many at home peeked through their fingers as if expecting the Devil himself — old Beelzebub — to appear to do battle with the popular Christian prophet.

Thomas Flood talked to God, and God answered him.

Surely their fears were justified: was he not announcing the end of the world? This was the revelation, the Apocalypse, Thomas Flood had promised them. It was the moment his Parousia Crusades had been leading up to. They stared enraptured at his leading man features, his aquiline nose, long upper lip and jutting black eyebrows, and opened their hearts. They listened intently to his instructions for their survival. It had come to this, as he had prophesied: a war to the death between the powers of heaven and the awful armies of hell. He reminded them that hell was a crowded place. They telephoned in their pledges.

Flood's powerful voice rose another carefully calibrated notch. He was no longer praying, he was preaching, his stern gaze conducting autopsies on their souls.

"Friends, let me be clear here: I am talking about Judgement Day. We have been preparing for it during our Parousia Crusades, and now the time, the most awful time, is just about at hand. It is coming, I promise you! We are taking our Lord's Crusade to that Babylon, that Sodom and Gomorrah, of homosexuality and devil worship and Jewish pornographers — yes sister, yes brother — to the smut capital of sin, San Francisco! It is there that we will make our stand for Christ. Yes! We will assemble our Christian Armies there for the great and final battle between the forces of good and the forces of evil as the Lord instructed us. Remember old Isaiah and prepare yourselves, my friends, for as it says in *Isaiah*, 'Behold the day of the Lord cometh, cruel both with wrath and with fierce anger, to lay the land desolate: and he shall destroy the sinners out of it.'"

He paused, and the camera switched to a clean-cut band of women who played a selection of Christian rock. It gave the flock at home an opportunity to admire the brightly coloured set, and to see the hope in the eyes of the giant studio audience.

Cut back to Flood, a longer shot. He stood alone on stage, his arms lifted in the 'V' for Victimhood sign that was his signature, and continued. He rolled the magnificent lines in his mouth, savouring them for his audience:

"For the stars of heaven and the constellations thereof shall not give their light: the sun shall be darkened in his going forth, and the moon shall not cause her light to shine. And I will punish the world for their evil, and the wicked for their iniquity; and I will cause the arrogance of the proud to cease, and will lay low the haughtiness of the terrible!"

They thrilled to his battle call. In a nation beset by rebellion, terrorism, hunger, riots and all manner of natural disaster — a nation seemingly on the brink of collapse — Thomas Flood had an answer direct from God. By the end of the programme they had pledged a record sum to support the Warriors of Christ who would be descending on San Francisco. It would be Armageddon. (Perhaps some hoped the trolleys would be spared, but they were hushed by souls made of sterner stuff.)

❖❖❖

After broadcasting, Flood liked a cigarette. He was sweating and his broad shoulders were tight. He left the studio after thanking his co-ministers and the tech staff and walked outside into the bright Los Angeles sun; a tall ramblingly constructed man, a handsome patrician. There was no weakness in him, but he was tired, and he allowed his usually erect military school posture to slump. Upon his features was the satisfied but genially puzzled expression he showed only to the Lord; it differed sharply from the burning sincerity he projected in the blue lighted cathedral of the air.

In the campus-like green courtyard of his own Parousia Foundation complex he had caused a garden to be built with a variety of sweet-scented trees and exotic flowers. There was a small pond alive with golden carp, a Mission oak, and a carved wooden bench, and it was there Flood headed to have his cigarette and settle the day's accounts with the Lord.

He stared at the water and flowers, and the high battlements guarding the fortress of his ministry. The sun made his eyes, weak from the studio lights, water, so that it might have seemed to an onlooker that he was weeping. He stretched his legs, concentrating on the polished toes of his expensive loafers as he sucked in the welcome nicotine.

— You ask too much of me, master. I could feel their fear and anxiety coming at me in waves. This country is about to bottom out, and they know it. But the pledges were very strong: $460,000 in two hours!

The voice answered him, as it always had:

— The people are frightened.

— So they should be. But why must I be the one to lead them?

— Because you are... plausible. They created you. They own you.

Flood opened his eyes and threw his cigarette into a discreetly placed stone ashtray. He heard members of his staff leaving the barn-like television studio and chatting as they strolled the garden paths. They'd be eating their lunches sitting on the benches around the pond, but he was not embarrassed about falling to his knees for an impromptu chat with God.

— Lord, I am thy servant with every sinful inch of my being. But why?

— Why what?

— Why me? Why must I be the warrior to lead this Crusade? If the end is near, why can't I be allowed to spend the remaining time atoning for my own sins and praying for your forgiveness?

— Because you *are* my servant, stupid, and this is how it works. Don't whine. You have several lifetimes to spend in my service. I am angry with San Francisco. I am a jealous God, and the people there worship other gods. You are my tool — the hammer with which I will smite them.

— There is no forgiveness?

— None for those who follow false gods. And none for hypocrites. Unless you follow my direction without hesitation I will keep you turning on the wheel.

— But...

— Don't forget, I have all the time in the world.

❖❖❖

Thomas Flood returned to the sweetness of the world, with its soft warm breezes, exotic fragrances, and bird song. He stood up painfully, his knees stiff, and smiled at the members of his staff who were looking his way. Let them think his public prayers were ostentatious off-camera. Who could hear the Lord but him? It was the spirit that seized him. When the voice spoke, he knelt. When he wanted the voice to speak, he knelt.

He strolled through the garden, nodding affably to his staff of technicians, fund assistants, secretaries, junior ministers, child care workers and security people, keeping a sharp eye out for temptation.

For a man like him, temptation was everywhere. He knew *Les Jardins des Delices*. Oh yes, he was a sinful, needful man, and because he knew this he could touch the hearts of his flock, who were all sinful and needful. So many shadows to slip between...

The world is sticky, he mused, as if a pot of glue had been

poured out over it, covering everything with the certainty of sin, holding everything to earth that wanted to fly up to heaven. A man could put his hand anywhere and it would up stick there; when he tried to free it, up it would pop with sin glued to it.

The topic of his sermon would be stickiness, he decided. When he broadcast tomorrow, he would ask his listeners to pray to come unglued. Flood chuckled at this impish thought, so unlike him.

"I want you to come unglued from the world," he would tell them. "I want you to detach yourself from everything that holds you to this miserable life. I want to give you wings that won't stick to earth, to this suffering earth from which we shall be released..."

Well, maybe that was going too far. He had a tendency to overreach himself. The voice talked to him and he transmitted it to the faithful, but sometimes his own ego got in the way of the transmission.

He walked into the tunnel that led to his offices, pressed his hand against the glass and spoke so that the voice print technology would open the steel security doors. Time for business.

XII
Healing and Dealing

Thomas Flood sat at a massive mahogany desk in his dark, imposing office, looking across the room at the seventeenth century pulpit the workmen had installed the day before. It was tall and ornately carved with cherubs and vine leaves and gargoyles. It had disappeared from a church in Vienna during the war, and turned up only recently in a Sotheby's catalogue. The television audience would never see it, of course: too ornate, too sensual; but he enjoyed the feeling of power it gave him. Standing behind its soaring wooden bulk, he felt protected, one in a long line of prophets and preachers. He was most vulnerable below the waist, where the black thing, Asmodeus, lived, and the pulpit concealed it. Perhaps he would tell them the Lord wanted him to have the pulpit as a platform. Then what his flock would be able to see was the half of him they could have, the part of him that was able to heal them.

He pressed a button on his desk to summon his secretary.

When Mary Ruth limped in, he could tell the pain was much worse. She was a thin woman in her fifties with a blunt, mannish appearance and a perpetually sweet expression on her face. She had been with him for over twenty years, but her strength was failing. They would have to pray together so he could tell her he was letting her go.

"Mary Ruth, you are a treasure. The pulpit is magnificent, isn't it?"

"I think it's just beautiful, Reverend Flood. A work of art. When they unpacked it, I couldn't take my eyes off it. To think that some man with his hands and the grace of God could make such a wonderful thing!"

"How is your leg? You seem to be favouring it."

"Thank you for asking. I couldn't get much sleep last night, it hurt so much."

"Walk for me, Mary Ruth. Let me see how strong a hold the Devil has on that leg."

Flood watched his secretary drag her arthritic leg across the plush carpet, feeling a warm surge of the most unbelievable love well up in his breast. He frowned when he felt Asmodeus stir and stood up quickly, abruptly snapping himself from his stolen pleasure. Mary Ruth's set sweet expression was jagged with the effort of moving her leg. Flood touched her elbow and fell to his knees on the carpet, pulling her down with him before she was prepared. Her gasp of pain when her knee struck the carpet was gratifying and exciting. Gratifying because he'd been responsible for her pain, exciting because he could heal her suffering. He launched into prayer.

"Lord, the Devil has afflicted one of the least among you; this good woman who is my helpmeet in our great battle for souls is in constant pain! She can barely walk! She limps along like... a cripple, when her spirit remains as strong and pure as your tears! Send her some relief from the affliction, merciful Lord!"

Carefully, Flood reached out to put his healing hand on his secretary's lame leg. He didn't want to upset her.

"It is this leg, Lord! I pray that you will heal with your infinite compassion the lameness of this dear, blessed lady who keeps my life in order. It's hard for me to see her suffering so..."

His hand pressed into her thin leg. He heard her groan because of the pressure, and he exulted. He ended his prayer with a quote from Scripture: "Lord, I am not worthy that thou shouldest come under my roof; but speak the word only, and my servant shall be healed."

He stood up, feeling Asmodeus rising, and that was shame in the sight of the Lord. He helped Mary Ruth to her feet. Tears streamed down her face. Next time they prayed together, he would tell her she must retire.

"The Lord will provide."

"Thank you, Reverend Flood." She hobbled to the door, where he stopped her.

"Send down for Jack, Mary Ruth. I want to discuss the figures from yesterday. Something doesn't add up, and you know how I am about figures..."

The poor old mare is ready for the pasture, he reflected. *But where would he find a replacement so loyal and so discreet?* He needed people around him he could trust, but he wondered if trust had become a luxury for him. Love Everyone, Trust Yourself was not a bad motto to live by, right up there with Never Complain, Never Explain — Just Kick Them Where They Will Surely Remember It.

Jack entered on soft leopard feet, rubbing his hands together — a worrisome sign to Thomas Flood, who knew his treasurer's every mannerism. He had trained himself to remember and analyse each of them. He trusted Jack with the collection plate, but only up to a point.

"Remember *Ecclesiastes*, Jack: 'Watching for riches consumeth the flesh, and the care thereof driveth away sleep.' What did we take in after the Evening News yesterday, when everything was totalled up?"

"Round figures? $450,000."

"What happened to $10,000 of that?"

"What do you mean?"

"Your accounting was short $10,000. That is a lot of money to fall out of the plate."

"Oh. That's part of your personal budget line. It came out of yesterday's pledges."

Thomas Flood regarded his treasurer with a baleful eye.

Jack looked down at the carpet, over to the pulpit, and back down at the carpet. He was a small, shy man with a bit of a lisp. Flood had prayed over it without result.

"Your daughter, Reverend Flood. It was her monthly stipend."

"Blackmail. I have no daughter."

Jack sighed. He had been around this corner a few times before.

"Perhaps so. But you made a deal. You pay, she stays away."

"Yes, Jack, I made a deal with the Devil in my daughter."

"As a matter of fact, there was a letter from her."

"I won't give her a penny more."

"She's living up in San Francisco. She wants to see you."

"What for?"

"She says it's about her mother."

"A whore is a deep ditch: don't forget, Jack boy, what kind of woman her mother was. A *very* deep ditch."

"You haven't seen Robin in two years. Since before she went to Paris."

"I'll consult with the Lord and let you know. Meanwhile, I want you to work up some figures on the merger with our friends in Atlanta."

And Jack scurried back to his office, where he directed a staff of twenty number crunchers, most of them Pentecostals, in managing the Parousia Foundation empire. Because he laboured over his spreadsheets, Thomas Flood could kneel and pray, secure in the knowledge that his money was safe. The Lord's Treasury...

But before prayer, a nap. *I need my strength to address the Lord.* He pressed a button on his desk console and a panel opened behind him onto a large dressing room. Here he made up for his broadcasts and kept a narrow couch where he napped.

Often, he dreamed. Sometimes brief flashes of nightmare struck, and he awoke wondering if in these last days, the world had cracked open. He stretched out and pulled a blanket over his shoulders. Asleep, he watched himself stand up and walk, but no one saw him until he opened his mouth and poured forth hell and damnation. His wife, who often appeared in his nightmares, and his daughter, who seldom did, appeared before him wearing the white robes of angels but with their heads turned from his view. He spoke to them of hell and they turned eyes full of overwhelming defiant lust upon him. And he ripped the angelic garments from them in anger and they were transformed back into serpents crawling on their bellies on the ground...

And then it happened in his dream that he branded his daughter, that he stamped her back with fire to burn the Devil from her. But Asmodeus entered her and corrupted her... and he slew the great harlot, her mother...

Thomas Flood came awake with a dry mouth, his heart racing. He fell to his knees next to the bed and prayed for relief from the nightmares.

— I have tried to atone to her, Heavenly Father. But as is the mother, so is the daughter.

— Thomas Flood quotes Scripture. Don't make me laugh.

Did you forget this one? 'Inasmuch as ye have done it unto one of the least of these...' You violated her innocence. You burned her body.

— You made me who I am, Master.

— I'm sorry, I won't take the blame for you, even if it was a botched job.

— She wants to visit me. She wants to talk about her mother.

— Tell her about her mother. Explain.

— I've tried, but she won't listen. There is a devil in her.

— Don't argue with me. See her. Tell her again.

— Thy will be done. But what should I say?

— Tell her the truth, you pusillanimous hypocrite. You murdered your wife.

❖❖❖

Thomas Flood looked out over the studio audience, waiting for the singing to stop. He hated Christian rock, but it brought them in. They came to be healed — the hope in their eyes was almost blinding — but they also came to be entertained. They wanted theatre, and the Parousia Foundation gave them theatre — and aerobics classes, daycare, and sweatshirts — whatever they wanted, just so they came.

Flood himself preferred the simple old hymns — "And He walks with me, and He talks with me" — but that was part of the old style of churchgoing. So were sermons that offered no answers. The world had become a perilous place, and people demanded answers.

A technician attached a tiny microphone to the top of Thomas Flood's bright red tie. The music stopped. The eyes that were recognised across the globe, cold blue eyes that saw right through you, were staring straight at America, prime time, into its living rooms and bedrooms, into its wounded psyche. The rich baritone voice asked them:

"Why is pornography anathema in the sight of God and of all true Christians? The answer to this question is available to us right in the *Book of James*: 'But each one is tempted when he is carried away and enticed by his own lust. Then when lust has conceived, it gives birth to sin; and when sin is accomplished, it brings forth death.'

"Friends, lust comes into everything. It has many disguises... I'm going to relate to you a misadventure that befell a young minister of God to illustrate this important truth about the power of lust. The story is about the temptation that a young man is likely to fall prey to. Temptation is tricky, like old Satan himself. Did you know that in the dictionary it says that temptation is 'a thing that attracts' but then after that it says it's an 'incitement to sin'? No wonder it's confusing. We all like to go towards the thing that attracts, don't we? Whether it's..."

He paused to drink from a glass of tea at this point.

"...good for us or not. Whether it's right in the eyes of Our Lord and Shepherd is not something we consider when we're young and ready to find a life's partner. We see the raiment of the flesh and we are blinded. We are hypnotised by the sight of a well turned figure. Or so it happened to one young man — and some of you may already have guessed that this young man was me.

"Her name was Rebecca, straight from the good book, and she was attractive. Comely. She was a definition of temptation in her comeliness. She was fair, almost pale, and her hair was black as the crow's wing, black and glossy. And her eyes, well, they were jewels you wanted to look at forever."

Another sip of tea. He smiled benignly as they waited for him to resume. He had them now. He looked over the heads of the attentive studio audience as if he saw the angel Azrael approaching on a cloud suspended from the ceiling.

He resumed: "Rebecca became my bride, and I was the happiest young minister in the State of....well, just call it matrimony. Holy matrimony." Here they laughed, and he paused again. "But my happiness was built on the satisfaction of lust. Satiation was the rule Rebecca lived by, as I learned to my sorrow on our wedding night. I began to neglect my relationship with God. The marriage bed became a grave of lust for me. Now, some might say, if children resulted from this carnal union, why then the marriage is fruitful and that is all that need be said. But I knew my soul was struggling with the Devil. I knew..."

Here he paused and seemed lost in thought, as indeed he was. He was recalling the visitation of the Devil in his marriage bed, and the vision stunned him with its power. He was between Rebecca's thighs rooting there with his lips to taste her where he shouldn't, and the snake appeared from her fundament, the green terrible snake of lust struck and bit his tongue, his lascivious tongue...

He shook his head clear with a widening of his eyes. On television screens it was magnified, so he seemed to be struggling with devils inside. In fact, he was, but he smiled and returned to his story:

"She was like an addiction for me. I confess it and I attest to it... she was like a drug I had to have. Her sex — the power of her generative organ — aroused in me a lust of monstrous proportions...Let me tell you, after a while it got so bad that Rebecca just began to live in bed all day long, watching television and eating candy and waiting for me to come home from church. I knew something was wrong with our marriage, but I didn't know what it was. I was innocent before I married her! And the worst part was, that it didn't stop even when she conceived, even when her womb was full..."

He covered his eyes with his hand, and bowed his head in shame. The audience stirred at the sight of him struggling with such a concupiscent Devil. But the memory he struggled with was not of his wife's sin, but his own.

He was seven, small for his age. His Sunday School Class went to the circus as a reward for learning all their Bible lessons. Little Tommy Flood went dressed in shorts and a t-shirt and sandals. The circus was thrilling. A tent was pitched in a vacant lot in the small Indiana town where he grew up, and there were animals and rides and clowns.

It was the clowns that Tommy wanted to see. He went off by himself to look for them, impatient before the show to see the funny men. *But the clowns were cruel and scary and there was a snake charmer who held him and suddenly the snake was inside him...*

He was getting sick and for a moment he lost his train of thought. Get rid of the snakes, he told himself. Snap out of this.

"Yes, I was innocent. I didn't know about the temptation of lust and what the punishment for it might be. It was God's punishment that was visited upon us. He was so sickened by our lust that he struck Rebecca dead."

He could almost feel them shiver out in the blue cathedral of television land. He could almost hear the million intakes of breath. He had never told this story before.

"My wife Rebecca was killed by an intruder in our home. He raped and murdered her, and it was God's punishment on us!"

His glistening blue eyes widened dramatically. His head fell to his chest.

After lingering on him for a slow sixty seconds, the cameras switched to Flood's co-host on the Evangelical Evening News, the Reverend Bill Dalrymple, who was inspired to make a particularly effective appeal for Crusade contributions at this dramatic moment.

The studio audience saw Flood step off the brightly decorated set and disappear through a door. He was headed for the men's room to recover himself, or throw up. He was in sore need of guidance.

He hurried down the long hallway to the men's room, pushed the heavy door open, and found Jack at the urinal. His treasurer zipped up hurriedly. A warning buzzer went off in Thomas Flood's mind, but he ignored it, his crisis was so great. He stepped quickly up to the white urinal and unzipped himself before Jack could leave.

His eyes fixed on Jack's, he held his power in his hand and shook it mightily, daring his treasurer not to look at the serpent in his hand. The moment was too brief, but Flood felt a deep thrill at having shown his power to this insignificant servant.

"Excuse me, would you, Jack? I really came in here to pray."

Flood fell to his knees before the urinal and called upon the Lord.

— This is more than I can bear, Lord. How do I explain Rebecca?

— You got yourself into this.

— Help me.

— You're beyond my help.

— I'm helpless.

— You've told yourself the story so often you believe it yourself.

— I confess, Lord, I don't know shit from Shinola right now. I can no longer distinguish what really happened from my version of it.

— You never could. You're hopeless as well as helpless, but you are my servant. Get out there and finish your lie, for sometimes I am with you.

Thomas Flood had spoken with God. It was on his face when he returned to the set, a look of awed resolution. He faced the camera and offered up his account of his wife's death, skipped over his indictment, trial and acquittal for the crime, and picked up the thread of his sermon again:

"The man who came into our home and murdered Rebecca was a consumer of pornography... the police found a collection of *Playboy* magazines in his closet! A fiend of lust! You know the famous saying, 'Pornography is the theory, rape is the instrument?' The man who came into our home was injected with the poison of pornography— the word itself means 'the writing of whores'— unclean images! Unchaste cartoons. Foul stories..."

God spoke through Thomas Flood. He felt transformed.

"Pornography is noxious in the nostrils of God, and our ministry here at the Parousia Foundation has been selected by the Lord to lead a great crusade into the capital of pornography and heathenism, San Francisco.

"That's right: San Francisco, Sodom by the Sea. It's a city built on vice, on licentiousness. Just a hundred years ago the Barbary Coast was known throughout the world for the number of its prostitutes. Not for the number of its churches! The Lord warned San Francisco in 1906 with a great earthquake, but still it kept to its evil ways. Our crusade to save the soul of San Francisco will burn the pornography and scatter the Devil worshippers! Lust will be defeated by our crusade, and driven down into the fiery pit!"

He roared the last line, arms stretched skyward in a triumphant 'V', eyes glowing with a fervour that was money in the plate:

"Lust is the devil we will drive down into the fiery pit!"

XIII
Buddy on the Loose

Robin and Pearl Dollar were still asleep when I hit the street. They were curled together like cats. I was hungry, and after I took care of that I just walked around looking at things. Faces passed like blips on a screen, like they weren't human. My hips hurt. My ass leaked. But I was smiling.

You could say I was under a spell. *Killer.* I liked thinking that Robin thought I could kill her father. I guess she had good enough reasons for such extreme prejudice. With six and a half billion people on the planet chomping on Big Macs, one big-assed preacher wouldn't be missed. And people get up and salute killers. If I killed Robin's father, people would pay attention. I wouldn't be invisible then.

I was walking on the Lower Haight looking at the hippies and the dippies and the faggots when, lo and behold, a familiar face. I turned my head but he saw me and I had to go over to where he was sitting and say hello.

It was Anyguy, the old Indian who was watching out for my luck. His box had a couple of twenties, so the luck business was good.

"I can see you found that bad girl."

"She was only half of it."

"You jump right into things, don't you?"

"No time to waste. People say the world is coming to an end any time now."

"You're in trouble if you believe that stuff. Don't worry — I'm watching your luck. Take your time. Enjoy. The world won't come to an end until the serpent swallows the moon. That's a long time away."

"When the serpent swallows the moon?"

"When else?"

"I think if I listened to you I'd be too crazy to enjoy myself."

"You can count on whatever I tell you, Buddy."

"Tell me why you call yourself Anyguy."

"You call me that. My name is Inigahi."

"What does that mean in Indian?"

"One Who Lives Alone In The Wilderness."

I laughed. This old Indian was amazing.

"And here you sit on your ass on a busy street."

He shrugged his high old shoulders.

"Life plays tricks on you. Maybe you only think I'm here."

He winked at me and somehow, don't ask me how, he sent a line in my pocket with a hook on it and, presto, my last twenty dollar bill was in his box. His eyes were shut.

I started to walk on when he didn't open them, but he called me back. There was a serious look on his face that I paid attention to.

"Look out for blood in your eye, Buddy."

"What does that mean?"

"Remember what I said."

❖❖❖

Sometimes I thought he could read my mind. I had to think about hooking another wad of cash somewhere, and K. Farouk's pistol was in my pocket so there was the danger of having to use it. Blood. That didn't sit well with me, but I didn't have a choice. I'd spill blood to be able to afford expensive women. It was part of the bargain you made with them. No pay, no play.

There are some advantages to being invisible like me. One is when you're hunting pigeons. There are a lot of similarities between people and pigeons, I've decided, after watching them both. Pigeons go where the food is, and leave a lot of droppings. Pigeons like crowds. Pigeons are easy to get close to. They're watching, but they're easily distracted. A lot of them are fat and careless. And some are just stupid.

I stood on a street corner looking down Market Street like I was waiting for a bus, but what I was doing was waiting for the right pigeon. They came in waves down the sidewalks, and then there'd be the stragglers. I waited a long time until I spotted the right one.

He was a typical California richie. Loose jogging pants about to fall off his ass, and a t-shirt that said 'A Higher Power Within'. He wore a bag around his waist that looked stuffed with money. He was built, but I'm not puny, and he had a tan so dark you knew he didn't know the sun gives you skin cancer. A real asshole.

I just followed him like a ghost, looking for the right place. He turned onto Valencia and I was right behind him at the underpass. Nothing there but a vacant lot and some trucks.

"Get it out," I yelled when I was about a yard or so behind him. "Give it up, you asshole!" The pistol was pointed at him.

I thought he was going to run because his eyes looked scared wild, like he couldn't decide whether to shit or go blind, so I jumped on him and jammed the barrel in his chest to stop any ideas. He practically stopped breathing.

"Take that off," I told him, dropping the pistol back into my jacket pocket. I owned his ass now. No sense attracting attention. Just in time, too. A police car slid by, but we just looked like two guys standing there talking.

His hands were trembling but he got the bag unbuckled and handed it to me.

"What's your name?"

"Tom. Tom Stanforth."

"Never did like that name. Well, Tom, I'm not going to tell you mine, but you want to forget about me. If you tell anybody about this I'll find you and cut your hands off, and then your balls."

I was right about my pigeon. His wad was held together by a gold money clip. Probably a bigger thief than K. Farouk.

"You're probably a lawyer, aren't you Tom?"

"Yes."

"I ought to kill you." I was just joking, but Tom didn't see me smiling. He muttered something like he was surprised and we both looked down at his crotch. He was pissing his pants and looking at me. It was disgusting.

"Don't kill me. I won't tell anyone."

He was a pathetic asshole, just about ready to cry, and he made me feel dirty.

"No, I won't kill you. But one of these days you'll wish I had, with the kind of life you got ahead of you."

I made him take off his shoes and socks and throw them into the busy traffic and then I skipped off down Valencia Street, flush again.

❖❖❖

It was dark when I got back to the Hotel Napa. The sidewalk outside it was filled with bag brides, pre-ops, post-ops and TVs. The lobby smelled like people had pissed in it.

The bed was empty. Clothes were everywhere, the way girls do. No note. Just gone, and they left the lights on, the door unlocked.

Should have tied them to the bed.

Well, what did I expect?

Shit happens.

❖❖❖

I knew where to look for Dollar. It was the busy time at the Pussy Palace. A fat Mexican-American in a tight purple t-shirt threw down tokens for my hard earned money and I stepped inside the sleaze emporium. Sex fiends everywhere, looking at the magazines, watching videos, checking out the booth girls. Miss Dollar Pearl wasn't working the booths, so I stepped into a cubicle that would allow me to view the live peep show with my Pussy Palace tokens. The wooden barrier came up, and a Latina girl came to my window and stuck her hand out. I gave her five from Tom's roll and she stood there smiling and waiting for me to touch her big silicone breasts. I touched them but it wasn't a thrill. Real titties feel real. But I asked her if she'd seen Dollar and she stepped away from the window.

Dollar was across from my window letting a guy feel her ass. There were eyes in every dark booth, just eyes watching. Guys coming in their pants watching Dollar and the Latina.

The guy stuck his finger in her pussy and she jumped back from him, seeing me at the same time. I pulled a fifty off the roll and showed it to her and she strutted right over to me.

"It is you, Buddy Tate. Your eyes glow in the dark."

She wasn't surprised to see me.

"Where's Robin?"

"She had places to go, and people to see."

Somebody yelled from one of the other windows.

"I want to talk to her."

"Play with my titties or I have to leave you."

I cupped one off her boobs in my hand and felt the bounce, the jiggle, the firmness of real girl tit, not plastic like the Latina's.

"I need to see her, Dollar."

"I think you scared her a little bit. I know her. She was upset about what she told you."

The yelling got louder and she pulled away from me.

"What she told me?"

"It was a nice party, Buddy. Now the party's over."

She danced away from me and a hand came out to stroke her beautiful ass. She grinned at me and winked, and the wooden partition rattled down.

XIV
Buddy has a Vision

I turned on the television at the Hotel Napa looking for relief. The remote was like a pistol I pointed and punched at talking heads as they appeared. Channel after channel clicked by that way.

I got interested when I hit a news show where experts were talking for the millionth time about the Kennedy assassination. They said there was new evidence that Kennedy had been snuffed by Oswald, working with the CIA, the FBI, and the Mafia. Oswald's picture as a young punk holding a rifle came up again and again. His wife, an old white-haired Russian-American lady, was talking about how he was in bed. Seems he couldn't get enough. Used to drive her crazy.

Maybe that's why he shot Kennedy. Jealousy, because old J.F.K. was getting it by the truck load.

Oswald had done it. He had gotten the world by the balls and twisted. He had caused a hundred million heartaches. He was invisible too, and then he picked up that Mannlicher-

Carcano rifle and pulled the trigger and he was everywhere. The guy had to be one of the hundred most famous people of the twentieth century. If he could do it, so could I.

And then I saw it! I had the vision! It was *me* up there on the screen, talking with Ted Koppel. Amazing! When I clicked to the next channel, there I was on it, talking to somebody famous. No matter how fast I fired the control, there I was. In some of them I looked different — older, wearing different clothes — but it was my face on the screen. Everyone was looking at me, all over the world. Asking my opinion about things. All I really wanted was for them to say my name: *Buddy Tate,* and keep it in their minds, so when they saw me they'd really *see* me. I wouldn't be some jerk who was invisible, I would be *Buddy fucking Tate!*

I punched that control until my fingers got tired, and on every channel found more pictures of me. Sure, I wondered a little about how I got there, but I take it when it comes.... If I was crazy, so what?

I got scared when I stopped seeing myself. Suddenly I was gone from the screen, and there was Thomas Flood talking down to people who were kneeling and praying and dropping their crutches. Telephone numbers flashed on the screen asking for pledges.

I hit the control. But on channel after channel, I was gone, faster than a commercial for dog food. Just a blip on the screen, and then gone. It hit me in the gut and I just kind of rolled around in front of the television in pain while Robin's father talked about coming to San Francisco to clean house on witches and pornographers. I was sure he could see me rolling around in pain, but his eyes just looked right through me as if I wasn't there. His face filled the whole screen, and his mouth was telling me what to do. I shut off the sound, but big letters crawled across the screen:

It is never too late to save a soul.

I wondered if I had one, and if I did, was there any hope for it? But hell, what's a soul but another shuck that guys like Flood sold you? I didn't need a soul, I needed a clean hit — right between this mother-fucker's eyes. If I didn't exist on *his* channel, then I swore he wouldn't exist on any channel. I, Buddy Tate, claimed them all.

I watched, trying to chill out, as Flood fleeced the suckers. He was scary. The flying saucer people would surely grab him and take him up and away — just up and *away* — if I didn't get to him first.

I thought about him torturing and messing with Robin and I felt how easy it would be to snuff him. I just had to get close enough, and she could help me get there. Then the whole world could tune in on our wedding...

I must have been hallucinating: what would we *do*, married? Couldn't bring that in clear on my own screen. Static. Interference. Buy a house? Ride motorcycles together? Run from the law?

Maybe we'd even have a litter of replicas of ourselves we would have to beat so they'd be like Mom and Pop? Then there'd be a smelly old dog who'd find Robin's bloody tampax on the floor and chew it. Bills. Taxes. No thanks.

But I wanted to imagine a future with Robin. I hoped that the two of us would be doing something to get in trouble. I hoped we'd fuck like big bunnies all the time. Then I stopped that line of thought. Hope was for losers. Hopers are dopers, I knew that.

There was only Flood in the way of my future. Popping him would be as easy as taking the K.Farouk .38 from my pocket and firing it at the television face. *Flash! Bang! Phfft!*

Got him right in the wallet.

XV
Asmodeus Rising

Passers-by turned their bodies and skittered sideways through the knot of black men in leather coats on the sidewalk. The group of men had a microphone, and one of them was haranguing a little crowd of whites, blacks, and unemployed Mexican labourers in straw hats.

"This is fucked up! The white man lets his wife work because he is a faggot! You people hear what I'm sayin' to you? A good woman should be at home, down on her knees in front of her man, takin' care of her children. Bein' a real woman! The white man is evil in how he looks on women. That's right, that's right! He goes to porno stores and spills his seed on the floor. He goes there to look at our black women, who are there whorin' their bodies so they can put fine clothes on their backs. God is watching all this! God knows! The white man is poisoning and polluting the whole world and the people in it, but God is watching!"

A little of this goes a long way, Thomas Flood thought with professional disdain, listening from inside his limousine. He was one of Parousia's street corner preachers, this angry young black man. Couldn't think of his name. It didn't matter. There was something about his aggressive technique that worked. The man had a gift. He needed training, but he would be useful when Flood brought his great Crusade north to San Francisco.

"We've seen enough of him. Let's go to that hotel where you say Robin has been staying." His driver's name was Hopper, and he was chief of Parousia's security force. He had located Robin Flood at the Hotel Napa which she'd been seen entering at odd hours, and leaving at even odder times.

Thomas Flood had evaluated the risk of paying a surprise visit to his daughter in these questionable surroundings — or even coming to San Francisco at all until the start of the Crusade — and decided that he didn't care about the risk. He needed to see Robin for the good of his eternal soul.

Hopper pulled the limousine up to the front or the grimy Hotel Napa on Eddy Street and Flood jumped out quickly, dressed in blue jeans and a denim jacket with a baseball cap. He didn't think any other disguise was necessary. He moved quickly through the smelly lobby and stepped into the narrow old elevator.

The door to her room was unlocked, and he pushed his way in. Music assaulted his ears. So Robin was here in this messy stinking hotel room in the Tenderloin. In the heart of vice. He saw a television on the floor with a hole in the screen.

Robin was in the bathroom singing to the music. Her voice was richer than he remembered. He called out, but she couldn't hear over the music.

It wasn't Robin. It was a black harlot sitting on the edge of the bathtub painting her toenails, naked as the day she was born. She had just gotten out of the bath. The mirror was still steamed over, and the dirty water was gurgling down the drain.

"Who're you?" she said, so surprised she dropped the nail polish. Her taut breasts bounced with the movement.

Thomas Flood was stunned by her comeliness. *This daughter of Ham is a temptress like none other since Rebecca*, he thought.

He could feel Asmodeus rising and he blushed.

"What are you doing here?" she demanded, hands on hips.

"I'm looking for my daughter." His throat was constricted.

"Well, you sure don't look like my Daddy."

"Robin. Robin Flood."

"You're Robin's father? The television preacher?"

Evidently Robin had told this black whore bitch things that were private, after signing an agreement not to talk about him.

"I'm Robin's father, that's right," he replied for lack or anything else to say — he couldn't take his eyes from her dark tight nipples, the beauty of her breasts. Asmodeus cried out to be released.

"I'm Dollar." She smiled when she understood his predicament.

"Why don't I wait outside until you put some clothes on?"

"No, you can stay here. But if you want me to put something on...."

"I do."

"Don't look like your dick do, darling." She laughed, sounding like a sinful child.

"Please. Put your clothes on."

He backed out of the bathroom and stumbled over the broken television set, falling to his knees.

— You have set temptation in my way, Lord.

— Don't do this, Flood. I will strike you down for this.

The black harlot came towards him wearing a white fur coat, open, holding her hands out to him, her big lips smiling, the hair between her legs shaved so he could see the puffy

lips of her slit. Where the serpent lived.
— Do not do this, Flood.
— I burn, I burn!

XVI
The Blood in Buddy's Eye

I was in a serious wicked mood because I'd been dumb. I'd always told myself that I'd keep it light when it came to girls. They had holes in handy places, but they weren't people, not really. Just fucking holes who'd leave you.

But then I wasn't a person myself. Nobody knew who I was or what I had inside me, and until I made them see I was capable of doing something dumb. Like falling for a lesbian who fucked my ass and took off with something of mine. What did she take? That girl took my heart. If I have one. (I guess I do, or I wouldn't be feeling this way.)

Dumb. I didn't like it. It made me gloomy walking through the Tenderloin. It was another one of those god damned perfect California days, but everything was grey and black and puke green to me. On the corner ahead a man was talking into a microphone and I went towards his voice looking for a cheap laugh. It was a preacher all right. An African-American gentleman in a leather coat, suit and tie. A couple of big kabloonas also in leather coats stood on each side of him holding big sticks.

I listened for a minute to his rap.

"The white man will die out because his genes are weak. The white man has polluted the world so much that it is now having an effect on the male production of sperm. That's right! You won't hear this information anywhere else but right here! The male sperm count today is only half of what it was 30-40 years ago, and you know what that means. This trend keeps up, there won't be any human race! If Armageddon doesn't get us first, then the white man's pollution will get us later!"

I liked that idea a lot. I was almost cheered up by the idea of the whole world fucking and no babies coming out. Just in and out, in and out, and then, *presto*, one day, no more us.

❖❖❖
•

I knew something was wrong at the Hotel Napa when I opened the door to Dollar's room. There was a bad smell added to all the other odours the three of us had mixed in the bed.

I stood there just looking in before I stepped inside and pulled the door shut behind me. I was very quiet, holding my breath.

As a kid, you always know when something is hiding in a dark room. So you try not to breathe, you get down low, and you just listen. Then you can hear the monster breathing.

I got down on my knees and started crawling like a baby on the carpet, guided by the light from the street lamps coming in through the windows. The smell didn't mean anything to me until I thought *blood*, and just at that moment my hand slipped on the carpet into something wet.

I held my wet hand up and tried to see what it was. Then I pushed myself up, using an end table and the wall, until I found the light switch. The monster didn't matter now. My bloody hand prints climbed the wall.

Everywhere I looked there was blood. Even some splattered on the ceiling in a delicate spray. It was on the floor, the furniture, and the walls. There was a hand print on the window. The television I'd shot was still on the floor.

When you go hunting rabbits, you have to skin them before you can cook them. I never liked that part, so I stopped going hunting. He hadn't skinned Dollar, but her beautiful brown body was covered with her blood. She was on her back on the bathroom floor, her head jammed up against the toilet like a bird with a broken neck. I think her throat was cut, but I didn't kneel down to look. Her legs were spread grotesquely wide apart, one of them propped on the tub, and there was nothing between them any more but bloody meat. The bastard had cut out her cooch.

That fucked me up. Miss Pearl Dollar cut up like a rabbit fucked me up. I always thought I was a don't-give-a-shit kind of guy. I enjoyed pain up to a point — giving it, and I didn't mind taking it. We all have to. But Dollar was a friend of mine. She had a fine pussy, and she was generous with it. A real slut and a good lady, despite her games with Robin.

That taught me a lesson — one of those you never want to learn this way. I had feelings I didn't know about, hiding inside me, I was fucked up like never before. I sat down on the couch and there was blood there too, like the guy had started slicing her up there. Like they'd been sitting talking, maybe about the blowjob she was about to give him, when he sliced and diced her.

I couldn't cry — what was that about, crying? Whining about the bad deal the universe hands you is not in Buddy Tate's vocabulary. What I wanted was revenge, big time, like elephants stomping on heads bursting like cantaloupes and hydrogen bombs dropping in the swimming pools of richies:

burn their villages and rape their women, swing their kids against hard objects.

I got the courage to look at her again. I thought that maybe whatever she saw last would be imprinted on her eyes. I bent down over her body, not caring about the blood I was slipping in, and put my live eyeball next to her dead one.

We eyeballed each other from different worlds. Hers were dark and scared shitless. They said, "please-don't-cut-me-what-the-hell-are-you-doing-you're-killing-me-and-I-don't-even-know-why". Mine were seeing inside her head, but then I realised her head had stopped, and it wouldn't be starting up again. Mine was still going, but hers had stopped like a busted clock. I didn't see anybody in her eyes, so I closed them like the cops do in crime movies. Shut those baby browns and didn't cry.

I just sat there in her blood next to her, not giving a shit for what came next, until I began to feel like I needed a bath. I was smeared everywhere with her blood, and my clothes were clotted dark lumps when I took them off.

No disrespect to Miss Pearl Dollar, so I put a sheet over her and poured a tub to soak in. But I was freaked, and kept K. Farouk's special .38 on the sink within easy reach. I just sank into that tub and spaced out. Put my feet up and started talking to Pearl like she was still there. Maybe she was, I don't know...

"Pearl," I said to the bitch, "you were hot — and now you're not." That's how I saw it, on one level. I wanted her to say something back but I guess she wasn't up to being teased one last time. I got serious then:

"Miss Pearl," I said to her quite sincerely, wiping my eyes clear of soap, "I'm going to be missing you. I wish you could still talk, so you could tell me who did this to you. I'd drop the hammer on the mother-fucker."

But she couldn't talk. I wasn't going to say anymore, because maybe I was getting a little crazy. But I could hear just fine, and what I heard was the door opening. I picked up the pistol and put it under a washcloth on the soap tray.

No point leaving the safety of the tub. I thought about rabbits. My heart beat faster as the footsteps got closer. Each footstep pissed me off. I expected Jack the fucking Ripper, but it was the African-American preacher from the street corner who thought white guys were faggots with a low sperm count.

His face turned the colour of ashes in a burn barrel when he saw me sitting in the tub taking a splash while the blood-covered walls and tiles said to him there was an oozing body under the sheet on the floor.

"What the fuck?" is what he said. He reached into his leather coat pocket for something but I showed him the pistol and he stopped that. I was happy. How many times in life does it happen that you have the perfect comeback for an important question? When he saw it, he repeated himself: "What the fuck?" and stopped his hand. Showed it to me empty. He'd learned the drill somewhere.

"What are you doing here?" I asked him.

"What you did, white man. What you did! My eyes are not weak."

"Fuck you, I didn't kill her. I don't know who killed her. Maybe you do — or you wouldn't be here."

"I'm looking for my sister, you red-headed peckerwood. My errant sister."

"Look for yourself."

He bent down, keeping his eyes on the pistol, and lifted the bloody sheet with two delicate fingers.

He started to barf big time. I guess he was discovering his feelings too. Choked it back.

"You know her?"

His face got worked up. His black-tack eyes got glassy.

"Her *name* is Latisha, and she is laying down there on the cold floor and you are calmly taking your fucking bath!"

His hands made strangling motions. "*I didn't*," I yelled at him, pointing the pistol. He stopped.

"You didn't what, you albino cockroach?"

"Pearl was a friend of mine. She was a good fuck. I didn't kill her. I thought maybe you did."

"Your mother on a plate with rice, white boy!"

"Got no mother. What are *you* doing here?"

His eyes went dull. "I was called to clean."

"What's that mean?"

"Man tells me to go clean, I go clean."

His voice was tight, just like mine. We knew what was wrong.

"Look, I got the gun. Who gave you the call?"

"Fuck you. I can't say that."

"It's your sister that's dead."

"You killed her."

"No, I just fucked her. She was my friend."

"You son-of-a-bitch white asshole mother."

I was sick of his shit.

"Get down on your knees if you don't want to tell me who sent you. You're gonna join your sister."

"Careful now." He had some spirit, but I was going to blow his ass away. I didn't care.

He got down on his knees beside Dollar's white-sheeted body. "Next to my ear. Right next to my ear, white boy."

"Excuse me? I'll shoot you any place I motherfucking please."

"Let me pray then. Have some respect."

"Pray that you tell me. That's your prayer."

I stood up in the bath water pointing the pistol at him. It was a powerful feeling, like being God.

He was muttering something under his breath like "blood", just that word over and over, and then he lurched up at me saying it louder and it wasn't "blood" he was saying but "Flood!" I brought the pistol barrel down on his head, his face hit the rim of the tub hard, and he folded back down like a jack in the box. I climbed out of the tub and stepped over him out into the room that was painted with blood.

Blood, blood everywhere and nowhere to hide.

When you don't know what to do, go to bed, get under the covers, and pretend it's all a dream. It usually is.

XVII
Blood Ritual

Robin Flood stood on her penthouse balcony high above the Mission District surveying her playground. Her gaze was directed to the left, towards North Beach in the distance, and then it slowly swept the horizon to the Bay Bridge. The paradise on a fault line built around the Mission Dolores was, to her, still a place of enchantment from an Arabian Nights fantasy. Especially as evening fell — purple streaks in the sky, the lights coming on — she felt that anything could happen here, that here she could play any role.

Slowly, languorously, she disrobed, and let each article of clothing drop to the floor — where it found its own niche in the ankle-high sea of clothes, books, shoes, art supplies, photographs, and the technodetritus of music and memory that undulated and billowed through the rooms of her Bernal Heights penthouse.

She sat at her make-up table to assess the damage wrought

by her over-the-top encounter with Buddy Tate, and to prepare for what promised to be an extraordinary evening.

The invitation propped against the mirror was on heavy expensive paper edged in what looked like dried blood. It said:

> The Society of Spectacles invites your
> participation in a Blood Ritual
> 9pm Tuesday
> Atelier, 346 Saint Street, SF

And in the lower right corner, in reddish ink, Laura Aurora had written her name in flowing calligraphy.

Robin applied white eye shadow to heighten the effect her startling eyes created. She used lipstick to make her lips and nipples glossy. When she stretched her new tattoo twinged and she was reminded of Buddy Tate.

"Buddy Tate," she said once to the person in the mirror, imitating his flat, vaguely threatening western voice. What she saw in the mirror was someone she didn't know, someone who could fall in love with Buddy Tate.

The mirror saw through her and out the window.

She stepped out into the balmy evening in a black leather cape, soft on her skin like her high black boots. Beneath her cape she wore a short black vinyl dress, cut low in the bosom.

She walked down Mission Street without looking left or right, feigning obliviousness to the eyes she attracted. Tall palm trees were spiky against the bright night sky. The homeless were everywhere, sprawled in every other doorway. Entire forlorn families waited on street corners for a ride to nowhere. Cripples, drunks and beggars were sentient obstacle courses stretched out in odd patterns over the coloured tiles of the sidewalk. A Mexican motif predominated. They were the 'helpless ones' to journalists — an ever-expanding population abandoned like old appliances by the Republicrat Party in the mid-nineties, when things first started going wrong.

She was walking past a large, ugly Evangelist Church with a skin of rough concrete and a tall skirt of wooden fencing, past posters announcing revival weekends and visiting ministers, when she saw a series of posters that frightened her. It was her father and his eyes seemed to be following her. There was to be a Crusade. He was coming to San Francisco.

She hurried past, not wishing to read any further. Gloom spread through her body, slowing her footsteps. She came at last to a loft building in a street named Saint, north of Market, and climbed the high stone steps to the first floor. There were buzzers in a row and the third one said 'Society of Spectacles'.

She pressed it and was buzzed in, stepped inside and looked up at a steep flight of stairs. Waiting at the top was a tall man who beckoned her to ascend. He watched as she climbed, and she didn't take her eyes from him. He had a broad red-lipsticked smile, a silver bone in his nose and silver chains running from his nose to earrings in his left ear. A large white feather hung from his other ear. He wore blue eye shadow and a black silk scarf around his shaved, tattooed head. His pierced nipples poked through openings in the studded black leather vest he wore. When she lowered her gaze she saw that fishnet panties cupped his bulging basket. He wore dark stockings, black vinyl boots with stiletto heels — and he carried off this improbable costume with insouciance. It was the way he stood, the fun in his eyes.

Robin thought he was the most beautiful man she'd ever seen. He was erect and muscular, and lines of energy streamed from his green eyes. He obviously knew who he was. Robin recalled a Zen Buddhist description: 'He had attained his skin'. And tattoos covered most of it, she noticed as he loomed over her.

She was three steps from the landing where he stood when he extended his hand and took hers, pulling her up faster than she expected, towards the light in his eyes.

"Robin?"

She lifted a puzzled eyebrow. "Yes."

"Laura told me about you. You met at the Spiral Dance."

There was a rustle of leather behind them and then Laura Aurora was holding out her long-nailed hands to Robin, pulling her close, smiling, her sharpened fangs glinting in the artificial light. Robin liked her musky smell and the pressure of Laura's small hard belly against her own flat abdomen, the older woman's bare breasts soft against her smaller buds. She wore leather and there was a riding crop stuck in her belt. A black motorcycle cap sat like a crown on her long blonde hair. Robin thought she had the incredible beauty that came from a life lived on its own terms.

"You've learned something," Laura Aurora said, peering into Robin's eyes, hands on her shoulders.

"I got a new tattoo," Robin shrugged.

"Something more."

"I..." She looked up at the man with the silver bone in his nose, who smiled reassuringly.

"This is Baron. You will be great friends but nothing more than that for a while. Baron is my husband."

"I didn't know man born of woman could look so *interesting*."

"Baron is the entertainment at this party. He's the star of our ritual. You'll see. Come."

Laura and Baron ushered Robin into a large room that was massive and mysterious to her. The wide board floors were dark and rough from a century of holding machinery. Chains, leather harnesses, dried herbs, mistletoe and ropes hung from heavy exposed beams. Long black curtains covered the wall at the far end, framing the space. Tall candles provided illumination. Incense was burning. She heard the light tap of drumming behind the low hum of conversation. Two dozen people — women, men and the shades of genderfuck between those illusory poles — stood in clumps talking. There were no chairs. Leather, rubber and PVC in subtle fantasies of black predominated, setting off bare arms, breasts, and thighs like jewellery. Beauty joined with outrage to reclaim the primitive — although Baron seemed, to Robin, to have set the standard for presentation of self.

She stood alone, wrapped in her cape, watching Laura Aurora greet newcomers with ebullient charm, thinking, *she is not protected like me, she can be this way because she knows who she is*. She thought this without envy, and with growing admiration.

Baron walked about the large room with the grace and presence of a gladiator about to enter a contest on another planet — say, Venus. His expression was amiable and benign with old friends, lovers and strangers alike, but his large liquid eyes mirrored other realities.

When what sounded like New Century chant was played on the sound system, Robin had the sinking feeling that something religious was going to happen and that she would not be able to escape. This desperate feeling, based on so much doleful early experience, was nearly always reliable. It was quickly followed by a sense of acute embarrassment for the people around her, who were about to make fools of themselves.

In the minimalist kitchen area she found soft drinks and fruit. She sipped pear juice and stood listening to the people around her, trying to imagine what roles they played outside the walls of this temple. In her father's house only he celebrated God. Here, everyone was a celebrant.

The talk, as it usually did, turned to certain themes of common interest: sex change operations, vampires, AIDS and its victims, the helpful attributes of various gods and goddesses. Robin had mastered the art of listening, and she also heard what was being said in a whispered antiphon by the same voices. They said nature was angry and people were going crazy, that something big was coming, that this was because there was no recognition of the sacred.

Conversations trailed off. An anticipatory hush fell. People were gathering around Baron, who hung from a rough wooden cross, wrists and ankles strapped to it with leather thongs. Steel needles pierced his scalp in a crown of thorns, and blood streaked down his face, which offered a look at transcendent peace.

Robin stepped back, stunned. In her confusion she was torn between feelings of awe and terror at the blasphemy. Her mind, so clouded by conditioning, was split by a lightning bolt of recognition. She stood mesmerised as she watched Laura conduct the ceremony of transformation, barely able to breathe.

Laura Aurora caught the blood that dripped from Baron's forehead in a silver chalice. She rubbed her naked breasts against his feet and legs. Taking a knife from her waist, she cut his panties from him and exposed his heavy penis. It was thick and veiny with a head like a ripe plum set in wiry black pubic hair.

On his lower belly was the face of a Japanese demon with open mouth, from which protruded... Baron's penis, the demon's tongue.

Laura moved around the cross in a subtle dance, shaking her breasts and looking up at her crucified husband as he came erect. She rolled his heavy balls in her hands and suddenly squeezed down hard, so that he gasped. Robin looked for a hint of pain on his face and saw only pleasure. Acceptance.

Laura licked Baron's balls and took each one of them in her mouth, leaving bright spittle in his pubic hair. He was hard by then, fully and triumphantly erect. Laura slapped his penis with her open hand and only flickering tension in his neck betrayed his pain.

Robin had moved closer, so that she was standing about three feet from Laura and she could smell their perspiration and sex odours. She felt the urge to rub her own crotch against a pole.... Her breasts felt heavy under the vinyl.

Laura held Baron's erection in her hand like a trophy. It was fully eight inches long and so thick Laura's hand barely fit around it. It was being offered to the celebrants: eat and drink of my body. No one stepped forward.

Laura licked the underside of Baron's shaft and then closed her lips around his heavy meat, her cheeks swollen with the effort to swallow as much of it as she could. She moved her head back and forth exciting him so that he gasped. Hearing this she stepped back from him and turned unexpectedly to Robin.

"Join us," she said, kissing her hard upon the lips. As if in a trance, Robin stepped forward and kissed the bulbous plum that crowned Baron's penis. Her wide mouth opened to admit this plum, while her tongue pierced the slit and she tasted his salty-sweet pre-cum. She pulled away only when Laura said, "Don't make him come, please. That's for me."

Robin stepped back, not daring to look at those who had watched her sucking Baron's cock. She knew she had crossed some boundary line and would be different henceforth. Bolder.

Laura put her husband's penis between her breasts, pressing the soft flesh around it, and he began to ejaculate into the air. She caught most of his emission in the silver chalice she had previously filled with his blood — gout after gout of sperm — while he screamed his ecstasy into the still temple. No one moved.

Laura, drops of semen on her face and breasts, held the chalice in the air and put it to her lips. Robin watched intently, now envious of her new friend, as she drank the mixture down without removing the chalice from her lips. When she lowered it, her lips were dark with blood and semen. She smiled.

She was magnificent, a high priestess of redemptive lust.

A low cheer went up and Robin watched the faces around her. They looked as if they had been struck by an experience of overwhelming power, a look Robin had seen on the faces of snake handlers and people so possessed they babbled in tongues.

She felt weak. The ritual was both beautiful and barbaric, transgressive and redemptive, and it had touched something inside her that the Christ story had never reached. She had no idea what it meant, but it was powerful, both in its initial impact and its resonance in her being. It was a feeling like seduction. She went to look for a bathroom, hoping to recover herself in private before having to talk with anyone. But there was no bathroom, only a restroom of the kind you find in schools and churches. There were four stalls separated by metal partitions and four gleaming white urinals. Above the urinals, signs had been placed: piss, blood, come, go.

Someone was in one of the stalls. Robin went down the line, but the only one that seemed clean was next to the occupied stall. She went in and sat on the toilet, hiking her skirt to her soft narrow waist. She never wore panties unless requested to for play purposes, so her bare buttocks felt the chill of the heavy white wooden seat. She felt flushed, and her clitoris was throbbing. Reaching between her legs, she wet two fingers with cold toilet water and brought them up to touch her sex. What she had witnessed released something in her, opened a door she had kept closed since leaving her father's church. It freed her, and it frightened her.

Her fingers probed into her sticky vagina and she sighed deeply. She was safe here in this cubicle. She could pray.

This is my prayer to the goddess, she thought defiantly. *This is who I will be from now on.*

Then came the old question: but *who* was she?

I am an animal. My sexuality is ravenous. My anger is enormous. I am she who masturbates in a strange toilet.

Her fingers moved faster, darting in and out of her vagina, rolling her clitoris between her nails, one finger exploring her anus, her left hand caressing her breasts.

There were noises in the next stall, so surprising Robin that she released a stream of warm urine, filling her hand and trickling hotly from her vagina and splashing into the toilet. Her nipples tightened.

There was a soft rap on the door of her partition. She didn't breathe. The door was pushed against and rattled.

"Robin? I think that's you in there. You smell like nobody else but you. Power pheromones. Open the door, okay?"

Robin numbly pushed the lock free.

Laura Aurora stepped in and pushed the door closed behind her. "You're doing the same thing I was doing. That scene turned up my thermostat."

Laura's usual benign smile was now a leer. Her fingers touched Robin's face, explored her lips and then her neck as if looking inside her skin for something lost. Robin trembled: this woman was a witch.

"I'm wet," Robin said weakly, "I'm hot." Words were inadequate.

"What did you think? I was nervous that I might do something wrong, but I think it worked out very well for the first time."

"It was breath-taking." Robin took her wet hand from between her legs and put it on Laura Aurora's thigh, moving it in wet circles up to the soft flesh of her inner thigh closest to her crotch. Her skin was soft over tight flesh. Laura's hands stroked Robin's short hair, snaking down her front to hold Robin's breasts as if they were doves fluttering to be released.

"It took your breath, my little darling? I'm glad. But did you *feel* anything?" Laura's voice was a hoarse whisper that trailed off.

"Passion," Robin said. "I felt passion. He was burning up and you were burning up."

"Kiss me, Robin." Laura bent over her and pressed her mouth against Robin's, who opened her lips to drink from the older woman's mouth. Taste of semen, dark taste of blood. An alarm went off: *what of AIDS?*

And the answer came: *This cannot be refused. This is part of the ceremony of my rebirth.*

The kiss was endless, and Robin's eyes closed, feeling Laura's hand between her legs, one finger in her vagina and another in her anus. She was enfolded in Laura's being as the narcotic kiss sent flickers of orgasmic delight to her every cell.

It wasn't painful when it happened and she realised immediately that she knew it would happen and she found that she wanted it immensely: the bite of steel at her neck, the release of the spirits of the blood. Laura drank from her like a kitten licking milk until Robin felt light as an angel.

"Who are you really, Laura?"

Laura stood up, licking her lower lip where a drop of blood lingered. "I'm anything you want me to be, Robin. Now you're part of me. I'm your mirror image twenty years in the future. I'm your Guardian witch. I'm the goddess Hera, wife of Zeus — who screws around a lot."

"What do you mean?"

"Think about it. I'm your friend, and there's one more thing I want to do with you."

Laura's hands took Robin's head and pulled it gently to her sex. "Do me with those lips, those sexy lips of yours, Robin."

In a dream, in a haze, Robin's tongue licked Laura Aurora's plump vulva. She took Laura's clitoris between her lips and pressed down, sucking and tasting the juices of the goddess.

Two fingers explored her narrow vagina and then she plunged her tongue in that succulent hole. Her hands grasped Laura's muscular smooth buttocks and pulled her close. Vaginal secretions burned in her nose as her mouth explored Laura's centre. Lust rode her bareback and whipped her so that her mind could make no images of what she was doing. When Laura's hot piss filled her mouth she drank it as if it were the pear juice she'd had earlier.

"*Fist me!*" Laura ordered, and Robin made a fist of her small hand and slowly penetrated Laura's wet cunt, letting it adjust as she pushed it up until her hand was half-way swallowed.

"*Fuck me, Robin!*" It was as if Robin's moving arm was what held Laura up. The partition shook with their movements which increased in intensity until Laura exploded: "*Oh, Oh, Oh, Oh...*" she babbled, with tears in her eyes, then hissed at the end like a cat and Robin remembered she was a witch.

They took their time at the sink cleaning up. Laura's bag contained make-up she shared with Robin, who sought to cover the punctures in her neck with powder.

"Is there somebody, Robin? Or will you play with us — with me and Baron?"

Robin frowned. Her back hurt. She could feel the tattoo bleeding.

"His name is Buddy Tate," she said it like a curse.

"Tell me about him."

"I am afraid of him. I want to hurt him."

"Why?"

"I don't know. Maybe I think he's got something I need."

"There are millions of pricks in the world."

"I mean he's got a part of me in him. So I want to hurt that part."

"What would you do?"

"I'd like to see him tied up and spread-eagled. Fucked by

Baron and every stiff prick and dildo in this place. Set his heart on fire, and, then when he was smoking I'd cut his throat and put it out."

"Whew. Your imagination is showing. And what did you do?"

"Fucked him in the ass with a dildo and left him wanting more. I disappeared because he said yes to something I asked him to do. But he's inside me, somehow."

"Don't worry. It's just infatuation. It'll wear off."

"He's not like anyone."

"What did you ask him to do?"

"I asked him to kill my father."

Laura Aurora paused and blotted her lipstick on a piece of toilet paper. She turned down the corners of her mouth in a doubtful arc.

"Why do you want to kill someone?"

"Not someone. My father."

Laura shook her head. "You are more complicated than I thought."

"I'm bad."

"Well, we're all bad girls here. We do things and believe things that most people think are terribly bad."

"No, I mean *bad*. Doomed to hell."

"You don't really believe that Christian stuff, do you?"

"It's hard to escape from. It runs in the family."

"Bible thumpers?"

"Did you ever hear of Thomas Flood?"

"Oh, no. Goddess, no! You aren't related to him — the Crusade against sex guy? Armageddon?"

"My father."

"Then you *are* bad." Laura said, giving Robin a hug. "*Very* bad." She stepped back with an appraising eye.

"I can't get away from him until he's dead, Laura."

"You got away from him in the bathroom. When I nicked

your throat and tasted your blood, you were... initiated. You're about to be reborn. You see, in a way, this gathering is for you."

"What do you mean?"

"Come on, I'll show you. Iolanthe is going to give birth."

Iolanthe was a pre-op with a wonderful smile, long dark hair and large breasts. Her penis was shrunken and still. She was lying naked on a long table, pillows under her head and her knees up in the birthing position. Robin and Laura watched with the rest of the gathering as Iolanthe's pretty husband breathed and grunted with her.

Laura Aurora whispered in Robin's ear: "Dominique is a big star in porno movies, you know. She was married to Star years ago."

Dominique's body was wrapped in chains light enough to allow free movement, and they were arranged so that her perfect breasts and buttocks were exposed.

Iolanthe's muscular thighs gaped wide, and she was straining her face red, puffing with the effort of delivery. Her groans grew louder and also more masculine, and Dominique busied herself between her wife's thighs. Her bottom wiggled enticingly as she assisted in the birth.

What she at last pulled forth, with the appropriate savage reverence for the ritual, was a large piece of bloody meat. She placed it carefully on Iolanthe's breasts and then left the table for a moment. When she returned, she wore a harness around her waist to which was strapped not a dildo but a blow torch. She took the bloody meat from Iolanthe's chest and held it aloft for all to see its dripping reality. Then she lowered it into the blow torch flame.

Meat seared, the smell of burning flesh rose in the air. In the silence there was only the gassy breathing of the blow torch. Stomachs turned. Someone screamed.

Robin felt people looking at her and remembered what

Laura had said, that in some way this ritual was for her. But it was for all of them. By it, Dominique and Iolanthe celebrated the birth of their love. It was sustenance for Baron and Laura Aurora, and for two skinny junkie girls who knelt before Dominique and opened their mouths like hungry birds. The meat blood of the cannibal sacrifice ran down their chins and trickled across their parsimonious chests. They chewed and sucked noisily and Robin felt her stomach protest again.

But Laura Aurora smiled, a mother lion watching her cubs play with a piece of antelope meat. She gave Robin a satisfied, slow wink. The gesture had the oddly endearing effect of half shutting her other eye.

"Just another night at the end of time," she said.

"What do you mean?"

"This is the year a lot of people like your father say is the last year of the world. Judgement Day is coming."

"Well, it may be *his* last year."

"You're dangerous, Robin. You've made your eyes opaque, so I can't look inside."

Before Robin could reply, *I'm afraid of what you might find*, Baron appeared wearing a turban through which blood still oozed.

"Life is beautiful when you wear a crown," he said, beaming and flashing his perfect white teeth. He was three or four sexes at home in the same body, operating with a self-confidence Robin had never encountered. He was happy, she saw. Truly happy.

Laura Aurora kissed her husband and knelt to take Baron's strap-on dildo into her mouth. The rubber glistened wetly after she'd paid her tribute. She stood, wiping her lips.

"You look like you're praying," Robin told her.

"This is more fun. I like to take advantage of every opportunity. 'The wheel might not come round again,' my grandmother used to say."

"My grandmother must have known your grandmother."

"My grandmother was Russian. She was a radical — a believer in free love. People thought she was crazy." She laughed. "Don't tell me our genes don't control us — we even inherit our desires."

"I don't think so. I'm not like my father."

"Your mother then?"

"I suppose so," Robin agreed, thinking: *such a slut*!

"You see? It's a good thing Baron and I don't have kids!"

"Men are different."

"The poor bastards are cursed by testosterone poisoning. Except for Baron. He is always on the sunniest side of every street, aren't you, darling?"

Baron smiled at them indulgently. With his bloodied turban and nose bone he might have been a maharajah or a head-hunter.

"What's your secret, Baron?" Robin asked him.

"Secret?"

"You're so cheerful."

"I'm lucky."

"You mean you wear a rabbit's foot and throw salt over your shoulder?"

"No, I know who I am, and I know what I want. That's lucky."

"So?" She wanted more.

"So, knowing what I know, I can do what I want to do. Simple."

"Doesn't it hurt?"

"That's the best part of it." He turned to watch a young woman pass, gazing longingly at her callipygous buttocks. He looked to Laura for her permission. Laura sighed and nodded.

Laura and Robin watched as he whispered in the woman's ear, grinning like a schoolboy sharing a joke. She touched his arm in response and followed him to a whipping post, where he bound her wrists and fastened them above her head. Three or four people gathered to watch as he snaked a cat-o-nine-tails across her plump, protruding buttocks, reddening them with graceful, loving skill.

"I'm a dreadfully jealous bitch," Laura Aurora admitted. "He always asks if he can play with someone else, but I'm afraid that one day he won't."

"Is it worth it?"

"Robin, I'xve tried the rest. Believe me, Californication is a state of heat like no other. But I've got the best, and I'm holding on tight."

"I think Buddy Tate would fit right in here," Robin mused.

"Your assassin?"

"I can't stop thinking about him, but I'm afraid to see him again. Does that sound crazy?"

"I hear it in your voice. Watch out, Robin: passion will drive you like an out-of-control car, I know. It happened with me. It wasn't with Baron, it was with a woman. We nearly killed each other. We would have driven off a cliff together if I hadn't escaped."

"I don't know what I'm getting into, but I'm getting into it, I think," Robin said, sounding rueful.

"Don't be so gloomy. The Castro Street Fair is tomorrow night. Come with us and we'll have some fun."

XVIII

The Castro Street Fair

Laura Aurora's positive nature recognised no obstacles to the daily realisation of her destiny. Nor was she conscious of the oppressive weight of humanity when it reached critical mass, as it does every year at the Castro Street Fair. She liked crowds, in fact, and as far as she was concerned, the best place to be in a Halloween crowd was at its centre. She located this as just beneath the ornate overhanging marquee of the stately movie palace, the Castro Street Theatre. That was where she had arranged to meet Baron.

But she and Robin were now three blocks from the Castro marquee, on a side street, and there were thousands of people in masquerade between them and the centre of things. Walls of noise and flesh. Beer-drinking werewolves and heavy metal hell.

Robin, who didn't at all relish the idea of being pressed up against — squeezed through — so many distorted and even disturbed strangers, had dressed down in basic survivalist black: leather vest, t-shirt, jeans, boots. But she wore a white cat mask with long whiskers.

Laura had worn one of her basic costumes too, but it wasn't self-effacing black she chose. A white garterbelt and sheer stockings drew attention to her legs, her best feature; tight red satin panties revealed the bulge of her pubic mound, and emphasised the beauty of her ass. A black leather corslet strained to cover her breasts. Her mask was home made, from a life-sized photo of her face.

Robin regarded her new friend with proper awe.

"You are fearless, aren't you?"

"I still get scared, but not so much anymore. Mostly I'm scared of wasting time. So I do what I want. I suppose someday it'll catch up with me, but meantime, I will have had some fun."

"I wish I could look at it that way."

"I look at it one day at a time — and it works."

"Was it your grandmother?"

"Oh yes. But my father, too. My mother was scared of her shadow. She let me down. I decided I liked men better. Poor bastards don't know what hit them when I come along."

She smiled at men passing near them, her eyes challenging them. "This is fun," she said. "Wild women on the loose — and a big party!"

"I don't know. Not my kind of fun, I guess."

"I love it. The noise, the lights, the spectacle. The idea of all these different people gathering to celebrate a pagan holiday. It brings out the exhibitionist in me."

"From what I've seen, it doesn't take much," Robin jibed.

"Well, why should I hide my real self from people? If you feel good about what you've got, show it off! You won't have it that long, anyway."

They turned to avoid a pack of costumed devils pushing their way through the growing crowd. There were sirens sounding and giant lights thrown up at the sky. The roar of 10,000 throats.

"How are we going to get through this?"

"I don't know. But I know Baron is waiting for us on the other side of this wall of people, so we're going to *have* to go through it."

"You're going?"

"Yes, and you with me, little one. It'll be an experience."

"But they won't move. How...?"

"Oh, yes they will." She unbuttoned her leather corslet to expose her full breasts. A piercing in her left nipple glinted. Her nipples hardened in the cool evening air.

She strode forward, parting a muscular nurse in a short white uniform from her bandaged and bloody patient. The crowd parted and she didn't hesitate. Robin followed, holding her hand so they would not be separated.

"It always works. I learned it when I was in college. It gives me more power than men get with an Uzi."

Robin was astonished to see that Laura was right. Her bared breasts acted as an open sesame on the thickly milling crowd. When a young man saw Laura's breasts aimed straight at him — coming at him as if to go through him — he gulped and ducked out of the way, his gaze locked on her bosom.

Over Laura's shoulder Robin had a fisheye view of humanity, and tried to control her fright about what she saw. At Halloween, people chose scary masks to represent or mock the dark sides of their lives, and Robin thought that many of the masks were more revealing than their wearers imagined.

They pushed forward, never pausing for fear of losing the next opening and being crushed in a whirlpool of demons. Robin saw the faces of men leering so that they seemed mask-like, and hands reaching out to almost touch Laura's breasts before she dodged and pushed into the next opening, the next crevice.

"They love us, Robin," she shouted over the noise of the crowd. Her voice was exultant, a scout in a new land.

"They want to touch you, Laura," Robin said, feeling panicky about Laura's bold display. But more than to touch, they desired to photograph, to tape Laura's breasts for instant replays and reruns throughout eternity.

Japanese tourists with faces like fat silly children shoved them at Laura's breasts, and when she side-stepped them they claimed their trophies anyway with video cameras. Because of the Evangelical Evening News, Robin knew that television was a soul-stealer; and these little cameras in the hands of amateurs horribly multiplied the opportunities for theft.

But her mask protected her, she followed, and the crowd continued to part. Fingers that Laura eluded grabbed at her, but she twisted away. It wasn't the men she minded so much, or their childish awe at seeing Laura's breasts on public display, it was the glimpse she had of her fellow beings *en masse*. Their gestures were coarse, and the expressions on faces not masked were frightening.

Maybe, she thought, *I am a snob. Too many people. My father lives on crowds, I can't. They want too much from you.*

In the middle of their passage, when she estimated they were half-way to their goal, they appeared to be trapped. Laura had stopped to pose for a newspaper photographer and the crowd had closed up all exits. Surely this time they could not escape, for the bodies were pressing against them, all the flesh forming a wall, hands reaching out...

"I love the attention, don't you?" Laura shouted, giggly with excitement.

Laura absorbed the energy coming at her from the crowd and used it to make herself stronger. Robin felt herself being drained, losing what little identity she had forged for herself from scraps found here and there. She was being swallowed by a 10,000-

legged beast that acted not on passion or instinct, but on something more primitive: the rhythm of blood, of hearts beating in unison, systole and dystole, *whup, whup, whup*....

She owned nothing, not even the moment. She was a drop of saltwater in a tidal wave, and it wouldn't have mattered where the wave took her. She felt herself being pushed and pulled by the crowd — movie stars and monsters, bikers and bad girls — holding to Laura and helpless in the uncontrollable, claustrophobic human wave.

The wave tossed them up at last under the marquee of the Castro, and there stood Baron, the centre of attention to the people immediately around him. He wore a short leather tunic, the feather in his ear and the bone in his nose. There was a whip in his hand, and a wicked look in his eyes.

Someone was dancing on the hood of a Cadillac parked before the theatre. He wore a ballgown that glittered in the marquee lights and a long blonde wig in *bouffant* style and he was trying to dance in eight inch spike heels. The crowd good-naturedly spurred him on with their applause, and then he threw himself into a sea of waving arms and was carried off, to be replaced by the next entrant in the follies, a black boy covered in silver paint, no more than sixteen and flaming. Laura embraced Baron and he stood with his arms around her watching the entertainment.

When the crowd began chanting for a woman to dance on the Cadillac's hood, Laura saw her opportunity and stepped forward. Woman had arrived.

Hands helped her up onto the hood and she stood there for a minute gazing down at her subjects, her naked breasts thrust forward, wearing a defiantly seductive smile. She shook her breasts and rolled her hips, and when she had their attention she spoke in a loud voice:

"I am your girlfriend. I am your wife. I am your lover. I am the eternal woman! My dance is hers — and it is sacred!"

And she began her intoxicating dance, moving slowly at first as the crowd clapped the rhythm, then faster, until she was almost whirling. She danced, and she looked out over the crowd — her audience — with the eyes of Salome. She danced, and the collective energy of the crowd moved in her. She was eternal. Her gestures had been there from the beginning — each turn of her wrists, each movement of her hands, each shimmy of her breasts and hips, each offering movement of her pelvis and her thighs.

"Go! Go! Go!" the crowd screamed as she danced for them, her breasts bouncing and her hair flying, a look of ecstasy on her face.

Baron moved close to the Cadillac so that, at the climax of her dance, Laura could dive into his arms. Robin was enchanted.

"I guess I got too wild," Laura gasped, exhilarated.

"You are never too wild, my darling," Baron assured her.

"I wasn't the dancer — I was just being danced."

Baron and Robin hugged her. "Let's find some place to sit down before I fall down," Laura said.

XIX
Baring Her Bosom

They managed to push their way through the crowd to a coffee shop not far from the theatre. Magically, there was a table for three next to a window overlooking Castro Street, which swarmed with darting beauty and contrasts like an aquarium full of tropical fish. The coffee shop was warm and noisy.

Laura moved her chair so that she could watch the street. Baron lounged regally, content in himself and cheerfully patient in the intervals between actions. Robin stirred her *cafe latte*, recovering her individuality, such as it was, thinking that so far friendship with Laura was a series of initiations taking her further away from her father and deeper into herself.

A small boy with black hair cut in a pageboy brought water to the table. He asked Baron about the silver bone in his nose.

"It's beautiful," he said admiringly.

"That's what it's for," Baron told him. "Just to be beautiful."

Robin sipped her coffee. When she looked up again, a

video camera was being pointed at her. The bearer of this bad tiding was a young woman with frizzy brunette hair and a distracted look. Her body was hidden in a costume: she was a nun, asking for confession. She addressed Laura.

"Wow, that was something. You were a goddess out there!"

The woman's enthusiasm buoyed Laura. "It's simple but effective — your costume."

"It's my sister's habit. She really is a nun."

"Well..." Laura cocked an eyebrow at the camera.

"Oh — can I interview you? I have a show on cable, and we cover all kinds of wild things. Alternative ways of seeing things, from modern art to modern primitives."

"What do you want to ask me?"

"Throwing yourself topless into a crowd like that took a lot of guts."

Emboldened by her dance, Laura seized the opportunity to address San Francisco. She was impish: "I suppose I could talk about my tits."

"Would you mind... showing them while we talk?"

Laura looked down at her bosom and slowly undid the loops holding the corslet over her breasts. Baron watched benignly. Robin pushed her chair out of camera range.

Laura Aurora held her breasts in her hands for the interviewer and cable viewers. Delicately, she pulled on a nipple ring to make her brown nipple stand up. When she spoke her voice seemed to issue from her breasts.

"You have to start somewhere to educate people about the power of sexuality. Why not breasts? If you think about it, naked breasts can't be exploited as easily as clothed breasts. What we hide, we fear or we covet, don't you think?"

The interviewer wasn't prepared for Laura's thoughtfulness. Serious talk wasn't the point of her show; exploitation was.

"Yes, but... why don't you tell us why you went topless to

the Castro Street Fair?"

"It was an experiment to prove how powerful a woman's breasts are. It doesn't hurt that I'm an exhibitionist, too."

"Nobody tried to grab you?"

"A few tried, but out of 10,000, that's not bad. I think that if every woman in California went topless, in a few weeks people wouldn't even notice tits, any more than a guy with no shirt."

"But wouldn't you be afraid of being touched all the time?"

"No more so than I would be of someone I didn't know touching my cheek, or my hair."

"I don't know. I don't think I could do it."

"Scared the boys might go crazy?"

"My breasts are pretty large."

"No comment, darling. Why don't *you* show us?"

She blushed. "No...I don't think I have the nerve."

"Maybe it's because you underestimate your power."

"Were you always outspoken like this? I mean, how did you grow up? What did your mother say about you going topless?"

"I grew up in a world of tight women in tight dresses getting tight, dear. They did not approve. My mother saw her breasts as assets, and you don't spend your assets."

"Sounds like Orange County to me."

"Actually, it was a little farther south. Republican country — knee deep in reactionary doo-doo."

"Things have changed since then."

"Not so you'd notice, where I grew up. Those people would vote for Hitler if he could be brought back in a blue blazer and khakis. And if he could be, they would!"

"So — they would be shocked if they could see you now?"

"Well, fear and shock are all they've got to hold on to. This is a pretty scary country right now for those kind of people who are scared of breasts. The economy is the worst since my grandmother's times, there are nuts with bombs and germs and nerve gas running around killing people. We've got earthquakes and plagues and floods and it's just driving people crazy. These are toxic times, fearful times."

The interviewer was getting nervous. Opinionated breasts were too bizarre for her show. She tried again to bring the conversation to an upbeat conclusion:

"I don't really see what going topless has to do with all the dreadful things that have been happening in the world, but I think it's wonderful that you've been willing to share your views *and* your breasts with us...."

She hurried off, on the track of oddities less opinionated.

Laura chuckled. "I don't think she liked what I had to say."

"But the camera liked what it saw, and that's what counts, isn't it?" Baron said.

"I guess that was another segment of my fifteen minutes of fame. Next time they can focus on my ass. Wait till they hear what I've got to say about *that*!"

XX
The Hot Spring

Fascinated with her new friends, Robin agreed to accompany them to a secluded hot spring in the mountains. They would soak in the hot pools and lie naked in the sun. There would be interesting people, good food, perhaps even a few rituals. This was the real California life, living well in defiance of the customary order of things.

Robin thought Dollar would enjoy a holiday, but she wasn't to be found. Maybe she had gone to visit her family, in yet another attempt to make peace with them.

Baron chauffeured them in an old blue Volvo station wagon decorated with stickers and dents. Robin sat in the back seat with Laura, who held forth on a variety of topics while stroking Robin's thighs.

Without telling Baron, they had shared some mushrooms.

"You know just where to touch me," Robin sighed, her attention concentrated on the parts of her body Laura was exploring. Laura's fingers delicately traced the outline of

Robin's slit, moved in wave motions around her clitoris, and entered her vagina.

"There's nothing like being played with in the back seat of a car," Laura breathed in Robin's ear. Robin spread her legs wider, propping her feet on the front seat. She saw Baron watching them in his rear-view mirror and smiled guiltily at him. He winked back.

"Want to join us, darling?" Laura invited her husband. Robin wanted him to say yes, but he demurred.

"There's plenty of time to play when we get there. But you two have fun."

He steered confidently around the endless switchbacks that took them up into the cool mountains. The air was dry and fragrant.

"I'm floating," Robin said dreamily. She snuggled cosily against Laura's bosom, waves of sensation splashing between her legs.

"You were born to be played with, Robin. You're so creamy and juicy..." Laura moved from the seat to the floor of the Volvo and plunged her head between Robin's thighs. Soon Robin felt the most incredible licking, magnified by the effect the mushrooms were having on her, so that the pleasure seemed to build and build with no imaginable end. What kicked her over the edge was looking up to see Baron watching them in the rear-view mirror.

❖❖❖

They arrived at the hot spring in the late afternoon and went immediately to the room they'd reserved. It was on the second floor of a sprawling old building with porches running its length on both floors.

They undressed and prepared to go for a dip in the warm

pool. Robin felt some initial trepidation at the prospect of appearing naked before strangers, She was not unhappy with her body — it was tanned and toned, and her tattoos and piercings highlighted its beauty — but she felt shame about her scar, even if it was covered over with Star's design. She envied the unaffected self-confidence Laura and Baron projected both clothed and nude. Laura's body sagged a little, but Baron somehow defied age. It was his bearing, Robin thought. The mushrooms let her see that he was a warrior from an heroic age on another world. All he lacked was a spear, but on their way up the long path that led to the bathhouse and pool area he found a piece of gnarled manzanita he used as a staff.

Soft, warm, fragrant breezes flowed over her nakedness. Nearby someone played a flute. The tall trees rustled dry leaves. It was like entering the Garden of Eden, with happy naked people everywhere. Of course she was used to seeing strange women naked in locker rooms, but here were naked men of all shapes and sizes, sitting and lying around on large wooden decks as if nakedness were the natural order of things. She followed Laura Aurora and Baron up the steps to the warm pool and slipped into the water. It was silky and full of minerals. Men and women stood and sat in it, their bodies like silver ghosts viewed through the water.

It was like returning to the womb. Silence was the rule, so the only sound she heard was the slapping of the water against the stone sides of the pool. A man moved slowly through the water cradling a woman floating on the surface, swirling her slowly in circles while she lay back in complete trust. Laura read Robin's mind — they were sisters of the mushroom — and cradled Robin against her breasts, pulling her over the surface of the water, which was kept at body temperature. For Robin, it was like amniotic fluid. She was warm and protected and fed and loved, and, she realised: *It is always like this —*

miraculously beautiful, all the time. I just don't allow myself to see it. But this is the way it always is: soft breezes, flowers, lapping water, gentle, loving people.... If only she could see things this way all the time, she might be convinced of the truth of this perception.

Everything was holy — but not holy like her father meant it. Whole. Complete. Of a piece.

❖❖❖

Dinner was vegetarian and delicious. They sat on the deck outside the dining room with a view of the dark ridges of mountains at dusk. In a clearing below, two deer foraged.

"I feel so relaxed I could melt," Robin said.

"You were cut out for this life," Laura replied. "Don't you think, Baron?"

"She certainly looks happy."

Robin blushed at this. Happiness was not an attribute she felt comfortable with. Satisfied, sometimes, but happy?

"I don't believe in happiness."

"You will when we get done with you, honey," Laura joked.

"When you were pulling me through the water, I felt that I was experiencing things as they really are — and then when we came out, I lost it."

"If you saw it once, you can always get back to it."

"How?"

"There are all kinds of ways. Drugs..." Here she smirked at the little secret they shared — "sex, ritual."

Robin thought of the crucifixion of Baron as a turning point in the growth she felt inside. An upside-down ritual.

"I'm still digesting what you did with Baron on the Cross."

"It's all in the realm of magic," Laura Aurora said. "The tattoo you got from Star was meant to have the effect of helping

148 Dark Matter

you to realise your own individual magic. That's what body modification and ritual is about."

"Shall we tell Robin about tonight? Or just blindfold her and take her along?" Baron asked.

"I don't think Robin is ready to proceed on that level of trust," Laura replied, reading the reluctance on Robin's face.

"What's happening tonight?"

"There's a ritual in the mountain lodge. A shaman with great powers will be leading it for some people who've come just to see him."

❖❖❖

They had to climb through the manzanita to get to the mountain lodge. They each had flashlights, and so did the shadows who climbed on the zigzag path ahead of them and after them. The stars were out and the moon was coming up to illuminate the inky blackness. Robin's breath burned in her throat with the exertion of climbing. She could hear Laura's rapid breathing on the trail behind her. Baron was striding far ahead, using his staff to help him stay balanced.

The mountain lodge was a simple teahouse structure, most of it a deck so everyone could be outside. The view was of a valley and mountains in the distance. It was a clear night and the universe was displaying itself in the form of billions of points of light winking down at them.

The deck was crowded with naked brown people wearing piercings, feathers and leathers. Unlike the more restrained group at Baron's crucifixion, these people were talking animatedly and showing off the art work on their bodies. Lamps gave off a soft ochre light. Fireflies twinkled.

Robin was introduced to most of the people in attendance. These were pagans, modern primitives, people who celebrated their bodies, and of course Laura Aurora counted them all as old friends. Everyone had a piece of news for her as they walked around. People spoke often of the shaman from San Francisco who would perform a ritual of the body for them this evening. One of Laura's friends had heard that he was a homeless person, a beggar on the streets. Another was heard to say that this man was a shape-shifter. He appeared in various places playing different roles — whatever you required at the time. He was a Native American whose body manipulations made him an elder of the tribes. Someone else said he was the resident ghost.

A haunting tune, gay but monotonous, was struck up on a portable electronic piano, and the gathering hushed. Once again Robin had the disconcerting feeling that she was about to witness a religious ceremony, but this time she looked forward to it.

A white-haired Indian in his sixties appeared among them. *Where did he come from?* Robin wondered. One minute he wasn't there on the deck, and the next minute he was the centre of attention. He wore a tight leather corset so that he seemed wasp-waisted. He wore a garter belt, fishnet stockings, high heels, a gold watch and an amulet around his neck.

She thought of Baron. Obviously he and the shaman had something in common. The shaman bowed to the four directions, taking from a leather bag at his waist a pinch of something he sprinkled around him, and around a bench. Next to the bench a table held a number of small glass globes.

When the shaman moved, he made a jingling sound. Robin's jaw dropped when she saw what was making the sound. He wore two ampallangs through the head of his penis, and his scrotum was distended so that it hung half-way down his thigh. Later Laura would tell her that his testicles were solid brass.

His big-nosed face was imperious, but Robin was surprised to see that he was missing a tooth when he called out to someone inside the lodge. A dark man in his forties with black curly hair entered, wearing only a black leather pouch for his sex.

"It's Markus Bloom," Laura whispered into Robin's ear. "He's a friend of ours — someone I'd like you to meet."

"What's this ritual about?"

"Exorcising demons."

Markus Bloom lay prone on the bench. The shaman tied his wrists with black silk cord. Lighting a taper, the shaman used its small flame to heat the inside of the glass globe he picked up. The heat created suction when the open neck of the globe was applied to Markus Bloom's back. Slowly, as the music played, the shaman applied a dozen heated globes to Bloom, with each one raising a large bump of flesh. It must have hurt, Robin thought, but Bloom made no sound.

As a finale, the shaman then took a stick and began to play on those cups, with piano accompaniment electronically tinkling up to the stars. When he finished, the crowd applauded delicately, and he bowed with great dignity. After he had removed the globes from Markus Bloom's back, the shaman moved around the deck greeting people. The ritual, although mild next to Baron's crucifixion, made an equally strong impression on Robin. She left Laura's side and went over to the bench where Markus Bloom sat. His heavy-lidded eyes and the dark circles under then gave him the look of a satyr, she thought.

"Who are you?" he growled.

"My name's Robin Flood"

"How'd you get here?"

"I came with my friend Laura Aurora. And Baron."

He was intimidating her with his rudeness, and she didn't

like it; but she couldn't just walk away. She had to ask.

"What do you want?"

"What was it like?"

"The cupping?"

"Yes — the cupping."

"Like holes were being drilled in me with lasers."

"Oh."

"What's the matter?"

"It didn't seem to hurt you."

"It's not the hot cups. It's pulling the devils out."

"What do you mean?"

"He means that when you've lived as long as we have, you're bound to attract some negative energy you're better off not carrying around." It was Laura, who was accompanied by the shaman. She leaned down to kiss the surly Markus Bloom, and turned to introduce the shaman to Robin.

"Robin, I'd like you to meet Inigahi."

"What you did was beautiful," Robin said to him.

He grunted, looking sceptically at her. What was wrong? Why was he staring at her without speaking?

"So — you're Robin, he said at last, almost mournfully, as if he'd heard reports of her far and wide. Laura Aurora caught the tone in his voice.

"Do you know Robin?"

"I've heard about her from a friend of mine, Buddy Tate."

"*Buddy Tate*?" Robin echoed disbelievingly. She didn't know what else to say. She felt disorientated. Buddy belonged to the city, to the scene they'd played out in the Hotel Napa. What would a shaman have to do with a bad boy like Buddy Tate?

"Have you seen him?"

"He's looking for you."

"He's looking for someone else, not me."

"He's not gonna give up." The Indian's certainty shocked

her even more. She was lost in the realm of magic. She had always before been able to keep the different parts of her life in separate, tidy compartments. Now everything was running together: what was going on?

Markus was interested. His dark brown eyes stared so intently at her she felt them pierce her defences. She looked away.

"Wait a minute. Is this Buddy Tate person a tall kid with long red hair?"

"Yes. Do you know him too?" Robin asked, staggered by this further evidence that the world was indeed magical.

"We had an encounter a few years ago. He was just a kid, but he stood out. He was weird, I guess is what it was, and usually I'm the weirdest person on the scene. It was just that once that we met, but I've never forgotten him. He's well-hung."

Robin sank down on the bench and Markus put his arm around her. Laura was talking with the shaman, who kept looking at Robin as if trying to make up his mind about something. He nodded his head at last, but Robin could see that he wasn't happy.

Laura sat on the other side of Robin and pulled her to her bosom. "I've convinced Inigahi to perform the ritual on you that he did on Markus." She stroked Robin's neck.

"What? Why would I do that?"

"Because it's the one you need to help your pain. He can draw those devils out of you. It's the next step in your transformation."

"But he doesn't like me. Why would he do it?"

"He says that he's watching out for Buddy Tate's luck, and that you're part of it. He has no choice. He says you have a lot of bad stuff in you that needs to be pulled out."

Robin let herself be led to the bench. Laura helped her off with her leather jacket. She was naked under it. She straddled the bench and lay face down while the shaman bound her hands. The wood was hard against her bare breasts, and she felt a chill of apprehension. She had lost control...

She closed her eyes and breathed deeply through her nostrils, hearing from far away the tinkle of the piano. She was more frightened than she had been since she was a child being punished by her father. But this wasn't punishment. This was healing, this cupped heat that bored holes into her being, heat that sucked at something lodged inside her, something hard that would not be moved made of loathing and fear. She felt herself trembling, but it wasn't *her* trembling, she was floating out of her body looking down on the shaman working on her, wondering why she didn't cry out. She felt her flesh rising in a dozen places, pulling at her tattoo, sucking her shoulder blades up like grotesque small wings. And still the thing inside would not let go, its claws hooked like iron in her.

The shaman removed the globes one by one, each one with a little popping sound that returned her in stages to her body, to the weight of her body, to the reality of the night. Then he slumped to the ground, exhausted by his effort of trying to pull into his own body the demon that lived in hers.

Robin wept. The people closest helped the shaman to his feet. Laura and Baron and Markus Bloom tended to Robin, who was limp, and sobbing something Laura didn't understand at first.

"Asmodeus in me, Asmodeus in me... *in me! in me!*"

XXI
Running into the Future

I woke up screaming in my head, with everybody dead. There was a monster in the room, and it was me. Me breathing like a monster, my tongue licking like a monster at the dry roof of my mouth. Monster me, monster mouth.

I was scared big time, but I don't dwell on things. Just make the next move. I had to take a morning crap but not in that bathroom. I had no heart to smell my stink mixing with the smell of Dollar's death stink.

So I packed my duffel and put the K. Farouk pistol in my pocket and left the Hotel Napa burning.

You know how it is when you don't feel like cleaning up. The room was a mess with blood all over the place and the bed like Custer's last fucking stand and bodies in the bathroom. I didn't feel like explaining it to anyone who might want to put me away. I found bottles of nail polish remover and alcohol and matches and made a party with some newspapers I threw on the bed. Just let the laws of physics take care of the rest. Then I took off down the back stairs and was history before the first alarm sounded.

The streets of the Tenderloin were nasty. I walked around looking at people's faces and getting more and more depressed. Every face I saw needed shoving in. Ugly faces that didn't see me.

Maybe I killed a guy. Maybe he was still alive and burning up, I didn't give a bat shit. But that didn't give them the right to look at me like that. Like I was nothing.

I headed up to Chinatown past its fruit stands, and then to North Beach with its fruits. I could hear fire engines.

Then I did feel looked at. I stopped before a store window selling leather jackets and cowboy hats and saw a cop car reflected in it, with the cop riding, shotgun staring hard at me. I walked on fast, and when I turned a corner they were gone, but the hairs were still standing up on the backs of my hands. Like a fucking werewolf, I wasn't used to being out in daylight, in the bright sun.

On the next block a line was forming at a bus stop. I looked around and there was the cop car, so I joined the line and kept my head down. The old lady in front of me on line said the bus would take us to a television studio, and I gave her the old ten carat smile. Television? Me? We were made for each other. The show was offering free tickets. I didn't recognise the name of the host, but I knew that inside the bus, inside the studio, there wouldn't be cops. It was funny: it took a hell of a lot to get on television, and nothing at all. I laughed and got on the bus.

It was a new talk show, one I didn't know about. They packed us in on tiers of chairs looking down at the set where the host would interview people. One of the cameras was right next to me.

The host was a porky guy who looked like he was pissed off

at everything. He came bouncing on the set, the applause sign flashed, we clapped, and the cameras turned to the studio audience to look at us looking at him. I knew a camera had shown my face on local TV before, but it wasn't a thrill. This was rinky-dink.

The theme of the programme was 'Predictions for the Year 2000'. If they asked members of the studio audience about that, and they came to me, I'd tell them the truth: the future's going to happen anyway, no matter what we say. The future's got it all figured out.

I watched for a while, and then I tuned out. The fat lady sitting next to me had an elbow in my ribs and I turned to tell her that. When I looked back to the set, there was my friend Anyguy. Dressed up, but it was Anyguy.

What was he doing on television?

The host said, "This is an honour, Chief... Inigahi?"

"I'm not a chief. I told you not to call me that."

"But you're a descendant of chiefs."

"My grandfather called himself a healer."

"And, I believe, your tribe lived around here. Isn't that what you told us?"

"I am descended from the Ohlone people, who lived here in peace until they lost their luck. Now there are no more full blooded Ohlones — my uncle was the last. I'm part Welsh, myself."

"Can you say a few words in your language?"

"I can't speak it. No one's alive to speak it."

I could tell Anyguy didn't like the host or his questions. I thought he'd probably pull out his knife and scalp the fat bastard if he wasn't treated right.

"They say that you have powers other people don't have. Some even say that you're a shaman."

"I can see into the future," Anyguy told him. He said it matter-of-factly, like "I have to go take a piss."

"That's a pretty big claim, isn't it?"

Anyguy had that 'look-out' look in his eye.

"Look, asshole, (they bleeped that, I'll bet) I don't say anything that's not true. You asked me to come on your show."

"Right chief. Suppose, since we've got a new century coming up, that you tell us a little bit about what we can expect."

"You'll lose your show," Anyguy said. He was sour.

"What?"

"I've said what I know."

Watching Anyguy on the set was just like talking to him on the street. He was mean-tempered and bull-headed. He could go toe to toe with Daddy, I think.

"Well, we'll worry about that later," the host said, but he looked nervous.

"It's gonna be bad. Worse than this century. A lot of hungry ghosts riding straight at us."

"What do you mean, ghosts?"

"Dead people walking. Blinking their eyes. What do you think I mean? All kinds of evil things are coming."

"Sounds like you agree with a lot of fundamentalist Christians."

"I don't agree with those bastards about anything. I said ghosts will be coming — not angels."

"Well?"

"What?" They were practically yelling at each other.

"Is that it? Ghosts are what you see in the future?"

"I said *lots* of them."

There was a break and they hustled him off. I hurried to catch up with him. He was surprised to see me.

"What are you doing here?"

"Staying off the street. What the hell were you doing on television?"

"They paid real folding money. $500 to talk to the old Indian and make fun of him. I guess I set them straight."

"Jesus. You were only on five minutes."

"I told them something for their money, didn't I?"

"Ghosts. Jesus Christ."

The sun was bright on the sidewalk outside the studio. A limousine pulled out of traffic and stopped at the curb in front of us. He opened the door just like he owned it, but I figured transportation for him was part of the deal. He waved me in, and climbed in beside me. He leaned forward to rap on the partition and we took off. He sank back into the leather and closed his eyes. "I hate television."

"Television is God."

"Shit you say, boy."

"I want to see my face spread across the biggest television screen in the world. Someday — this is my prediction — they're going to hang one in space, maybe from the moon, so the whole world can watch it. And you know what? It'll be my face that's on that big screen, and everybody in the world will see it."

"Let's say that happens..."

"It *has* to happen. Don't forget, you're watching out for my luck. That's what the future holds for Buddy."

"But what would you say?"

"You mean once I'm up there? Once I'm famous?"

"Tell me."

"Don't worry, I've got ideas." But I knew I didn't.

He just looked at me a long time, like he was reading in my eyes what I hadn't said to him yet. He was waiting, and he had the time.

"You remember that hot girl, Dollar?"

"I guess I do."

"I found her cut up in the bathroom at the Hotel Napa. Somebody cut her bad."

He groaned. "Is she dead?"

"She's way past dead. He cut out her cooch."

He groaned again, like there was a creature inside him.

"Who's he? Who's the son of a bitch who did it?"

I told him about Dollar's brother then, and what he'd said. "Flood."

He shook his head. Shook it again. "That preacher?"

"I got to kill him, Anyguy. That's the way the future has to go. It'll be like stepping on a big bug."

"She wants you to do it, doesn't she?"

"I'm sure if Dollar could talk, she would want me to."

"I mean Robin Flood. She wants you to."

"How'd you know about that?" I felt a chill run down the back of my neck and I sat up straight on the plush leather seat. We were driving through a park, past a giant old building with marble columns. I didn't want to hear his answer. He had me spooked. He had my head turned around the wrong way.

"She told me herself."

"And just when did she do that?"

"Last night, up in the mountains. That's why I have this limo. I've been travelling."

"Tell me where she is, and I'll go talk to her."

"She doesn't want to see you, Buddy. I don't know where she went."

I knew it didn't matter to him if I didn't believe that. He wouldn't tell me no matter what I did. I knew he had made up his mind.

"So that's the long and short of it? She wants to stay clear of me?"

"She's got something holding onto her insides. I tried to get it out, but it is very strong."

"Her father."

"That's the way I see it."

"I guess there's no way around that, is there?"

"You've got blood in your eye, Buddy."

"You want his scalp as a souvenir?"

"I want his dick in a mayonnaise jar."

I was ready as I ever would be. He dropped me off at the bus station and I took the next bus south, headed into the future.

XXII

Pagan Goddess

Look out, Thomas Flood, Buddy Tate's comin' at you.

Knowing you're going to kill someone that everyone wants killed is a very pure feeling. Figuring out exactly how to do it is confusing. In LA I took a taxi to North Hollywood, which is where the Parousia Foundation had its offices and church and television studio. We drove around until I found a cheap motel not far from Thomas Flood's stomping grounds. It was a semi-sleazy neighbourhood with a lot of bars and pool halls, but when you walked by the buildings of the Parousia Foundation, there everything was kept up just right. The grass was clipped, the hedges were trimmed, and everything was freshly painted.

I walked around the whole operation a couple of times and didn't have a clue what to do next. Then, outside a building I spotted a big sign for 'TV Studio' and followed it to what must have been the entrance. It was closed, but there was a big board with announcements on it — signs telling about the Crusade for San Francisco that was coming up, and signs for classes and workshops, and then a schedule for the Evangelical Evening News. Flood was going to be in the studio tomorrow afternoon. Free tickets were offered, so I went to get one. At least tomorrow I could go see what would be involved.

I went back to the motel and took a nap, and dreamed about Robin. She was kissing me and turning me on but when I reached down to feel her pussy she was cut up like Dollar. I woke up with a hard-on I felt bad about. Even after a cold shower it wouldn't go down all the way. I got dressed and went out to take a walk, led by my dick on a midnight prowl.

I don't like bars because boring people get drunk in them, but where else do you find girls in a strange neighbourhood? The first and second places I walked into were Spanish, and the next one was full of faggots, but then I got lucky. The guys sitting around the bar drinking and talking looked like Christmas was coming. Maybe they were just happy it was pay-day, but they were grinning and punching shoulders like high school kids. Even though I didn't see any women, I ordered a beer and sat down. You could tell something was going to happen. It was the way the bartender was nervous about giving me a beer. Everybody was expecting something.

When she walked in I knew right away she was what they were expecting. She was something all right. Every man in the place watched her strut down the bar. They each said hello, or whistled. She was probably Spanish, but she was wearing a red wig. She had a narrow waist, big ta-tas, and an ass to file in your memory book. You could tell she was a hooker by the way she looked at them, as if she was figuring how long this business would take. She was dressed for action: halter, skirt, boots.

"Hey, Marcy, me first!" an old guy at the end of the bar yelled, and everybody laughed. It was a party and she was the cake.

I wondered where it would happen. There was a dark room off the bar with a pool table. That would do.

"I'm in a hurry," she said impatiently. "My babysitter's on overtime now." She took off her little red jacket, put it on the bar.

"Maybe we should draw straws," one guy said, like we might go one at a time and wait for our turn. Dweeb didn't get it.

"First, I want my money," she told them. "First things first." Wallets were out in a flash. The bartender headed for me, but not to ask if I wanted a refill.

"This is kind of a private party. I'm closing up."

"How much to join the fun? Or maybe just watch?"

"You have to ask Marcy."

"Here's a twenty to put in the pot. That'd be about it, right?"

"Yeah, I guess so. But you have to be a gentleman. And wear protection."

Gang bang. I know that PC lesbofems are horrified by the thought, but it's just a woman's power, natural and inborn, being used to raise some cash. A fair deal for all. With a gang bang with a whore, not only is the price right, but the woman's right. She has got to be hotter than a pistol and cooler than a rock if she's willing to take on fifteen guys — that's how many I counted heading into the dark pool room — at the same time. Everyone knows what it's about, and the schedule is pretty strict: get on, get off, no bullshit, here's your twenty, thank you ma'am.

Of course there's male bonding. Guys like teams. Makes them feel secure to have their best buds with them on important occasions, sharing life's little joys — like Miss Marcy. With Marcy, they could play a team sport again. It says something when you think that one woman is the equal of fifteen horny guys.

They could be boys together again enjoying a woman the way she was built to be enjoyed. No romantic muss and fuss, just the old in and out. She would strut home with a good day's pay.

Someone turned the light on. A bare bulb over the pool table.

The bartender locked the door and it was quiet. Marcy counted the money on the bar slowly and methodically, putting it in piles. When she was satisfied she had enough to make it worth her while, she said, "Three at a time only. Everybody has to wear protection. No kissing on the lips. And I don't like pain." She bent over to unzip her boots and I saw her bare ass.

I joined the dog pack following the bitch in heat.

Marcy climbed up on the pool table and put her knees up, bracing her feet against the edge. When one of the guys brought his rolled-up coat for her to use as a pillow, she adjusted her wig before putting her head back, and let this glazed look come over her that I remembered from my times with LaDonna, my whore back home. She was powerful.

"All right. Who's first? I hurt my leg on my bike yesterday, so be careful of that."

Zippers came down, and the guy who'd suggested drawing straws was first in line. He acted embarrassed, but you could see he was so hot to get his dick wet nothing else mattered to him. He was a dog, that's all he was. His tongue was hanging out — but it's not easy, being first.

You could tell he was self-conscious, climbing up on the pool table with her, but he couldn't help himself. After all, his pants were down around his ankles, his white ass was up in the air, and he was first up at bat.

Somehow he got it in. She sighed, and turned her head for more cock. A tall guy knelt on the table and was able to reach her mouth with his rod. She French-kissed his purple knob. I was standing close to them, enjoying the sounds she made:

the guy rooting in her cunt, big hand on her boob, jiggling it, the beautiful wet sound of pussy giving and taking, and her slurping as she sucked the tall guy — she was amazing.

It was like a race to see who'd be in the old swimming hole first after that. Shoes clunked to the floor, pants came down, guys stood around rolling rubbers on their weenies.

The guy who went first grunted and got down, and somebody else climbed on. I couldn't see Marcy's tits because hands were constantly squeezing them. Everything flickered and flowed. I'd concentrate on one scene, stroking myself, and then something else would happen. Marcy worked hard and gave value for her money.

I had something special in mind, so I waited my turn with her. Watching's not fucking, but it can get you hot. Fifteen guys, young, old, fat, thin, in between, going primitive over a hot slut on a pool table is not a scene you're ever likely to forget. Just the sounds and the smells made you happy to be alive, a man with his dick in his hand.

She said only three at time, but I watched her take on six at a time and barely work up a sweat. She was on her knees on the green table on top of a hairy guy with his dick up her cunt, while a muscular black dude knelt behind her with his meat buried between her cheeks. She had a dick in each hand and was giving head to two more at the same time. She was sweating and breathing hard when they let her breathe, but you could see in her eyes that it was touchdown time.

I wanted her ass so bad I thought I'd snap the condom waiting for it to be free. When the black guy climbed down from the table I saw the brown target of opportunity winking at me and I couldn't stand it. I climbed up on the table, put my arms around her waist and grabbed her tits for grips so I could shove my johnson into glory.

God damn, it was just like hot butter. I shivered, it felt so good. I could feel the hairy dude's meat on the other side of the wall of flesh separating us, and it was like Marcy wasn't there, that she was only a tool we were using to rub our big ones together. Close as we all were, though — she still had her hands and mouth full — we only touched through Marcy.

I moved back so I could watch her butt cheeks as I moved the big red one in and out, in and out. They were plump, white, and tattooed with just two words, one on each cheek: Pagan Goddess.

I put my hands over the words and pulled her hard back against me. The muscles of her asshole milked me and I couldn't hold back anymore. I came like King Kong.

I was wiped out. She was still going. Guys were standing around with their dicks at half-mast sneaking peeks like after a football game. They were faggots, just like me. But I guess that's what it was about: all men are faggots at a gang bang.

XXIII

Buddy in the Lion's Den

When I went out for breakfast the next day the streets were crowded with buses. It was the faithful, come from all over Southern California to see Flood and show off their illnesses on the Evangelical Evening News.

Their lumpy bodies and hopeful faces and bright clothes made me sick, but I realised that if I wanted to get close to Flood I had to look like them. I'd have to behave like them. Just pretend I'm somebody else, and not Buddy Tate.

After breakfast (huevos rancheros for under $3.00, a bargain), I walked myself to a Salvation Army not far from my motel and bought some bright clothes that I looked like a stupid golfer in. A Spanish-American gentleman gave me a haircut so short I could feel the sun on my scalp burning it.

When I thought I could pass for a hypocrite, I walked over to the Parousia Foundation and joined hundreds of people in lines like ants waiting to get into the auditorium of the studio. While I waited, I kept my sunglasses on so people wouldn't see what I was thinking about them. There was tons of security — suits watching the lines, cops in uniform, even a helicopter in the sky.

A favourite fantasy of mine is to shoot down helicopters — one of the favourite weapons of the Republicrat police state, Daddy says. I always laugh when one of them crashes. One less eye in the sky.

There was a metal detector and more guards but I walked right in. I was just another stupid golfer. I was early enough that I was able to get an aisle seat not too far from the stage. Sat down next to a pregnant woman wearing a blue maternity dress.

Sitting next to her was a face I wouldn't forget. He was the dweeb from last night's gang bang who went first. No wonder he'd been in a hurry to get his ticket punched, I thought. Seeing the size of his wife's belly you could guess he hadn't had anything more than a charity hand job in months.

Everybody keeps fucking secret, but then when it's big belly time, they're saying to the whole world: we've been fucking!

She had giant jugs sitting up there on top of her belly. She hadn't noticed it, but one of them was leaking, and there was a wet spot below her left nipple. I imagined how hard they would be with milk in them. I wondered how I could touch them without her noticing.

They could make me a hypocrite on the outside, but inside my head, I was still Buddy Tate. I started to get stiff, so I looked at the stage, where the set of the Evangelical Evening News was big and bright and full of technicians getting things ready. It was like a rock show when they started. Loud music, hymns from a choir in white robes. Maybe the Rolling Old Bones would come on. People were getting excited and waving their Bibles in the air. It was a big auditorium. Thousands of people waiting for one man to come on stage. For a minute

I felt depressed that it wasn't me they were waiting for, then I felt a surge of power and it didn't matter. Sooner or later I was going to shoot the man they were waiting for. Cancel him out — then they'd turn their attention to me.

Kill, my insides said. It was like there were headlines inside my head: *Buddy Tate Shoots Thomas Flood!* I was going to send the hypocrite from hell to his place in glory land with other great victims: George Wallace, J.F.K., John Lennon, Ronald Reagan, Bobby Kennedy. When the roll was called up yonder, he'd be there. Or maybe down yonder.

The whole place stood to sing a song that wasn't a hymn. I stood up and moved my lips while I stared at the wet spot growing under the belly's left tit. She caught me looking and looked down at herself and turned red as a beet. It was turning me on.

"In a sinful world swimming in pornography,
We stand up, O Christ, for common decency.
Stand up, stand up, for common decency!"

That's what it sounded like, but they didn't pass out the words. Everybody knew them by heart. The singing went on and on and the belly kept distracting me. I can't be let out in polite company. If the fight song hadn't ended when it did, I might have reached out to stroke that belly.

Saved by the Reverend Thomas Flood from my dirty mind.

He came out fast holding his arms up in the air and lifting his eyebrows. He started the show with a prayer, which is handy for getting your audience to see things your way. After the prayer he sat down with a sidekick and they yakked about gloom and doom in the news. Since I wasn't in it, I didn't care about the news. But then he started on pornography and I sat up straight and paid attention. He was talking about leading a crusade to San Francisco, and he sounded pretty excited.

I looked around me and the faces were mean and stupid.

They'd follow him in their buses to what he called Sodom by the Sea and burn the Pussy Palaces and lynch the faggots. Punish the perverts.

The belly had put her hand over her breast to cover that wet spot. She looked like she was pledging allegiance to Flood. No matter how hard I stared at her, she wouldn't look at me. I didn't exist. I saw her husband checking me out and I winked at him and he sat back and watched the show. He remembered me, too.

I couldn't stop myself. I moved my arm so that it brushed against her big full titty. Five points. She still didn't look at me. I moved my arm up and down so that I could feel the full shape of it. I thought I should stop, but I couldn't. I did pull my arm back and try to behave when she looked at me like she was begging me to stop. Pleading with her eyes.

I guess she knew she was trapped. Her husband wouldn't defend her, and she was too self-conscious to stand up and be the centre of attention. I could molest her all I wanted.

Before I could put my hand on her leg I forced myself to pay attention to Flood. I had business to do. If I let myself be distracted I'd miss the right moment. I didn't know what I was going to do, but I wanted to be ready for it.

They made a general call for sick people in the audience to come up and let Flood lay his healing hands on them and I decided I should go up. I was sick, wasn't I?

I walked down the aisle with a bunch of cripples and old people, hating every step but forcing myself. The lights up there were brighter than I expected, so I guess I looked stunned climbing the steps to the set. It was the right look — a stunned golfer — for the role I was playing. There was a very long line, and it was a big stage. I looked into the audience for the belly, but the lights were too bright. Tried to decide what to say to Flood if I actually got close to him. Should I tell him

I had AIDS and that he had given it to me? Should I tell him I fucked his daughter and haven't recovered?

It might be my only chance to get close to him. Maybe I could grab him and break his neck, but I doubted it. More than likely, I'd break mine.

I was close enough to watch him dealing with a black woman with breast cancer — a tough sell — by putting his hand on the top of her head and praying at the top of his voice over her. It was his phoney smile that made me want to puke: concerned, compassionate, we're all members of the human family, I am a do-gooder, so eat my shit. It's that kind of hypocritical smiley-face that is ruining America.

My eyes are easy to read. Call me paranoid, because I definitely am, but I thought a security guy sitting behind Flood caught a peek at what's inside me when we stared at each other. He was looking at me really hard like, *who is this assassin I'm going to have to deal with?* His eyes were dead like a computer screen — all business, and not a Christian thought mixed in. He was suspicious.

But then Flood beckoned to me, smiling that big phoney smile. I walked up to him and everything left my head when I saw the camera pointed at me. All I could think was, *television!*

All I could think was, is Robin watching me? Is Daddy?

Flood pulled me down into a kneeling position. He's very strong. When he touched my head I kind of resisted and he pushed it down with strong hard fingers — the same fingers that had hurt Robin. My face was practically in his fucking lap, on world television. Even in fucking Thailand they were watching me be submissive to this Nazi! There was nothing I could do! I had to eat it and swallow it and it was bitter.

I was a whore. I'd do anything to get blasted out via satellite to the whole world.

"My son," he said over me. "Do you accept your saviour

Jesus Christ?" All I could do was nod, with his hand pushing my head down.

"My son," he asked, "your affliction is of what nature?"

"I'm..." But he stopped me before I could say it by starting to sing in a loud voice. The choir picked it up and I couldn't say anything. I saw technicians scrambling and then the guy with the computer eyes was pushing me off the set and off the stage.

Backstage he hustled me into an empty dressing room and locked the door.

"Who're you?" I asked him, afraid he'd kick my ass before we were even introduced.

"I'm Mr. Hopper, and you are trouble, pilgrim. My job is to get rid of trouble."

He looked like he was getting ready to get rid of me in the next five seconds. I didn't think I could convince him I was just a stupid golfer. He pushed me down into a chair and I stayed. I was no match for him.

"I've got you now, little pilgrim. I'm thinking about hurting you just because you're trouble. But first, tell me your name."

"It's Buddy Tate."

He was behind me, standing over me, and then he grabbed my right wrist and twisted my arm up against my shoulder-blade hard. It hurt like hell and I was reeling like I'd made a bad mistake. He was something scary. So strong that I couldn't move my arm a fraction.

"You wanted something when you came here, little pilgrim, little rat face. What did you want from Reverend Flood?"

"I just wanted his blessing."

I heard the little '*swoosh*' of a lighter and he burned my hand with it for five seconds, stopped and asked me again. I wanted to tell him, but I'd bitten down on my tongue and couldn't get anything more out than to beg him to let me breathe.

"Just for a minute. Don't think it's a permanent right."

"Just be Christian with me."

"You wouldn't want that. This is easier than that, let me tell you, little rat face."

He burned me again.

"The cross is a symbol you haven't paid enough attention to," he said. "We're going to have to change that. We're going to have to save your soul, little rat face."

He made me scream for Jesus.

XXIV
"If thy Right Eye Offend Thee..."

Crosses.

Like everyone else here in the land of the duped and the home of the slave, I've stared at them all my life. In Christian America, crosses are everywhere you look. In churches, but also around the necks of pretty girls and beast bikers.

The crucifix rules, and it's dipped in blood.

I could never understand that. Think about it. Jesus was not just *killed* on the fucking cross, he was *tortured*. Nailed and stretched! It's sick, worshipping two pieces of wood used to torture people.

To me, wearing a cross around your neck on a gold chain is the same as wearing a miniature electric chair, or a noose. (Of course, if you're a wage slave in a suit, you do wear a noose around your neck...)

So it scared me that after Mr. Hopper got through banging and burning me I didn't see stars like in cartoons, I saw crosses. Dozens of little crosses wherever I looked.

My soul was saved.

When Mr. Hopper and his friends let me go I was barely able to stagger back to my motel room. Crosses everywhere. The management had put a sign on my door saying I could find my duffel in the office. I had to pay three days in advance if I wanted to stay. I was in no shape to argue with them. I needed to be somewhere it was dark.

I just hid in that room for days like a hurt dog. I slept a lot and tried to heal, but the crosses wouldn't get out of my eyes. If I turned on the television I'd see it through a moving field of '+'. I couldn't get rid of them. Even watching a porno channel, they were still there. I'd be watching a babe take it up the chocolate highway and tattooed all over that wonderful image would be crosses.

It was driving me crazy. After a few days I managed to get one eye clear, but a cross remained in my right eye, sometimes with a figure on it, sometimes not. I saw the world with a crucifix imprinted on it.

I tried to be calm. I needed some serious advice to see if I wasn't going crazy, but who could I talk to? Maybe Anyguy could have said what to do. Maybe Robin, too — but what did she care? She wanted something from me I wasn't able to do.

That left Daddy. I thought I could find him. But I didn't have enough money to make the trip back to where he was probably holed up — some trailer camp up in the hills of Idaho — but I had K. Farouk's most blessed piece.

I didn't have to go to them, the suckers came to me.

I was feeling better, still blinking my right eye, when there came (as they say in horror movies, and this was a horror) a rapping on my motel door. I opened it reluctantly. Before me were victims from the word *go*. It was a guy and girl all dressed up and carrying briefcases. They were Jehovah's Witnesses.

"Can we ask you some questions?" said the girl. The guy

looked like he'd never had a blowjob in his fucking life.

I smiled. "Come on in."

She looked at him and he nodded. I stepped aside to let them into the room and closed the door behind me. Click lock.

"What do you want to ask me?"

"We wanted to ask you some questions about how you see the world situation today. You know, it's a very frightening world in many ways..."

The girl talked. She was about my age, I guess, with plump cheeks and a smile like she'd caught you looking at her tits. She had a blouse full, so I looked at them and not at her mouth, which was saying crap that I wasn't hearing because there was a cross on her tit. She wasn't wearing one. My right eye was branding her tit with it.

"I think the world is coming to an end," I said. I wasn't joking.

That stopped her for a minute, but she picked up the thread again. "Then you agree that Armageddon is at hand?"

I pulled K. Farouk's pistol out of my pocket and showed it to them. They both looked like they'd been goosed at the same time. "For sure the world is coming to an end for you both if you don't give me your money. And your car keys."

I thought he might do something, but he didn't have the stones. She opened her briefcase and gave me her wallet. He reached inside his jacket and gave me his, along with the keys. He looked like he couldn't believe this was happening to *him*.

I could have done anything then. The cross was like a gun sight, and it was good to have the power again. They were scared and I could do anything with them.

"If you hurt us, your soul will go to hell," she said, like she was reading my mind.

"I'm not going to hurt you unless you make me," I promised. No, I wasn't going to blow them away. But I didn't want them following me. I went over to the phone and yanked the cord out of the wall, then sat down on the bed I'd messed up.

"I want you both to get undressed," I told them.

"What are you going to do?" he asked.

"First your shoes, then your pants, then your shirt. It's simple. You've done it a million times."

He got to work while she stood there watching him.

"Now you," I told her.

She took off her suit jacket without taking her eyes off me. She was nervous and it took a while to unbutton her blouse. She was wearing a lacy white brassiere and they were all that I hoped for when she took it off. Big and firm with pale pink nipples.

He had stripped down to white jockey shorts and he still had his socks on.

"Have you ever fucked her?"

"That's private."

"I bet she doesn't give you any. You walk around all day knocking on doors because of her. And then she doesn't give you any."

"We're not married yet," she said. She had a long white skirt on.

"The skirt, too."

"Please. Haven't you embarrassed her enough?" he whined.

It made me ashamed to be a man, looking at this dickless wonder. "If she doesn't take her skirt off, I'll shoot you."

"Please, Angela. He looks crazy enough to do it."

Her eyes were wet, but she wouldn't cry. She unzipped the skirt and pulled it off. White panties with a big bulge in them. The cross in my eye was tattooed on that bulge.

When she pulled them down I got hard for the first time since the gang bang. She had more hair on her snatch than most men have on their heads. It was lush and brown and unbelievably sexy just to look at it. This was a pussy I just had to pet.

"Come over here." She edged over to me like she was walking on eggs. I had to see it up close, to smell it, and play with it. I made her put it in my face. She smelled like soap, not like juices, but I rubbed my face in that bush and licked it and got some souvenirs between my teeth.

That was all. I'm not a rapist. Buddy Tate can find willing pussy any time. He doesn't have to force anybody. I just wanted a taste. Is that a crime?

"Now you," I told the dickless wonder. "Put your face in her bush. Do it."

He was scared of me and scared of her, so the way he did it was half-assed, but he did it.

"Now show her your dick." He pulled it out through the front of his jockeys, looking ashamed he had an erection.

"Look at it," I ordered her. "Now you two are going to get better acquainted. Touch it like you mean it."

Her face was all scrunched up like she was looking at a big dead rat rather than the penis of the man she was going to marry and have babies with. She started praying, "Our father who art in heaven, hallowed by thy name..."

I got up off the bed and motioned for both of them to sit on it.

"Put your hand on his dick, goddamn it." She did it. "Now — move it up and down." She handled it like it was a rattlesnake.

"You never learned how to be a girl, did you?"

I was disgusted with her, but the scene was turning me on. Watching does it for me. He didn't seem to be enjoying himself — it was like he was watching her wash his feet — but maybe he didn't know what to expect. Probably never jerked off in his whole wasted life peddling *Watch Towers*. Well, I'd show them another kind of watchtower.

They were both looking at me and not at what they were doing. I unzipped and let the big boy out of the corral. Put both hands around it and waved it in their faces.

"This is how you give a hand job," I told them. When she saw how big I was she couldn't help herself. I could tell something clicked down between her legs. Maybe it was like getting saved. I had her attention now. She was fascinated with the way my right hand moved up and down, how I played with my balls, then went up to the head for a squeeze. He watched her like she was turning into somebody he didn't know.

I gave it my best and it wasn't more than three minutes before I came in my hand. She had stopped touching him and was just staring. I could see the lust in her eyes replace the fright.

I was feeling crazed, and the cross in my right eye seemed to be getting bigger. But before I left them to sort it out I wanted to show them something.

I held out my hand to them. My hand filled with my own come running between my fingers and dripping on the floor.

"This is what it's all about. It makes babies. It's life."

I wanted them to remember this lesson. I brought my hand up to my face and licked up my own come. It was saltier than usual. I wiped my hand on the bedspread, zipped up, gathered up their clothes in one arm, picked up my duffel, and said good-bye, locking the door behind me.

Maybe, if I was lucky, I had saved two souls.

XXV
"...And Cast it From Thee..."

Driving is torture enough without seeing every truck coming at you with a crucifix printed on its grill. I thought I knew where Daddy had drifted to by this time of year, I just had to get there. It was a good little Japanese car the Jehovah's had loaned me, so I made good time.

I cut through the Restricted Zone of Nevada and headed north into Idaho through Boise and the Sawtooths up to the Bitterroots. Daddy liked to go where he could get away from people who want to tell you what to do.

Where the highway ends and there's just a couple of dirt roads and a convenience store and big-assed mountains all around, Daddy had found a place to hide. The guy in the store said there was a little trailer camp up the road, and I knew I was home.

It was a plain old beige trailer with some dead flowers in front of it, away from the other trailers. I didn't see Daddy's pickup, but I knew I had the right trailer because of the bumper sticker on the screen door: Live Free or Die. It was Daddy's motto.

I knocked on the screen door but the only sound was flies buzzing, so I stepped inside. It was basic bachelor: a couch and a television and an unmade bed, chairs and a table with beer bottles on it. It smelled like Daddy: sex, booze, cigarettes, guns. But the old block wasn't in his cave.

I looked in the refrigerator and found two bottles of Bud, three eggs, horse radish, a jar of mayo, bread, and a pint of vodka. In the coils under the refrigerator was the usual stash of home-grown bo-bo. All the comforts of home sweet home. I was hungry, so I fried up some eggs, made sandwiches and drank a beer. Rolled a nail and kicked back like a king, stiff and achey from the long drive.

I wondered what Daddy would say when I told him the adventures I'd had in California. He'd probably call me crazy when I told him about the crucifix in my eye.

I must have dozed off on the couch. When I woke up it was dark out. Maybe he'd gone off on what he called "manoeuvres" with his camouflage buddies up in the mountains.

There was no beer left, so I poured myself a vodka, and turned on the television for company.

A big mistake.

Thomas Flood was praying on the screen. A close-up of his folded hands, while his voice prayed hard about pornography. How the souls of pornographers would burn in hell. I wondered if Markus Bloom worried about hell.

"Certain well-intentioned people have asked, why am I striking so hard at pornography? Doesn't the world have bigger problems? Many, even some who call themselves Christians, say that it doesn't hurt anybody, that pornography is a so-called 'victimless crime'. But, my friends, the victim is Christ Himself! Saying that pornography is a victimless crime is like saying the filth will not soil your garments. Pornography has the curse of Onan on it."

I don't know why I didn't shut the bastard off. When I looked at him the cross in my eye was a gunsight pointed at his head. Someday I'd have a real chance at him, and there would be blood in his eye, blood covering his head. And I'd cut off his holy pecker and stuff it in his mouth.

I poured another vodka and imagined that. It made me feel good.

"Lord, the power of prayer is enormous, as we witness here every day on our show. We have used the power of prayer to heal the afflicted and lift up the godly. But now we must use the power of our prayer as a weapon — a shining sword — against the ungodly.

"Who is the pornographer? Who is he? We know he's a man, because the women in that filthy business are just like kidnap victims. They don't know what they're doing. Some man with his mind in the gutter led them down the garden path. Let me draw you a portrait of the pornographer: he's a fat man puffing on a cigar — and yes, many of these fat men with cigars are Jews! Surely I will not be accused of anti-Semitism if I point out to you that Jews — and Italians of course — run the pornography trade. The pornographer, friends, stands for everything that has gone wrong in America, and his home is San Francisco. We must march to that Sodom by the sea and establish our Crusade there. Armageddon..."

I tuned in and out of his rap, getting a depressing feeling that my punishment in life for my sins was to have to listen to Flood whenever I turned on the television. With him taking up so much TV time, there'd never be any room for me!

If I kept listening to him, I'd go crazy, but I couldn't turn off the set. It was like I was hypnotised. Like he'd put a curse on me by putting his goddamned cross in my eye. I finished the rest of the pint. I was beginning to feel it, because I don't drink much. I'm not a lush, I'm a lover.

"People often say, wouldn't it be more charitable, even more Christian, to forgive the pornographer? Or the Devil worshipper? Or the homosexual? To forgive the sinner? But we must stand firm when the ungodly can corrupt a whole nation! I think good Christians have a duty for righteous anger. My response to corruption is not to turn the other cheek. As it says in Matthew, 'If thy right eye offend thee, pluck it out, and cast it from thee!'"

Something clicked. My right eye *did* offend me. The cross in it was getting bigger. It separated Flood's face into four parts. It vibrated.

He was inside my head. Mr. Hopper and his friends had put him inside me.

I fumbled for the zapper and pressed 'off' but Flood was still there on the screen, praying, his face divided into four squares. Once when I was six a big fat tick got in my ear when I was sleeping. When I felt it in there sucking my blood it made me crazy. I ran around the house screaming that I couldn't get it out. Daddy put some lighter fluid on it and pulled it out with tweezers, each of its legs like a hook tearing my ear so it bled. But it was out, and I owned myself again.

I stood up because I felt sick and the trailer was tilting.

I made it to the bathroom just in time to chuck up my fried eggs into the toilet. When I could breathe again I pulled myself up to the sink, opened the medicine chest and found Daddy's straight razor, the one he'd taught me to sharpen for him.

I didn't want to do it, but I had to. With three fingers I pulled my right eye out of its socket, so determined to do it that I didn't feel the pain. I picked up the straight razor and cut through the muscles and tendons holding it in, and held my bloody right eyeball in my hand. It was slippery, and harder than I expected.

Then I cast the offending eye into the eggs in the toilet, and flushed it away.

Daddy found me in the bathroom passed out, face covered with blood, toilet paper stuck in the empty eye socket.

"You've done yourself some serious bodily harm, Buddy, that you will regret. It may be that you're not *compos mentis*."

I told him about the crucifix, about Robin, and about Flood.

"That son-of-a-bitch hypocrite Flood is going to take over the country. He needs to have his mail delivered to him by groundhogs."

"Well Daddy, stay tuned, because it will be me who gets the job done. It may take a while, but I'll do it."

"I believe you will. You turned out to be an ambitious boy after all. The world might hear from you yet."

XXVI
Bad Little Girl

When she was a little girl, before her mother died, Robin Flood dreamed that she was not only a little girl, but an animal, too. She liked animals, of course, as lonely children often do. Her favourite outing with her parents was a trip to the zoo. But her dream was recurrent: one night she was an ocelot, the next she was a fox. She was okapi, but she was also jaguarundi, otter, panda and racoon. She wore her little girl clothes in these dreams, but her face was furry, her nose tipped black. She was herself, but she was also something wild.

One day her parents, seeing her love for animals, decided that she was old enough to care for a pet. Robin asked for a monkey — but not just any monkey. She was very particular: she wanted a Japanese macaque, a small, delicate monkey with a pink face and sober, soulful eyes.

Robin named her new friend Emily and spent nearly all of her free time when she was not in school talking to her. Emily listened; her parents didn't. Emily was unusually intelligent and loving, but nevertheless there were times when Emily lapsed — when she was more wild animal than good little girl. One Saturday when Robin was eight, Emily wandered into a prayer breakfast father was giving and bit a few important fingers. Father was very angry.

When Robin came home from school, her father was waiting. He took her into the basement, where Emily was to be disciplined for being a monkey, and not a good little girl. It would be a lesson for Robin.

The basement was dark and scary. Robin liked to play down there with Emily around the great furnace and in the laundry room. It was a scary place but that was part of its appeal to them. It offered a taste of adventure.

Poor Emily! She was tied by her tiny wrists to a big clothes drying rack. She was chattering her teeth and making the high pitched sounds of alarm macaques make when they are frightened. She bared her white teeth in distress, her wet saucer eyes begged Robin to help her, but Robin couldn't.

Father was father, so he had to punish.

❖❖❖

You made me watch, father. It was a belt you used, and you hit poor Emily with it and when she howled, you looked at me. I knew that you could turn your anger on me. It didn't last very long, but my heart was broken. Then you made us kneel and pray that Emily wouldn't be bad again. When I went to untie her and pick her up she bit me on the chin and I didn't make a sound. I knew you would come back and beat her again.

I saw that cruelty was the worst sin. Deliberate cruelty. That cruelty made Emily run into the street a few days later, and she was killed.

After that happened I went into a little room inside myself and shut the door. I was eight, but I have always had a very strong will. I decided I would let no one in my room. I would pretend to be the dutiful Robin Flood, Thomas Flood's daughter, but in that little room I remained an animal. Emily lived inside me.

I watched you at my mother's funeral, father. I saw that you were posing. She lay encased in that rich wood and you postured, one hand on her casket, for the television cameras. She looked up at you with sightless eyes from the open casket, and you didn't say good-bye to her, you said prayers. *Prayers*!

I knew that you did not love her, that women frightened and disgusted you. I knew that you had been cruel to her because she was a woman and you did not know what that meant.

I hated you when I saw your cruelty, and it dried up my heart.

❖❖❖

You killed her. You knew that she was stronger than you, and you feared that she would devour you with her womanhood. So you killed her. But it was her sex you really wanted to kill. Her powers as a woman. Maybe as a goddess, if Laura's right.

I am the daughter of Aphrodite. We are all goddesses and gods, and your church says we are devils.

Your pathetic, cruel church.

❖❖❖

I am an animal. I am a goddess. I am my mother's daughter. I am not your daughter. I am not a good little girl any longer. When you killed my mother, when you burned me, you made me bad.

❖❖❖

Buddy Tate is an animal like me. His smell pleased me — it was hard winters in little towns, smoky sex and sudden violence. His willingness when I fucked him pleased me. The size of his cock pleased me. What he said and how he said it.

I have trouble with passion. It's too big an emotion to remain stuffed in my little room. If I let it grow there would be a meltdown.

And yet, I think I feel passion for Buddy Tate — and I'm afraid of it. Afraid that it will burn us both up.

You will chase me, father, and I will run, and that will be our history until the end. One day I will stop running and fight you. Or Buddy Tate will kill you for me.

I like to think that we'll cut your heart out and eat it.

Don't you understand that you have to die so I can live? Don't you understand that, until I see your mortal blood, I will never be whole?

❖❖❖

The last time I saw you, father, was the last time you hurt me. You'd sent me away to good schools, and for that I thank you, if for nothing else. I learned how not to be your daughter at them. I was in Paris pretending to attend classes at the Sorbonne but actually fucking my brains out when you called me home. You threatened to cut off my allowance if I didn't come. I was to make an appearance to demonstrate that you're a 'family man'. It was a big event — a convention of religious broadcasters, I think. Bible-thumping babblers.

I dressed in black, with pearls, but I left a small gold ring in my nose to signal my defiance of you. I knew I shouldn't, but I was a bad little girl. You wanted me to make an appearance as the Parousia Foundation's poster girl: the dutiful daughter who went to the best schools but was still a good Christian — so what were those liberals talking about when they said fundamentalists are uneducated?

But that little nose ring, symbol of my defiance, made you nervous. Your noble brow crunched up with scorn and distaste when you saw it. You reached out and took my nose between your strong fingers and you pulled my head down, forcing me to bow to you. When you let go, I was crying.

Those are the last tears I will ever shed for you.

❖❖❖

I prayed to the snake gods, do not let this evil man my father hurt me with his powerful serpent. Its head spat venom and its body was a muscle that could choke my heart.

❖❖❖

I swore that I would never see you again, but my dreams betray me. My nightmares will deliver me into your hands.

I must go to you one last time because there is a question I have to ask you: if my mother was bad, like me, how do you know that I am your daughter?

XXVII

The Prodigal Daughter

It wasn't home that she returned to, but an evangelical empire. The Parousia Foundation campus had multiplied like cancer cells beneath the ozone hole that had opened above Southern California.

The gatekeeper who led her through a maze of corridors and gardens into Thomas Flood's presence remembered her as a child with braces on her teeth. To play the prodigal daughter she'd removed her earrings and nose ring and dressed in simple, modest outfit of black silk. Her tattoo and the ring in her clit hood would protect her back and front.

The decision to come was her own. There was no one she could discuss it with. Dollar was still missing: hadn't been seen at the Pussy Palace in days. She called the Hotel Napa, but its number had been changed to a lawyer's answering machine — there'd been a fire. Laura and Baron were on a retreat in Big Sur and could not be reached.

Thomas Flood greeted her on the steps of the picture-perfect white chapel he'd had built to use for exterior shots to open the Evangelical Evening News. He held open his arms and she screwed up her courage and stepped into the strong circle they made.

She thought that he looked different than she remembered, as if television had somehow magnified the impression made by his good looks and erect, athletic body. She noticed that he was wearing makeup.

"How are you, father?"

He smiled, his eyes crinkling with the crow's feet of satisfaction. "We have prospered, Robin, as I prophesied we would when you were a child, and I started this ministry."

"I don't want my picture taken."

"Come inside to my office. We'll talk."

He touched her arm to guide her to the sleek building where his office was. She stopped her instinct to jerk free. The touch of his hand, his punishing hand, repulsed her, but she bore it. The sound of his voice made her heart clench like a fist, but she bore it. Her nightmares and dreams had driven her to him to ask one question. His answer might save them both.

He sat behind his massive mahogany desk and his secretary, Mary Ruth, brought them tea, staggering under the weight of the silver service while Thomas Flood beamed. It was a family reunion.

The ornately carved pulpit caught Robin's attention.

"That's beautiful. Eighteenth century, isn't it? Maybe Munich?"

He was pleased. "Vienna, they tell me. I see your education hasn't been wasted on you."

"No. I did an art history minor. Once I did a paper on the evolution of pulpit design, of all subjects to choose."

"Like father, like daughter. Do you think I can get away with using it on television? I don't think so."

"I haven't watched you that often, father, but I would say not."

"We hit 40 million households. It's a big ministry, Robin. Big Nielsen ratings. I should wait, I suppose, until you tell me why you wanted to visit here — but I'll say it anyway. Fools rush in where angels fear to tread, they say. There's a role here for you at Parousia. I couldn't wait to tell you that."

She was stunned.

He looked expectantly at her, as if he'd offered her the keys to his kingdom. She saw in his eyes what she had never seen clearly before: the pressure inside him was so great that it might erupt from any of a hundred places in his psyche. He was chillingly possessed. His demons were responsible for his charisma.

"I'm a minister without a helpmate, Robin. I won't marry again. Who could step into the role more naturally, than my own flesh and blood? Oh, I won't rush you into anything. But if down the road you could see yourself serving as my... what shall we say...?"

He waited for her to speak, allowing for the shock of his proposal to be absorbed. When she simply stared at the pulpit without speaking, he asked: "Robin?"

Her reply was a mumble, he thought at first, but he heard what she said. Her words struck in him a deep organ note of despair. Yes. He heard what she said: "*Am* I your flesh and blood?"

But he asked: "What?" He spun around in his chair so that his back was to her. He fought to control what rose up in him.

"I wanted to see you so that I could ask you. You said that my mother was a slut. If she was, how do you really know that I'm your flesh and blood?"

"I am your father."

Suddenly she was filled with an anger that etched her next words into the air as if she'd written them with a flame thrower: "*If you are my father, I hate you so much that if I could explode your head right now I'd eat what's left on a plate. And then I'd vomit your brains in someone else's face, some derelict. And I'd kiss his dirty mouth and fuck him in your Baroque pulpit!"*

When he spun back around his smile was crocodile sharp, and he sounded almost grateful for her anger when he spoke, "Shh, child, don't. Don't injure yourself and your immortal soul." He put his hands up, as if to ward off her attack.

"You have killed me inside."

Thomas Flood frowned and closed his eyes. He stood up slowly and walked to the window that looked out over the Parousia garden. Another golden afternoon was dying, its long crisp shadows playing over the carp pool. He wanted her to explain, but he couldn't bear to hear her answer. He knelt on the floor by the window to ask for guidance.

— She is the only one who can save me, and she reviles me. I will burn in hell without her.

— What do you want me to do? You're scheduled for hell in my book. She won't forgive you.

— Help me claim my punishment, Lord.

❖❖❖

He spoke to her.

"I am guilty, Robin. In my soul, I am guilty. There's something inside me that wants to come out, some foul thing that lives in me..."

"*You don't have a soul!*" she hissed at him, backing away. His kneeling frightened her. She watched him crumple slowly until his forehead touched the floor. He sobbed.

"It lives inside me. It has since I was little, since the clown put his snake in me and the snake grew and now..."

His shuddering sobs were so heartfelt she felt herself relax her guard. What was he babbling about?

"You killed my mother! You burned me!" she almost wailed, controlling her voice just in time. "You raped me!"

"Then punish me! Burn the thing inside me! Do whatever you want with me!"

He pushed himself up to his knees again and began tearing at his tie, fingers scrabbling down the buttons of his custom made shirt.

"Whip me!"

She felt cool and dry and hard inside. It was unique, hearing her father beg. She felt a perverse curiosity about how far he might go. She imagined black slime oozing from him, inky exhalations of evil billowing into the room.

He exhaled, she inhaled. What was inside him would be inside her then. Unless she forgave him. She tried to imagine punishment serious enough for his crimes. Punishment that she alone could administer there and then. Punishment so that she could forgive him.

He pulled his belt out of his trouser loops and held it out to her. She took it because of Emily. He had bared his broad hairy back to her, and she struck him with all her force with the buckle end of the belt, then dropped it. One for Emily, but nothing for herself.

She imagined degradations, but they would be no more than tokens, innocuous theatre. Shitting in his mouth would probably get him off, she thought bitterly.

"Use the belt as hard as you can. Burn me!"

Maybe if she could pull him down as he had her, hold him down as he had her, she could burn him, scald him as he had her. But what good would any punishment do? There was no forgiveness in her heart.

"Forgive me, Robin. Asmodeus can be beaten out of me. I can vomit him out, you'll see. Please, little Robin, I never meant to hurt you, or Rebecca. This devil inside me has its claws in my heart."

"Father, I wouldn't piss down your throat if your heart was on fire. There is no punishment for you but your own hell."

He looked up at her with cold, tired eyes. They were dry. Sadly, weakly, he stood.

"You are my daughter, and you are cursed. Your mother was a whore and I was weak with her, and when you came I hated you as the devil's spawn."

Then Robin wept. The question was answered. If he was her father, then for her to live he certainly had to die. She was too weak to punish Thomas Flood, but not Buddy Tate. He was strong. She could make him kill for her.

Buddy Tate, bang, bang.

XXVIII
Night of the Living Dread

In the country of the blind, the one-eyed king is crazy, somebody told me at the hospital. Maybe I got that wrong too. Hell, I was born with a crazy tendency in me and those crosses sent me over Niagara Falls in a lawn chair. I seriously didn't care. I was fucked up. No place to go but the end of the line. Homeless at twenty-two. I slept in a box in a parking lot that had been carved out inside an old movie house on Mission Street.

The marquee outside said 'El Capitan' but the inside had been bulldozed to make way for cars. Nobody left their cars there because it was too dangerous, so now there were just bottles and weeds and boxes and bundles and shopping carts full of shit. It was as safe a place as any to sleep. I was the one-eyed crazy king of the Mission, from 16th to 24th Street, from Valencia to Guerrero.

During the day I dragged my box out to the sidewalk and put an old pot out with a sign on it:

Willing to do anything you wouldn't do
Blind and homeless — please help out

I'd sit there on an old car seat I'd found, calm as a fucking Chinese Buddha, with my eye patch pushed up on my forehead showing the bloody cotton wadding the hospital had put in my empty socket. I kept myself clean and kept K. Farouk's pistol handy to use against the burners. (Kids had always done it for fun, but now there were gangs of vigilantes who drove around looking for helpless homeless to set fire to.) I made a few bucks a day just sitting there, but the competition was stiff, so my speciality was geeking.

That means, say, that if the landlord of a flophouse finds an old lady dead, and she's been dead in one of his rooms for a while, and, like old ladies do she's let her cat food dishes pile up, and the stench was perfume for maggots, that landlord might engage my services. And I'd come clean it all up, glad to be of service. A geek will eat anything...(just a joke!)

My life wasn't too bad. I had a lot of time to think. I'd sit on the sidewalk and watch the passing parade, laughing in the morning at the worker bees who ran past me on their way to the business graveyard. Zombies.

I tried to keep Dollar's dead eyes out of my head, but Robin was always there. I didn't know where to start looking for her — and if I found her, what would I say to her? *I fucked up?* Same with Anyguy.

I didn't do what I said I would, so I was nothing to them.

Hell, sitting there with my pot, I was taking bread out of Anyguy's mouth.

It was temporary, being homeless. I told myself that every day, while I waited for luck to catch up with me again.

Seeing life at crotch level seems to me just about right. It equalises everything. All kinds of people put money in my pot except for richies. I really hate them. The world at crotch level is divided between the people who feel bad for you and sometimes throw a quarter or a dirty job your way, and the people who never feel bad for you and who would step on your tongue if you put it out onto the sidewalk to catch flies with.

The worst thing about being homeless and fucked up was no sex. The second worst thing is dealing with crazies. They are all over the streets, like in that movie *Night of The Living Dead*.

Crazy people should never have to deal with other crazy people. It makes us anxious. Scariest of the crazies were the Vietnam vets. They were mostly great old guys when they were sober, but when they beamed up, watch out. One of them took a fix on me for some reason. He was a big dude with a beard. Word on the street said when he was really flying he'd claim two to three dozen kills in service. Put him together with some malt and some crunch and munch, and you had one dangerous lost soldier. His name was Big Mac.

I stayed out of his way because whenever he saw me he got belligerent. I didn't want the rocks in his head banging against the rocks in my head.

When I had my run-in with Big Mac, I was in a pissy mood. Lonesome, maybe. I needed to get laid. What I had in the pot wouldn't buy a hand job in a dumpster. I was sitting inside my box in the El Capitan homeless shelter when I saw him coming.

He was juiced and yelling, "Kill! Kill! Die! Die!" Staggering at me like a monster movie. There was a full moon just coming up — the El Capitan had no roof — so maybe that was it. I took out K. Farouk's .38 and cocked it and yelled back at him:

"Get back, Big Mac! I'll shoot your ass!"

I showed him the pistol and it slowed him for a minute, but the motherfucker thought he was Goliath and kept on coming. Anything short of a missile wouldn't have scared him.

So I aimed for the leg. Missed — which is why Daddy

always says aim for the belly. Shot again and hit him, but he kept on coming, really worked up now, so I jumped up and ran, out of the El Capitan and across Mission. Cars almost hit me, but people ducked like they'd rehearsed all their lives when they saw me running at them, a blind man with a pistol.

Stopped in a doorway to catch my breath and put the pistol in my pocket. When I walked out on the street again I forced myself to go slow and keep to the shadows. After a while I felt calmer, but more weirdness was waiting for me when I got to Market Street. It had to be the full moon.

I was just standing on the corner waiting for the light to change, minding my own business. I was headed for the Castro where they were crazy, but about sex, and maybe I could peddle my ass. Innocent, just your ordinary homeless victim on the street.

A little woman in a blue dress and a vinyl jacket walked up and stood behind me waiting for the light. I was hyper-aware and could feel her eyes in my back, but I didn't turn. Just crossed the street fast, figuring I could outdistance her. Half a block later she's running after me, yelling something I couldn't understand. I turned to figure it out and she yelled it: "You think you're gonna get away with it, but I know I can do something about you. You're a child molester, and I'm gonna have you arrested!"

Child molester? I was still not full grown myself.

She's screaming this, on the south side of Market Street, just after Valencia. People passing by must have thought it was an argument between homeless people. I couldn't tell them I'm not *that* crazy, so I really picked up the pace. She followed right after me, yelling and carrying on. If a cop car had come along then, good-bye Buddy! I had to break into a full-out run to escape the loony bitch.

I ended up on a traffic island near the Castro with busy traffic on both sides of me. I don't like to play in traffic, but it felt like a refuge because there were no people on foot nearby. And what better place to peddle my ass? I was so horny I'd let some faggot suck me off so I could go find a good looking girl like Dollar to fuck. I was so desperate to get off the street I'd take the first offer that came my way. If you had a taste for real raunchy rough trade, you'd put the brakes on for Buddy Tate. Where else but on this traffic island on a full moon night in San Francisco could you find a crazy, one-eyed homeless man who's hung like a stallion?

Naturally I stood there for a long time. I had a full basket under my tight old street sale 501s, but maybe people could sense the harder bulge of the .38 in my pocket. Knowing pigeons, I figured that under the influence of the full moon there'd be one who'd put himself at risk. All it took was one.

A car passed me, slowed down and backed up. A grey BMW with vanity plates I liked: IAMTHEONE. I looked into the car when the window was rolled down. There's always that first excitement when you're about too see someone you're going to have sex with. When you're expecting a stranger's eyes to look you over and you see a familiar face instead, it's a kick to the heart. It took me a minute to put the right name on this face, but the circles under his eyes reminded me. It was that pervert pornographer, Markus Bloom. Long time no see.

"Buddy! It's Buddy Tate!" He was giggling like he was high on something, but I was glad to see him at that low point in my life.

"What are you doing here?" I said back, and that made him giggle even more. He nodded his head in the direction of somebody in the front seat. I looked in closer with my eye and saw a woman, nothing more than a skinny bag bride.

"Same thing you are, by the looks of it. Getting my fix."

"I'm not having much luck."

"Well, you look kind of wild. Get in the back, come on."

I hopped in and slid across the leather seat, to sit behind the skinny whore he'd picked up, so I could talk to him.

He held up a finger that was wet and gave me a big grin.

"Smells good, doesn't it Buddy? Sweet smell of pussy. The owner of this aroma, this pungent whiff of sublimity, is Tinker Bell, whose acquaintance I have just made."

She wasn't bad looking in the dark, but I couldn't see much. He was playing with her as he drove, you could smell it.

"Come home with us, Buddy. We'll have a little party."

"Three's a crowd, isn't it?"

"Oh, there's more than three. Other guests are waiting at my apartment. Tinker Bell is the party favour."

That brightened things up.

"I'm glad I came to California," I told him. "This is the promised land, like they say." Things were definitely looking up.

"Yes, it's a wonderful illusion, this town. Full or wonderfully depraved people bent on having a good time."

"You just got me out a jam, Markus. I'm glad you saw me."

"It was fate, Buddy. But what the hell happened to you? What happened to your eye?"

"I see fine."

"Buddy, you have a patch over your eye. You smell bad. This is your friend Markus Bloom asking you."

I thought about it. I hadn't talked about what happened to anyone but Daddy.

"It was a girl I can't get out of my head, Markus. That's what happened. I went from being a man who knows his own mind to a puppet. I'll tell you all about it someday."

"Give me a name?"

"The girl?"

"Yeah."

"Robin Flood."

That stopped him. For some reason I could tell he didn't want to talk anymore. He said something light:

"Women are waves in the ocean, Buddy. You'll see tonight."

He put the pedal to the metal and knocked my head back.

XXIX
Play Party

Buddy Tate

I, Buddy Tate, thought I'd died and gone to heaven when I walked into Markus's party. It was dark, but the first thing I saw was a big room filled with mattresses and a bunch of people getting friendly with each other, taking off their clothes, kissing, sucking. I just gawked, like I'd walked into a movie. There must have been twenty couples.

Markus stood there, looking at the scene before us, a grin on his face. His hand was around Tinker Bell's neck, just stroking the back of her neck. He winked at me.

"I guess the clinic didn't do us much good, did it, Buddy?"

I got a kick out of Markus. He was who he was, just like me, and he didn't say sorry every time he had a lech.

"Big party," I said, my eye glued to the scene before it. I watched as a woman pulled up her skirt and a naked woman tongued her clit. I could just move right in, slip it to that bare butt girl before she could turn around...

Markus must have read my mind. Even Tinker Bell could.

"There are rules at this play party, Buddy. You have to be cool. You have to ask permission before you touch..."

He had more to say on the subject, but I interrupted:

"I can handle myself, don't worry."

"...and in your case, you have to be clean. You need to wash up. Over there's my private bathroom. You just take yourself a tub and don't come out until you feel like it. There are other bathrooms for party players. You can wear one of my robes if you want to get out of those clothes."

Markus Bloom couldn't do enough for me. I was grateful that we had sealed our friendship with a hand job back at the clinic.

His private bathroom was big enough to park a car in. White tiles and black marble and big shiny mirrors. A giant tub. Markus liked good living, but I didn't think he was rich. I had the feeling that he lived from temporary to temporary, just like me.

After a bubble bath I shaved and looked for myself in the mirror. I liked what I saw. Ready, willing, and able.

I looked good. Yeah, just one eye, but with one eye I could see what I needed to see over, under and around. I was clean and smelling sweet. One minute you're on the street, and the next you're a party favour at an orgy — the kind you only see in porno films. Maybe I had gotten my luck back.

Like Daddy used to say to me, it's a great life if you don't weaken.

I put on one of Markus Bloom's bathrobes and went out to join the party.

And what a sight it was. For the first time, I missed not having that other eye. Every direction I looked in was flesh — tits and ass and floppy dicks. I didn't know where to start sniffing for a piece.

Then I found out that Markus had taken care of that, too. I didn't recognise her without any clothes on. She looked like a boy who'd decided to play being a girl. Tinker Bell, the other party favour. Her titties were almost a handful, and her pussy was shaved.

"You look human now," she said, like she was relieved.

Her eyes and nose were red, and she was sniffling.

"You look like a drug addict to me," I replied.

"Don't give me a hard time, Buddy, please don't. I need this money. Just let me do you."

"You're too skinny." She just wasn't my type.

"Please, Buddy. Markus sent me over to you. Said I should get you fluffed up. I'll do anything you want." Whining.

"There's a party going on."

"No, it hasn't even started yet. People are just getting acquainted. Come on, just tell me what you like and I'll do it."

I didn't even like her, but the flesh is weak. She was a gift — how could I refuse? Long time, no nookie.

"You can hurt me if you like," she said. She was begging me. Hurting wouldn't turn me on, but her willingness was.

I wondered if anybody was watching us the way I liked to watch. It had to be that somebody was, I guessed. I hoped so.

Well, I said to myself, *let's see how far she'll go*.

Start with her mouth. I moved my finger across her lips, making her open her mouth, and stuck the finger in. Her tongue was skinny just like her body, but it was wet and suctiony around the finger. I stuck it in further and she gagged, but I never felt her teeth. I looked in her eyes to see if she resented me doing that and all I saw was curiosity. I owned her. I could do what I wanted with her. Then Markus would pay her and she could go dope.

I put my hands around her neck and squeezed just for a minute, feeling her pulse strong against my hands. She wasn't scared. Her body was bony everywhere, but her skin was soft, and when I pinched her nipples they stood right up. I twisted them and pulled them hard and she bit her lip, but she smiled.

She was turning me on. Old Blind Bob was poking up through my robe. I used two fingers to explore her pussy, jabbing them up her while I bit her nipple. She rode my hand, rubbing against it. She gasped when I put a finger in her asshole. It was tight, just right tonight.

I pulled it out and pushed it into her mouth for her to clean with her lizard's tongue. The same with the fingers in her pussy. She licked them like a cat. She was a challenge.

She was like a doll, a fucking doll. Nothing got her excited, so that made me push things to the limit. She was beginning to feel like a responsibility, gift or not. Girls always are.

"Use your hands," I ordered her. "Play with it."

She grabbed the pole that I had stuck into her belly with both hands and skinned it back. She was good at hand jobs, so good it made me want to get it wet. I didn't even have to tell her what to do. She dropped to her knees and opened wide. It was a tight fit but I slid it in, grabbing handfuls of her hair to guide her with. That lizard tongue flickered around the head and pushed inside the tip and I felt a jolt of electricity behind my balls.

"Use your teeth," I told her. She was good: they came down like gates on my prick, sawing it and chewing it. Looking down at her face full of me, she looked a lot better than she had at first sight.

"Now, no teeth," I ordered. And just like that, her mouth was tight and wet and slippery. I held the back of her head and pumped into her mouth, fucking her face and getting more excited as I jabbed it down her throat and felt the wonderful ripples of pleasure at each stroke. When her eyes bugged, I pulled out fast and she gasped for air. The smell was like she'd vomited and swallowed it. I didn't care. She wasn't running away. I owned her.

She had gotten my dirty mind to working overtime. I pulled her into the bathroom and locked the door behind us, dropping my robe. I was going to make this bitch scream.

I still didn't see anything more human than curiosity in her eyes. She had done that before, all that we had done in public. I wanted to make her feel something, because *I* wanted to feel something.

I made her lick my balls and clean my crack with that lizard tongue, and then told her to stick two fingers up my asshole. When she got it open I told her to stick her tongue in there and let her fingers fuck me. I was getting hotter, and my excitement seemed to be sparking hers.

It was time to fuck her. I pushed her down on the tiles and pulled her skinny boy butt up to me, ramming it up her cunt and riding her. I gave it everything I got, and I thought I'd split her in half before she made a noise, and then another one.

"Oh," she said to the floor. "*Oh, oh, oh...*"

Near us stood the sink cabinet. I opened the door under it, and reached inside, hoping to find a tool. It was there, like I hoped. I left her for a minute while I plugged in the hairdryer, and then plunged back into her.

The hairdryer was what did the trick. I held it about two inches from her skin and just moved it over her body. Up her bony vertebrae, melting them. Over her skinny buns. Her neck and shoulders and arms, everything getting red while I just kept pumping, knowing I was in control now, and that this was what she wanted. She was noisy.

The hairdryer was still whirring when I put it down on the tile and pulled out of Tinker Bell. She collapsed on the floor and I pulled myself up, holding onto the sink. The mirror made me look huge. It distorted me. And my wet penis was like a club. Looking at it in the mirror I suddenly realised I hadn't worn any protection. I was so horny even for a skag like Tinker Bell that I had forgotten. What a dickhead.

Good thing I hadn't come. Some people thought that if you came, you increased your chances of getting something. The same people said the best thing to do was take a leak right after. I decided to do that.

Walked over to the toilet to piss but I couldn't get the boner limp enough to pass urine until I stood at the sink and poured cold water on it.

I looked down at Tinker Bell. "I'm so hot, Buddy Tate. Cool me off, would you?" She was pleading. She wanted a shower.

The first gush hit her flat chest and then I sprayed it over her body. I had a lot in me. I just kept pouring it over her, and then into her mouth when she opened to drink. It was one of those endless pisses that satisfies the soul.

Markus Bloom

Markus Bloom loved play parties. He was being a good host when he sent Tinker Bell to Buddy. He sincerely believed in his own religion of Eros. His motto was, "Where proud perverts gather, there is my church. There I shine."

He used the word pervert often, using it and other words in ways that reversed their traditional negative meanings. Since he considered himself an artist of sex, he thought almost all the forms it took should be encouraged and celebrated; he believed that the body and erotic energy might be used to attain even higher states of consciousness — even to explore spiritual realms.

To keep his own healthy, boundless degeneracy fresh, he changed the sexual roles he played almost weekly. One week he bottomed, the next he was a lesbian, the next he was a top, then for a month he'd play husband; he never tired of the endless dance of sex. He categorised nothing except his own reactions.

For him, pornography was the literature and film exploration of the most mysterious and holy of human activities. He often quoted the great pioneer pornographic film-maker Lasse Braun, who told an interviewer, "As a pornographer, I have cast my lot on the side of love."

Markus quoted Braun often, as he went about his business spreading pornography in all its forms like a *fin de siècle* Johnny Appleseed. Creating it, producing it, manufacturing it, distributing it. With Quixotic ardour he championed what television Jeremiahs like Thomas Flood said America feared most.

Consequently he was a celebrity in great demand in the San Francisco neo-pagan radical sex underground where all the fun happens. His idealism inspired those less bold, and challenged the censors, preachers, pundits, repressers and suppressors he called the 'No People'. Like an evangelist of lust he spread his erotic gospel by writing books, publishing magazines, making videos and CD-Roms, staging erotic festivals and throwing the best play parties in the City of Perpetual Indulgence.

Wherever Markus went, he was accompanied by an entourage of porno starlets, pretty boys, and eccentric women of wealth. At first glance, Buddy Tate seemed an unlikely friend for Markus to add to his circle. Buddy was extreme. A genuine bad boy. But there had been an instant mutual recognition between them in the clinic — and the *size* of that snake he kept in his pants!

Everything he'd heard from his friends Laura Aurora and her consort, Baron — and wicked little Robin — confirmed his first impression of Buddy: here was Priapus, son of Aphrodite and Dionysus. Buddy was unique. Markus looked forward to educating him, perhaps smoothing over the rougher edges.

It was about time for the party to start. He stood at the door welcoming latecomers. They were neo-tribal — modern primitive, biker, swinger — pierced and tattooed and costumed. The liveliest spirits in a defiantly sex-positive community.

He'd never had a taste for rubber before but his interest was piqued with the arrival of a small, slender woman in a black rubber bra, tight rubber corset, and black rubber boots. At first he didn't recognise her because of her mask of tight black rubber.

It was Robin Flood.

Laura Aurora

It was a play party with ritual overtones that began when Laura Aurora, topless — and matchless at ritual — walked onto a stage area to one side of the crowded mattress room. She called the gathering to order:

"There are more non-violent subversives out there than there are anywhere in the country," she declared, adding, "and we have more fun, don't we?" The crowd of celebrants roared. They were sitting or lying languorously on the mattresses in various stages of undress, in various configurations of partners, toying with each other but no more. They knew the order of events: first came the story circle, in which participants were invited to tell tales of their first sexual encounters.

Voices spoke up in the crowd. A woman told of her first encounter with a vibrator. When she was a teenager, she'd found the old fashioned implement hidden in her mother's closet. She nearly electrocuted herself playing with it, but she discovered the joy of vibrators. Other women had vibrator stories. A man related a story of crawling into a storm drain as a ten year old and being able to look up women's skirts through an iron grill in the sidewalk above. The stories were intelligent and sex-positive, and they loosened the crowd up, making each person feel a part of a benign group organism.

Then Laura, assisted by Baron in full regalia, cast a magic circle, bowing to the four directions and invoking the goddess. After the invocation, the love games began.

Robin Flood

Robin talked with Markus Bloom, who admired her costume and what the rubber did for her breasts, and walked past the orgy room into the kitchen. She poured herself some juice, ate some celery sticks, and listened to the conversations around her. The rubber was warm, but it had the desired double effect of hiding her and making sure everyone saw her. Restless, she walked outside for air. An iron staircase descended into an airshaft which led to the party's dungeon, and a cloakroom. She took it. In the largest room a naked man was lying prone on a hospital gurney being fisted by a 'nurse' in white uniform who had unbuttoned her crisply starched blouse to expose her breasts. She moved so that their tips rubbed against his body. A woman was tied to a pole wearing only a garter belt and stockings, while a man in leather who didn't have his heart in it stroked her lightly. There was a row of black leather slings, with no one in them. Stocks of contraceptives and Crisco filled one low table. The space was set up for comfort, safety, to be both intensely sexy and yet cosy. Safe harbour.

Robin was on the run; the shadow of the hawk's wing was over her face. Like a hunted rabbit she dived into any hole she could find. After rejecting her father, there would be no more cheques from the Parousia Foundation. She could not go back to her apartment. She knew her father would set his dogs Hopper and Thumper on her and she feared being snatched and put in some mental institution run by her fellow Christians until the Crusade for San Francisco was over. Or Armageddon.

She lived underground, with friends who had a spare room or a fold-out couch. She dressed like a leather boy when she went roaring down evening streets on her Harley. She disappeared into the shadows of the Mission and North Beach, where she came out in public only on stage, as part of a vampire-lesbian strip act called Tragic Magic.

Like her, Robin's colleagues in this act were young and well-educated and good looking, living in one of the most pleasant cities on the planet. And their most fervent ambition was to strike a meaningful blow at the consumer capitalist business culture that was eating souls everywhere. Their duty as artists was transgression and the re-establishment of ritual.

In addition to taking their clothes off and rubbing their bodies together for horny men, the members of Tragic Magic wrote poems and performed them while blood flowed over their bodies. They ate together, partied together, and slept together.

Robin had come to Markus Bloom's play party because, after a steady diet of women, she wanted some dick. She was hungry for a man's hardness — bone and muscle and gristle and alien psyche. She went back upstairs, not feeling part of anything and wanting to. Markus was gallant and lecherous, coming to embrace her when he saw her standing in the kitchen by herself.

"Can't find anyone, my poor pussy? I can fix you up. In fact, how about *me*?" He leered, lifting his eyebrows like Groucho Marx, and she laughed.

"I don't know if I'm ready for you, Markus. You're big game."

He laughed, flattered; she stepped away from him and went to play voyeur in the orgy room. She stood against a wall, letting the beautiful scene before her define itself in her vision. Everywhere was movement and laughter and soft moaning. The low soft lighting made skin and hair glow. It was a democracy of lust, of body types and tastes.

She was looking for a come-fuck-me man with a lean hard body like Buddy's. Across the room standing near the door, Markus Bloom was talking with Laura and Baron. Not six feet away from her a tanned blonde with very white teeth was giving head to a muscular young man who was masturbating her. They were so hot and so beautiful, orgiasts near them stopped their own moves to watch. They applauded when he proved able to perform auto-fellatio. "Hey! Check this out!" the girl cried. Not far from them, an oblivious threesome flowed together — a man pleasuring slender twins with arts he must have learned elsewhere than in America, Robin thought. She was sweating lightly inside her corset and boots. Trickles ran between her breasts. The rubber pressed firmly against her clitoris. No one approached her.

She saw a familiar face and smiled. It was Captain Stump, Laura's friend, whom she'd met at the Spiral Dance. She saw his merry eyes and his fringe of black beard first. He was naked, and his stump was buried between the thighs of an overweight black woman, who sucked the toes of his foot. She was operatic in her appreciation of the pumping stump.

Everywhere she looked Eros reigned; but there was no one for her.

Markus Bloom

Markus couldn't get Robin out of his mind. He suspected that she had that effect on most people. Seeing her in the rubber outfit made him appreciate the appeal of this fetish for the first time. It was an impervious second skin, tightly displaying while concealing the wearer's body. He had his pick of any number of women at the party, but he'd given himself to all or them before. As he grew older and expanded the number of his conquests, along with the number of things that stimulated his sophisticated appetites, he was more demanding — but never jaded.

Seeing Robin by herself, he decided to try again. He would be perseverance plus.

"I think you're looking for someone, Robin," he whispered in her ear.

"You're right, Markus."

"Will I do until he comes along?"

"This is your lucky night."

He led her to an unoccupied mattress covered with blankets in the corner and pulled her down with him. He stroked her thighs and pressed the hard palm of his hand up against her crotch, feeling rubber's soft resilience. Her firm breasts felt firmer when toyed with through rubber, but her ass felt more elastic. It was like caressing her with gloves on.

But his interest in rubber stopped there. He had no early sexual associations with it. He unzipped the corset and tugged it down over her breasts, slick with sweat, and over her ass, peeling it like a condom from her body. The mask, rubber bra, stockings and boots stayed on. His hand stroked her pussy and then he buried his face there, drinking the nectar that ran onto the blankets between her ass cheeks, using three fingers to probe her sopping wet vagina while pushing a little finger in and out of her slick anus.

She wrapped her slender thighs around his head and grabbed his curly hair, rubbing herself against his strong, hungry mouth — then, just as vehemently pushing his head away.

"I want it in me, Markus. All you've got. Take that famous prick of yours and just shove it up to my lungs. I'm juicy for you, *oooh*, Markus, I'm so juicy..."

Dirty talk drove him crazy. Robin was thrashing about beneath him like a crazy woman while he struggled with his zipper. At last unzipped and unbuckled, he pushed his pants down to his knees, braced his feet, and shoved the happiest part of himself up her tight little cherry-red cunt.

He fucked her with the intensity of a teenager getting it in the first time. That was half his secret. The other half was Taoist sex magic: he could have as many orgasms as she could, but without ejaculating.

She met his every thrust with her own, lifting her firm buttocks from the blankets to screw herself around his crowbar erection. Without losing rhythm, they changed position and she was riding his delirious pole up and down, milking it while his hands played with her black rubber breasts.

She was a goddess astride him, her long finger nails raking his sensitive nipples, pulling his nipple ring. He felt the blood on his chest and then she was leaning over him, arcing her body so she could lick his blood.

She drove herself to orgasm, her eyes squinted shut and her bloody mouth open in a rictus of ecstasy, her tongue licking her lips. She was grunting and moaning, sobbing in a strangled sort of way as he massaged her breasts and then pulled her head to his for a kiss.

Her open mouth descended on his, but then her head jerked back, as if she had seen a ghost. She stopped moving.

"Robin?" he asked, but she didn't look at him. He thrust himself into her to get her attention, but she was limp, a doll he bounced. He twisted his head to see what she saw.

Buddy Tate stood over them, with Laura beside him. They were both naked, and Buddy had an enormous erection which Laura was stroking with visible delight.

Buddy Tate

I walked around the party in Markus's robe with a hard on

and an idiotic smile on my face. It was like I had discovered a secret society of people who thought about and dreamed about the same kind of nasty stuff I did. Only it wasn't nasty to them. I've watched a lot of people do wild things, and most of them have this really selfish look are on their faces when they are getting off. Not these people. The look on their faces was like they were sharing something.

I guess they were. For sure I wasn't.

That big room just wouldn't let me go. It was like watching the Bay waters at night. Rise and fall, in and out. I saw Markus headed into a corner of it with a girl who was dressed in black rubber. He never missed a trick.

People wore some kinky stuff. I went around the edge of the fucking-ocean to the kitchen, and standing in the middle of it was a big guy with a bone in his nose who looked like he was having a good time. I couldn't believe what I was seeing. Not only did he have a bone in his nose, he was wearing chains, leather, high heels, lipstick — the whole nine yards and more. His butt was bare, and he was tattooed all over. What was weirdest was that he was wearing a strap-on dingus like the one Robin busted my cherry with. Was this guy confused, or what?

I turned around so he wouldn't see I was laughing at him. Then I thought, who the hell are you to laugh at anyone? Buddy Tate is the weirdest here.

There was a stairway down to the basement off the kitchen. I went down it in bare feet to look around. Fat women showing their tits hanging up coats, and in the next room people hurting each other.

I'd heard about this, but I didn't believe it.

A nurse with her arm up some guy's ass. Ouch.

A woman with a fine butt was getting it smacked with a ping pong paddle. Double ouch.

I was headed back upstairs when I saw the man with the

bone in his nose coming down, followed by a big blonde showing her tits. She had a whip. It looked like there was going to be a show, so I stayed to watch.

There were chains hanging from the ceiling, with leather wrist straps. The blonde bitch stretched him up on the chains till he was standing on tip toe in high heels. She flicked the whip a few times, and then gave him a good crack, but he didn't flinch. He kept a smile on his face, like now he's getting what he came to the party for. Crack!

I guess I was seeing the real thing, because other people stopped what they were doing to watch for a minute. I didn't get it. It was too weird for me. Being hit with a whip has got to smart something fierce. They could be fucking. But they both seemed to be enjoying themselves. His ass was getting red and welted. She stopped and moved her hand over what she'd done, then picked up a different whip, a smaller one. Crack!

The small whip got his attention. He kept smiling, but now he was wincing, and little sounds were coming from him. She gave him two dozen of those, and he was feeling something.

When she untied him, he kissed her, a hot one, and they stood together like a king and queen. That's when she saw me watching them with my johnson sticking out of the bathrobe.

I was surprised when I looked down. Something about the whipping had gotten to me, I guess. Maybe because they were looking so hot because of it, and so close.

"That's the best compliment we've had all evening," she said to me, her hand stroking his ass and the dingus he wore.

"I don't get it — but you know, whatever rings your chimes."

She kept her eyes on my prick, and I wondered if I was about to get lucky. She was older, but good looking, with sexy saggy boobies.

"What don't you get?"

"Doesn't that *hurt?*"

"I think that's the idea. Did it hurt, Baron?"
"Perfectly, my dear."
"I just like it straight," I said. "That's all I need."
They laughed, but I didn't think they were laughing at me, but at the word 'straight'. Or the idea. I think they were too bent to imagine how good straight could be.
"Don't mind us, we're just having fun."
"Like I said, your idea of fun..."
"I'm Laura Aurora, and this is my husband..."
"Baron, I know."
"And who are you?"
"Buddy. Buddy Tate."
She lifted her eyes off my cock at that news. I got that powerful feeling that she knew who I was. It's like a rush.
But she didn't say anything, just looked at me hard as if she was trying to piece something together.
"I'm a friend of Markus's," I told her.
"Yes... He's talked about you."
"Low down and dirty, probably."
"What about your eye? He didn't tell us about your eye."
"I can still fuck with one eye, if that's what you mean."
So far she'd noticed I was a big prick with one eye.
"I believe you."
"Okay."
"Why did you come here tonight?"
"Just looking for a girl."
"Any special girl?"
"I guess not." I wanted to say you'll do, but this was a lady.
"Are you sure?" She was grinning at Baron and he was grinning back. I didn't get it. These people were over my head.
"Hell, I don't know what you're talking about."
"Come on, I want to show you something upstairs." She took my hand and I followed her upstairs to the fucking ocean.

She led me straight to where Markus Bloom was being ridden like a merry-go-round horse by a girl in a rubber bra and not much else. I could see Markus's dick going in and out and the sight stiffened me up so Laura noticed and grabbed me. She had a magic touch on my dick. I didn't see the rubber girl's back until she bent over to kiss him. She had a tattoo with a big snake in it, and dragons.

"Peekaboo," I said. "I see you."

XXX
Blood Wedding

"You are obviously some shy of reality," I said to Robin when everybody had left and we were alone on the mattresses with the sun coming up. "Part of you is just not here, I think."

"I'm real, Buddy." She was curled up facing me, wrapped in a blanket. Those big blue eyes were smiling.

"Real is something that's sure, like fucking."

"Well? We did that, a few times. My little spot's been rubbed raw."

"Markus probably did that."

"Are you jealous of Markus? He's not as big as you."

"I'm happy to hear you admit it."

"But he can last longer than you."

"He's got more money and two eyes, too. I'm not jealous of Markus. He took advantage, but he's my buddy."

"Buddy, it felt so good to have you inside me. I didn't think I'd ever feel you again."

"It hasn't been that long since you and Pearl ganged up on me." Then I told her the bad news about Pearl.

"He did that to her?" Like she didn't believe it. She sat straight up and big tears ran down her face. "Hold me, Buddy."

I just held her while she cried, a first for me. When she stopped, she took my face in her hands and looked at me. I knew what was coming next.

"What happened to your eye? Is it...?"

"It's gone. Rotting in a septic system in Idaho." I told her about the cross in that eye, about going home to see Daddy and Flood. How I failed and that's why I hadn't looked for her.

"I wish you had."

"I promised you I'd kill him and I didn't. I like to keep my word."

"He's coming here to San Francisco with his fucking Crusade."

"I know, I saw his posters."

"He'll be preaching at a different place every night. There'll be chances...."

"I can't do it."

She froze on me. I let go of her. She was like wood.

"What do you mean?"

"I tried getting close to him in a crowd. All I've got is a .38, and he's got good security, you know that. I don't know what I can do. I'm not a sniper."

"We'll make him come to us."

"How?"

"Leave that to me, if I can get him alone, you'll do it, won't you?"

"I'll get it done, don't worry."

"Then we're free. We'll find some place to hide."

"I won't hide. I want everyone to know it was Buddy Tate who killed him."

"But then you'll probably be in a prison, and I'll be alone."

"It's got to be that way."

"Why?"

"Because that's the way I always thought it would be."

"Buddy?"

"Yeah?"

"Do you think we're crazy?"

"Yeah, we're crazy. But so is everybody else."

She put her head in my lap, gave Mr Penis Head a goodnight kiss, and went to sleep. The shades were pulled, but they were glowing with the sun. There was a space between the shade and the window moulding and through it I could see a sliver of blue sky.

I couldn't sleep. All I could do was to sit with her head in my lap watching that sliver of blue sky. This was new for me, watching over somebody. Being able to touch her cheek or her full lips with my finger, or push her hair back. She didn't wake up when I did that. Who was she? I didn't know. Just some gaga girl with good aim. She knew where to shoot me, so I wouldn't even know where I'd been shot. It had been like that from the minute we met at Star's.

It didn't make any sense. Feeling like this was strange because I knew I didn't give a shit about myself, but she was different. I had to care for her. We were hot in bed, but this was something else.

I thought about escape. I could always put a pillow under her head and slip out the door into the blue sky, and *vaya con Dios*, Robin. But I knew I wouldn't do that.

Daddy used to say, "Tell the truth to yourself, even if you wish you hadn't." So I told myself the truth through the hours of that morning when I watched Robin sleep. She had put her hooks in me just like Flood's goon Hopper had put a cross in my eye. For the first time in my life with a girl, something else was more important than the fucking. And that was dangerous. You start thinking like that about a girl, and it's ball and chain time.

I tried to think where I slipped up — where I let something besides sex make a difference, but there's no one time that you notice. As usual, it was just one thing leading to the next, like following a ball of string unwinding in front or you. You kept your head down and followed the string and didn't even notice when it led you into the cage and the door slammed behind you.

I never had any choice in the matter. It was all decided before I came along. I wanted to be noticed — that's how it started. After that, everything was 1-2-3.

It was like my head was stuffed with all that had happened, and there was more to come I had no choice about. Thinking wasn't going to change that.

I fell asleep sitting up, not thinking.

❖❖❖

I was in a red room with Robin. Everything was red, so red that I could only look at her, and her face was glowing, like she was lighted from inside. We were getting married, and I was happy about it. That was when I knew it was a nightmare, so I tried to wake up, but I couldn't. Robin took off her dress and she was covered with tattoos, even her titties. She was pierced everywhere, not just the usual places, but on her thighs, her shoulders, at her collar bone. We kissed and she bit me with pointed teeth so that the blood filled our mouths together. I wanted to fuck her real bad, just drive myself inside her and stay there pumping steady, but when I touched my prick it was slick and slimy and cold. I looked down and saw that it was a snake, and I saw Robin's reaction at the same moment. She ran to a big window and climbed up on the sill so she could jump. I tried to catch her but I was too late, and she was falling — and then I was, too, because there was a cord joining our wrists...

❖❖❖

She was straddling me, shaking me.

"Buddy! Wake up. You're making the most awful noises."

She was naked. No tattoos, no piercings like in the dream. Just the nipple ring I kissed when she lowered her num-nums to my mouth. Bigger than bite-size, and firm.

I could tell that what was waking up lower under the blankets wasn't a snake.

"What time is it?"

"Just after midnight. You've been out all day."

"When did you get up?"

"Hours ago. I cleaned up a little. Had something to eat. Talked to Markus."

"Where's he?"

"Getting into some mischief, I think. He won't be back for a few days. The place is all ours."

"Is that all you did? Just talk?" I couldn't believe that Markus hadn't taken advantage again. I would have.

"Well..." She smiled and looked like she was deciding something.

"You can tell me. Markus is my friend."

"I'm a bad girl, Buddy. You know that."

"Bad girls are the best."

If I was jealous at all, her telling me made it all right. Dirty stories were a turn-on.

"He wanted to fuck me, but I'm still sore. You know how he is. He won't stop until you give him something. He was playing with my ass, sticking his finger in, while I was making coffee in the kitchen."

"Did it feel good?"

"Oh yes. It always feels good when my ass is played with."

"Did he stick it in?"

"No, I didn't want him to. I just wanted my coffee. Coffee is my addiction."

I was getting impatient. "Well, what did you do?"

"He was all dressed, ready to go out. But he unzipped his fly and showed me that big thing he stuck in me last night. 'Just suck it a little,' is what he said. I didn't have to do anything. He walked over to where I was sitting at the kitchen table and stuck it in my face, skinned back and ready. So I gave him a coffee suck."

"What's that?" Maybe a little jealousy flared up here.

"I kept some warm coffee in my mouth so when I sucked him it was warm. He came right away."

"Did you swallow?",

"No. From now on, that's just for you. I made him come in my coffee cup. Then he drank it."

"You're a slut. You are some fucking whore slut."

She licked her lips and winked at me. Those hooks were in deep. She was my kind of girl in the whole universe, which I guess is what they call love.

I threw off the blankets and showed her my erection.

"How about a coffee suck for the big boy?"

She shook her head. "No, I have other plans for us. Come on, get up. Let's take a bath together."

❖❖❖

The big tub was full of bubbles. She had put candles around Markus's bathroom for light, and they made it feel like a cave. There's something about the privacy of a bathroom that makes it sexier, sometimes, than a bedroom. I got in the tub and buried myself in bubbles, while Robin played with make-up at the bathroom sink. When she was ready she came to me. She'd put lipstick on her mouth and nipples, and edged the red with a thin black line to make her puffy lips stand out even more than they did normally.

"Now you," she said, holding up a lipstick. "Remember that big 'X' you drew on Star's window?"

I held still while she put lipstick on my mouth. The stickiness was like sex, and when we kissed in the bubbles we rubbed the stickiness all over our faces. In the warm water we flowed around each other, touching every part underwater so that I couldn't tell where I left off and she began. Or we'd copy each other — when I played with her boobies she'd play with mine. I got enormously hard, like a tower, and it stuck out of the bubbles so that we both laughed. She'd touch it, or put her tongue in the tip for a minute, but the idea we both got into was just to play in the water. When she had to pee, I told her to do it in the water, and put my hand down there to feel the piss jet erupt against my wrinkled fingers.

After a while we stopped, and just leaned back, kind of folded together, and she said some words like a ceremony over us:

"Let him kiss me with the kisses of his mouth:

For thy love is better than wine.

My beloved is unto me as a bundle of myrrh,

That lieth between my breasts."

"What's that?" I asked her. "It sounds like poetry."

"It's from the only section of the Bible I like. Since this is about as close as we're going to get to a wedding, I wanted to say it to you. There's one more line."

"Set me as a seal upon thine heart, as a seal upon thine arm, for love is strong as death."

I said the words over to myself so I wouldn't forget them. Set me as a seal upon thine heart... This was serious juju she was doing. She was marrying us so I could never escape, and it was all right with me.

"Buddy, don't ever say love to me, that's all I ask."

"I won't."

"And don't be surprised at anything I do."

"I won't."

She moved, and I didn't see what she was doing. When I looked, I saw that the bubbles around her were turning red. She had a fearsome look in her eye and she was holding up a razor blade. She'd cut herself, and now she was going to cut me.

"What are you doing?"

"'Trust me, Buddy. Hold still for me."

What choice did I have? She leaned over me and cut my neck and kissed where she cut. I could feel her sucking, her soft mouth and pointed tongue drinking my blood, licking me.

I never expected being cut and bleeding would turn me on, but it did. The tower was up above the bubbles again, and the bubbles were turning red. It occurred for just a flash that maybe I was going crazy, letting all this shit happen, but what did that mean? I was crazy already.

Robin moved away from me in the tub and climbed the tower, a bloody lipsticked grin splitting her face. She stood and lowered herself slowly on it, the wet heat of the water sloshing into the tight wet heat of her cunt. She had a fierce look on her face when she'd swallowed me whole, and then that look changed into surprise. She was moving up and down on my root, and the water in the tub was slopping over the sides, and then a tidal wave slapped me in the face and she fell back. The tub was shaking and I saw the water jump out of the toilet and back in. I reached out and grabbed Robin but she was slippery and I couldn't hold onto her. Dust and plaster dumped down on us. The medicine chest opened and bottles and jars came banging out. I was bounced up and down in the water and banged my elbow.

When the shaking stopped, most of the water in the tub was on the floor. Red covered everything, like in my dream.

"Earthquake, Buddy. Just like he predicted."

"Who predicted?"

"My father. I think he's arrived in San Francisco."

XXXI
End Times

Buddy Tate

Robin ran to the window with a towel around her. I was king of the jitters: everything was jumping up and down inside me, my guts and my heart were bouncing like superballs, my eyeballs were jiggling. I staggered and limped to a television set and punched it till I got all the news. That bitch Mother Nature had taken a club to San Francisco. There were pictures of fires, collapsed buildings, and people like me acting jittery and crying.

Then Flood's face was zoomed in on. He was on the news, with a Chinese-American reporter in the background telling us that Flood's Crusade for San Francisco had begun with a bang. He was speaking in a big stadium, standing in front of a huge cross that sparkled with blue and red lights.

"Nation shall rise against nation, and kingdom against

kingdom and there shall be famines and pestilences, and earthquakes..."

Robin came back from the window. "I can't see much. It's smoky out there. I think there's a crack in the building across the street." Then she saw who was on television.

I was glued to Flood. He was foaming at the mouth and people were cheering. She sat on the couch with me, knees to her chin.

"Our nation is divided into many pieces and we see them falling apart before our eyes, The Kingdom of God is fighting against the Kingdom of Evil..." I zapped the son-of-a-bitch off.

"We're the Kingdom of Evil, Buddy. He's talking about us."

"I figured that. Looks like the Kingdom of God has a whole lot of people in its army."

"My father's flock are sheep. They're in the big city now. There are wolves running in the streets."

"He's got Mr. Hopper and his nasty friend. And a lot more like them. They know how to put a brand on you."

"I'm not worried about them. They'll do what he says, and I think I can get him to come to us."

She was shivering, so I put my arms around her.

"How?"

"He wants my forgiveness, and for that, he's willing to accept my punishment." She smiled, showing blood on her teeth.

"Bang bang?"

"I have a better idea. It's what will make him want to come to see me — anywhere I say."

"What is it?"

"Let it be a surprise. You'll be there."

I wanted to know more, but she closed up and just sat huddled in the corner of the couch, thinking about something. Things were a mess in the kitchen. Pots and pans and cans and boxes all over the floor and the counters. I found something to eat and went to clean up. It was ragged work shaving. I put a band-aid on my neck to cover up Robin's cut and got dressed.

I was feeling panicky, like K. Farouk's pistol was the only thing in my life I had to hang onto. There was a whole list of things I didn't want to do banging around in my head and making me crazy, and only one thing I wanted to do: run.

Robin Flood

Buddy's gone. But I knew he will return.

Alone, I listen to my heart, and shiver at the earthquake inside. *Dah-dum, dah-dum, dah-dum.* Blood I came from, blood I go to. I ride on blood, my body a temporary channel for the river of life, a red liquid tide surging against the elastic boundaries of veins and arteries. Down the surging rapids of this eternal torrent I am hurtled, a small black boat on a river of pain and desire.

I drank his blood. I begged him for his death finger, and he gave it to me. Buddy Tate is mine.

Now I desire, and desire is dangerous for me.

Laura Aurora

Buses full of crusaders in bright colours streamed into earthquake-stunned San Francisco from the south and east. The buses were seen parked at City Hall, at Fisherman's Wharf, at the Embarcadero, and down Market Street. Thomas Flood's frightened, anxious, proselytising armies piled out from them to roam the streets of the stricken city with Bibles in their hands. Innocent irrumators and J.O. Jocks in the Castro were accosted by squads of middle-aged women and elderly men who had been directed by Flood to surround and harass the obviously degenerate. People with piercings, tattoos and strange haircuts, people wearing black leather or not enough clothes, were to be confronted by the wrath of the godly. Serious and persistent persuasion was to be applied.

When Laura Aurora first saw these pilgrims on the streets of her scrambled city she winced at their tight, mean faces. But she knew there are many paths up the mountain, so at first she was inclined to be charitable toward the invaders. Then in North Beach an incident outside a strip club reminded her that the Indians who welcomed the first Pilgrims soon came to regret their charity.

A crowd of onlookers had gathered around six elderly men and women in bright polyester who were screaming Bible babble at young stripper outside a strip club on Columbus Avenue. Laura knew the young woman from pagan gatherings. She belonged to another coven, but she was an enthusiastic apprentice in S/M circles. Her name was Sheba, and she looked especially pretty in bondage, Laura recalled. Sheba and Baron had done a scene at Markus's play party.

She was engaged in a hopeless debate with Flood's crusaders, who were preventing her from entering Babycakes, her place of worship. She tried to speak to them of the Goddess, but they shouted her down with their dirty-minded craziness.

"Exploitation of the flesh is a sin! Lust will drive you down to the fiery pit! We are trying to help you save your immortal soul! Cover your nakedness and accept Jesus as your saviour!"

Sheba covered her ears to block out the foulness of their exhortations. Then she was inspired to respond with her righteous flesh. Barred from the temple where she was worshipped, however crudely, as a manifestation of Aphrodite, Sheba decided to perform her dance on the street for the Warriors of Christ who confronted her. Her eyes flashed with bold defiance.

She shook out her long blonde hair streaked with the colours of the rainbow and it cascaded down her back. She opened her leather jacket and offered to their shock and dismay the sight of her quivering young breasts, which swayed as she began to move her hips. She stretched her arms up and moved her hands and fingers in intricate patterns.

Her street dance drew men as if by magic from blocks around. The men pressed against in against Christ's Warriors, angling for a better look. Although fond of dancing naked in public, Laura decided not to join Sheba's protest.

But it gave her an idea.

Thomas Flood

Thomas Flood loved helicopters. The snicker-snack of the turning blades, the glorious feeling of descending from the heavens as if on a wing and a prayer, elated him.

The Parousia helicopter, a big Sikhorsky, clattered over the low white cityscape of Sodom by the Sea toward a rally Flood had called at a Triple-X establishment known as the 'Pussy Palace' aka the Erotic Exotic Exploratorium.

Flood sat by himself gazing out over the city he'd come to conquer. He fondled a relic in his pocket, a good luck charm. A sow's ear in a silk purse, he smiled to himself, fingering the leathery object. He had cut it from the whore's body, from the black whore he'd discovered in the Hotel Napa.

His team, headed by Hopper and his disgusting associate Floyd Thundergaard, universally known as Thumper, sat behind him talking about strategy for the Pussy Palace rally.

While he fingered his sow's ear and the buildings and streets *whooshed* by beneath their feet, Flood talked to the Lord.

— Lord, I have done thy bidding. Our armies have fallen on this city of lust. Tonight we will bring the conflagration to an egregious den of iniquity.

— This will show them. They laugh off my earthquake?

We'll give them fire.

— Lord, sometimes you scare me.

— I told you: I am a jealous God. These people need a lesson. It's the Kingdom of God or else.

— I am your instrument.

— This is the big one. Don't screw it up.

— Your anger fills me.

— It should. I'm pouring it in your ear.

— My daughter is down there somewhere. She has hardened her heart against me, and accused me of monstrous things.

— Don't bother me with your personal problems.

— I know I am fallible and weak, Lord, but I need your help with her! I will be nothing unless she forgives me.

— Don't bullshit me. You know you can't lie to me. It's going to come down on your head, and she's the key to the crash.

— Why does she hate me?"

— Why shouldn't she? I hate you.

Flood broke off his prayer. Sometimes these prayers went nowhere. When you talked with God you had to be prepared that sometimes he wouldn't make sense.

He shouted back to Hopper: "What kind of coverage do we have lined up?"

"One network, two locals so far. The bonfire will be what they want to get. That's what they're coming for."

The bonfire would be the highlight of the Crusade for San Francisco: half a ton of filth burnt in the street while he preached The End. That would strike fear in their hearts.

He felt a surge of power, God-like power.

Markus Bloom

Markus Bloom was not the kind of self-hating, pasty-faced pervert pornographer who would allow a dark angel like

Flood to fall upon his beloved city without fighting back. He confessed to many weaknesses, but he adhered to a strict code of right and wrong: Eros was right, and the God of St. Augustine was wrong.

Like Sheba in North Beach before her strip club, Markus made his stand at the entrance to the Pussy Palace, his cohort a bevy of porno beauties, transvestites, leather dykes and heavy players. Word had spread in the radical sex underground of the City of Perpetual Indulgence that guerrilla theatre was going to be employed against the invaders. Dozens of defiant degenerates swelled the ranks of Markus Bloom's army until they were able to ring the building with a human wall. In their motley uniforms of leather, chains and dungarees they were a formidable sight, and people kept arriving who wanted to join them and confront the fanatics. A militant party atmosphere began to develop.

Markus left his post and walked across the street to the dumpster that city fathers had provided for the purification of sexual images by fire. Some of them were probably his own creation, he knew. The television cameras were being positioned around the big dumpster, and men with walkie-talkies darted about looking up at the sky. Markus heard a helicopter.

He approached one of the technicians to ask where the director was. There was going to be a counter-demonstration protesting the book-burning. The man ran off, and soon an impatient young man wearing headphones and carrying a clipboard strode up to him.

The director kept looking skyward, and the noise of the descending helicopter grew steadily louder.

"What demonstration are you part of?"

Markus turned and pointed to the growing wall around the Pussy Palace.

"We're the people they hate, these Crusaders. What Flood is

going to burn in this dumpster is our art."

The director was sceptical. "You're shitting me. That's *smut* in that dumpster. I saw it."

"And you know it when you see it, I'll bet."

"Yes, of course. But what are you doing to do? There's not going to be a riot, is there? I'll have to move the cameras, and they're set now."

Markus smiled at the director's nervousness. He pushed it: "Just to demonstrate that one man's smut is the next man's delight, what we're going to do is remain in front of the Pussy Palace and get really comfortable. Then, as the spirit moves us, we're going to get down and dirty, do you know what I mean? We're going to play some games you can't show on television. But you know what that means: you won't be able to show the Pussy Palace. There'll be no contrast. Just an evil preacher with a big bonfire, and us yelling and..." — he paused for effect as the director got the picture — "and...slurping."

He giggled inappropriately, as if he saw the joke and the director didn't. The director glared at him, and turned his attention to the roof of the nearby building on which Flood's helicopter had set down. The noise was deafening.

Markus Bloom returned with a simple message: "These people would like to burn *us* in that dumpster out there! What do you say we turn the other cheek? In fact, why not *both cheeks*? Let's show them what they're missing!" He giggled happily.

Markus began to remove his clothes. Soon everyone was tugging and pulling and slipping out of clothing, and a wall of naked flesh three or four bodies deep stretched around the Pussy Palace.

Naked, they began to cavort. The television cameras were quickly pointed their way, for pictures never to be broadcast. Powerful lights illuminated a living frieze of satyrs, nymphs, and maenads guarding the temple of Eros. It was a bizarre sight in a city of bizarre sights, but it was instantly upstaged by the entrance of Thomas Flood.

He was being scooted in a golf cart to a cherry picker that would lift him and an aide above the dumpster filled with smut. The massed ranks of the Warriors for Christ parted for his cart, many or them shouting Bible verses. Some wept at their proximity to Flood. They surrounded the dumpster as the cherry picker lifted him over their heads, singing "Stand up, stand up, for decency."

He stood above them like the Angel of Death, his head thrown back, looking skyward. Hopper stood behind him, scanning the crowd and keeping an eye on the perverts. Microphones whined, and Flood's voice boomed over the P.A. system:

"We have arrived here with our armies, as we said we would. We are here in the heart of Sodom struggling against the Kingdom of Evil. We have brought our Crusade to this wicked city, and we have brought the cleansing fire with us! Let it start fires all over this suffering land!"

His face was a stern mask looking down upon them. His right hand was jammed deep in the pocket of his sober, elegant suit. He peered across the street at the heathen demonstrators ringing the Pussy Palace.

"These are *their* works!" he shouted, indicating the dumpster and then pointing to the naked degenerates moving in obscene rhythms before the neon-streaked building. Hopper produced a torch and handed it to Flood, who held it aloft and pronounced:

"Let the fires of a righteous God consume the filthy, graven images of a degenerate city!"

He tossed the torch into the dumpster, the contents of which had been soaked with gasoline. *Whoosh*! Flames roared twenty feet into the sky. The Warriors for Christ screamed their approval. The perverts howled. Onlookers coughed and cheered.

"Let us march!" Flood exhorted his followers through the leaping flames and smoke. "Remember: they walked in the midst of the fire, praising God, and blessing the Lord!"

The funeral pyre of pornography lighted the night sky. Charred bits of erotic imagery fluttered down on Christian heads.

Thomas Flood was lowered, and he climbed into his golf cart. With Hopper driving, and surrounded by a squad of Warriors, he approached the pagan front line.

Markus Bloom stepped forward to meet the invaders wearing only a formal smile but looking as regal as Atahualpa. He was accompanied by a lissom mocha pre-op with perfect breasts and an equally perfect cock. Behind them stood a tall dominant everyone knew as Lady Terrence wearing a corset and tall boots that were being shined by the tongue of a fat former Jesuit priest dressed in only a motorcycle cap. Nearby, leather dykes aired their Amazon chests and pretty boys in white jockey shorts were kissing. The outrageous tableau teased the cameras.

Thomas Flood stood in the golf cart so that he towered over Markus. He found that he was nervous before the sinful.

"Get out of my way. I'm going in there," Thomas Flood ordered. Television crews scrambled, trying to record the oncoming confrontation between the powerful televangelist and the proud, naked pervert without showing forbidden skin.

"This is holy ground," Markus said calmly. "It's also private property. Fanatics and puritans are not welcome."

There were shouts of approval behind him.

Flood decided to try another tactic. Sensing the potential in the confrontation, he played to the television cameras.

"The gates of Hell are guarded by the dogs of smut," he proclaimed. "He challenges me because I just burned his children

— the pornographic products of his twisted mind. He is of the party of Evil."

Markus Bloom was at a loss for a moment, as if even his sophisticated mind could not comprehend the bullshit he was hearing. The television cameras focused on the way he chewed at the corner of his mouth, wondering how to respond to such craziness on national TV. After all, he *was* naked. Then it came:

"Hold it," Markus said. "This is a simple case of attempted breaking and entering. A man in a suit with a gang of zealots trying to trespass on somebody else's church and disrupt their worship."

Markus crafted a good sound bite, radicals knew; but Thomas Flood was not prepared to be challenged. He had imagined the ungodly would flee before him. He squeezed the sow's ear in his pocket and wished that he could kneel in his chariot and consult with the Lord. He sensed that it was the most crucial moment of his life, and he was unprepared. But how, after having led his legions to Sodom, could he back down from this clever, naked pornographer?"

"You profane the word church!" he began, but realised he was spluttering. The naked man's debauched eyes bored into his like hot sensors. Flood had no choice but to return the intense stare. He knew that he had to avoid looking down at the man's nudity in the eyes of the cameras.

"All right," he said at last. "Open those doors and get out of the way!" His command was delivered in the deep, solemn tones he used during his televised miracles, but Bloom simply giggled.

"You're not coming through us," he said.

"I will roll right over you!" Flood thundered in vain.

"Go home now, back to your television life."

Flood sensed danger. Why was this pervert so self-confident? Why wouldn't he get out of the way? Why was he smiling like *he* had the upper hand?

Then Bloom was speaking again, pointing at Flood.

"Beware false prophets!" he said. "This man is a false prophet. His daughter is one of us, and she hates him — for good reasons."

Flood felt the blood leave his head. What was happening? What was this pervert saying? Robin? *Oh, not Robin!*

Sensing that it was his finest moment, Bloom kept the story he told TV America simple and almost Biblical in its purity. His theme was the hypocrite unmasked. How the mighty holy conceal their crimes. Murder. Child abuse. Cruelty. Insanity. While he spoke, he fixed baleful eyes on Flood, who stood with bowed head, stricken — suddenly transformed from righteous crusader to accused criminal before a national television audience.

When Bloom finished, the cameras were turned on Flood and reporters yelled questions at him. He shook his head, disorientated.

"These are lies, of course," he answered mildly. He shook his head again and looked around him, squinting into the lights. Behind him the flames were at their height. "I deny these filthy accusations." But there was no conviction in his voice. He touched Hopper on the shoulder and the big man backed up the golf cart and turned around. The Warriors for Christ were silent as he passed through them, charred confetti raining down on him.

When the crowd of perverts saw Thomas Flood retreating, they set up a raucous cheer. They sent their champion forth, and he had conquered. Stunned that he had prevailed, Markus Bloom accepted their congratulations and kisses. Then, as their naked guerrilla general, he led them forward against the retreating enemy, chasing the crowd of Pharisees from his temple, brandishing no weapon but his rampant erection.

Laura Aurora

At almost the same moment, across the city at Fisherman's Wharf, Laura Aurora led an unusual attack by pagans on the Crusade for San Francisco.

Laura's strategy was lifted from what she had seen Sheba do with her dance. A small army of witches drawn from the thirteen major covens scattered around the Bay area converged after dark on the Wharf parking lot, where ten Crusade buses were parked and their occupants had set up lawn chairs and card tables.

Laura surrounded the first bus in line with a dozen of the prettiest lesbian witches, and their tactics were repeated around the other buses. The Crusaders who stood near the door of the first bus looked with horror upon Laura's toplessness. She chose a woman her own age to approach first, thinking, *be gentle, I might have had to lead her life...* The woman looked more puzzled by the sight of Laura's breasts than shocked.

"What do you want?" she asked. Laura replied by stepping closer and kissing the woman lovingly on the lips. The woman jumped back, rubbing her lips.

But there was to be no dialogue, no debate with the deluded and the fanatical. Kisses were to be the only communication, and there was no appeal from them. Soon all the Crusaders had retreated to their buses and locked the doors.

The witches made a circle and set up a powerful chant to make the buses disappear. They cast a spell that worked, for the buses started up, one by one, and slowly rolled out of the City of Perpetual Indulgence, followed by the hoots and cackles of the victorious witches.

Thomas Flood

As his helicopter rose into the night sky above the flames of the bonfire, Thomas Flood imagined himself jumping from it and falling into the fire. Then the Lord spoke to him.

— The flames of Hell. How appropriate.

— I told you I was weak.

— You've failed me.

— I pleaded with you to let me seek my own redemption. But you sent me here. I did my best.

— Flood, you will have to die to redeem yourself for your sins.

— I asked her to punish me, to forgive me...

— I don't care what you did to her. I'm talking about this fuck-up. You'll have to pay with your miserable life.

— I don't care anymore. I am your sacrifice.

— Maybe we can make a martyr out of you. Maybe you can still be of use. Martyrs are always good as examples.

Flood bowed his head in surrender.

Timing is all. Hopper tapped him on the shoulder at that moment of utter resignation to his fate, a telephone in his hand.

"Reverend Flood, it's your daughter. She saw the television coverage and wants to talk with you."

Flood took the phone and put it to his ear as if it might contain a bomb.

"Yes?"

"Father, I saw what happened." Her voice seemed far away, although, he reflected, they might be flying over where she was. He couldn't think of what to say to her.

"Father?"

"Yes?"

"I'm ready."

"Ready?"

"I can forgive you."

He was flooded with a wave of gratitude. He put aside suspicion.

"Can I see you?" he asked, fearing she might say no.

"Oh, yes. I've worked out your punishment."

"What is it?"

"To follow in Christ's footsteps to the cross."

"To the cross?" His mouth was dry. She *was* his daughter!

"My forgiveness will follow."

"I don't know what to say. Where can I find you?"

"Come to 346 Saint Street tomorrow at 8pm."

"What is there?"

"It's a loft used by the Society of Spectacles. I'll be there. You must come alone, without your goons."

"And you will forgive me?"

"With all that's left of my heart."

"Why do I have to wait?"

"There will be an invited audience. People whose forgiveness you must also ask for."

"No. I won't do that. For you, I will suffer willingly. But not for the crowd. Please don't ask me to do that."

Silence on the phone. Did she hang up?

"Robin?"

"I'm here." Her voice was colder than ice on an open wound.

"Let it be just us, Robin. Please."

"All right. Come now."

"Now?"

"I'll be there in an hour. At midnight."

"But..."

"No more excuses." She hung up.

He looked at the phone, acutely conscious that he was held up — suspended in the sky — by a whirring machine, with a dead phone in his hand.

"Hopper!" he called, Hopper crept forward and knelt before his master.

"We're putting down somewhere. I'm going to see my

daughter."

"That's pretty sudden, sir."

"I'm going to get out and take a cab, when we're down. And you're not to follow me."

"Sir, why not?"

"You can't go where I'm going."

The silver bird lurched, and Hopper fell back on his ass. Flood suddenly felt light-hearted.

It was all to be, as he had foreseen. His life and his work had led him to the inevitable. He called upon the Lord.

— O my Father, if this cup may not pass away from me, except I drink it, thy will be done.

There was no answer this time.

XXXII

Exorcism

There was nowhere to run to. Between the earthquake and the future coming up fast there was no alley I could duck down.

I walked uphill and downhill, and people were out in the streets looking jittery. There was a lot of smoke, and sirens wailing. Somebody said there were fires in Oakland, somebody else said North Beach. The sun was going down and it was choked with smoke. Ambulances and fire engines charged through red lights.

I was on the look out for Anyguy because I needed some luck now, not to mention advice. I walked over to the Mission to check out the El Capitan homeless dump, and who was sitting on my old spot on the sidewalk under the marquee but Big Mac, with a big dirty bandage over his leg where I'd shot him. I didn't give a shit about Big Mac, but seeing him there helpless made me feel good. Like just by accident I'd done a good deed for him with that shot. I mean,

I'd slowed him down. Now he didn't have to scare people. He could enjoy life at crotch level.

When you get tired, you go home. But I was homeless, like Big Mac. If I didn't go to Robin, there was no place for me to go. Maybe she would be waiting for me, maybe she wouldn't.

She. She. She. She. She. *She.* *She*!

What happened to me? *She* did.

I was feeling so sorry for myself. I stepped into the street without looking and almost got hit, but somebody pulled me back by grabbing my arm. It was Anyguy, with a big grin on his face, just in the nick of time.

"I've been looking for you," I said.

"I thought you might be, Buddy. I've been having dreams about you. So when I was driving around I kept my eyes open."

There was a limo behind him, parked at the curb. I wasn't surprised. Nothing Anyguy did would surprise me any more. He was powerful in ways not yet recognised by modern science.

We got in the limo and he looked at me and slapped his knees. "That was some earthquake, huh?" He sounded happy about it, like it was another one or his tricks.

"It shook me up. I'm still shook up. Everybody is."

He chuckled. Heh, heh, heh, like that. "That's fine, that's just fine," he said, and he slapped his knee again.

"You're crazy."

"I've been praying for an earthquake for years. All of this was Ohlone land once, and my people were happy here. Soon maybe, it will be ours again. Let nature rip it up and start over."

"That'll take a while."

"Ghosts are patient people."

We stopped at an intersection because the street was full of running people yelling things we couldn't hear. The streets were jumping. It was a good time to be safe in a limousine.

"Where are you headed, Buddy?"

"That's what I wanted to ask you. I don't feel very lucky right now. When the earthquake happened, I was in a tub with Robin and she was sucking blood from my neck. I think we got married. So I guess I'm going back to her."

I told him she was at Markus's and he leaned forward to tell the chauffeur how to get there. He knew the streets of San Francisco like the back of his wrinkled old hand.

"Buddy," he said to me. "I've been watching your luck for a while now. I think you got some left, but tonight is going to be some serious agenda. You have a choice right now: get out of town, head for the mountains like your old man..."

I stopped him. "You know I'm not going to do that."

"Women get a hold on you if you let them."

The limo pulled up in front of Markus's, but I didn't see any lights on. I asked Anyguy to wait while I ran upstairs. My name was on the note stuck in the door, and an address. Saint Street. She'd signed it, and underneath added, "Come fast — Now or never."

I showed it to Anyguy and he sighed. "You're going to need all the luck you have left to get through tonight. I can see that. I'll take you over there, and then I'll just hang out."

"What for?"

"Nothing better to do, I guess." He shrugged. "I guarantee the luck I sell my customers — even if I have to cheat by helping out."

He drove me to Saint Street and parked down the block.

I ran up the stone steps to the door. There were three buzzers, and one said 'Society of Spectacles'. I guessed that would be where she was, and punched the buzzer a couple of times. The door clicked open and I climbed up a steep wooden stairway to another door.

I knocked, and pushed it open.

She was there in a white dress in the middle of a gigantic

room lit with candles. There was a fireplace with a fire in it that threw big shadows on the walls and ceiling, and on a man hanging on a cross.

I could have turned around and walked out and walked downstairs, I could have gotten into Anyguy's limo and scooted down the road. But I started walking toward her across the bare wood floor. We were married, weren't we? I had promised...

When I got close enough I could see the resemblance between them. His mouth was where her mouth came from. Their blue eyes you couldn't see into. There was a stool next to the cross. He'd used it to get on the cross, and she'd used it to tie his wrists with leather straps to the cross beam. She'd made him strip down to his white underwear, I thought at first.

"I started the party without you," she said. Her jaws were set and her lips were tight. There was a big knife in her hand, but no blood on it. Then I saw that she'd cut his suit off him after she'd gotten him tied up. It was a pile of rags.

I went over to look at him. I had to look up but it was like looking down on him, because I knew how this was all going to end, and he didn't. He remembered me and he flinched.

"Buddy's here now, father. We can start."

She had set up a video camera on a tripod to record her father's punishment. It was running the whole time we did what we did.

"My father believes he's capable of sending earthquakes to San Francisco to punish us. He's capable of convincing himself of anything."

"I know somebody else who thinks *he*'s responsible."

"Now he has convinced himself he's here to earn my forgiveness."

"Robin," Flood said. Hearing him talk for the first time made me jump. He was human, after all, not just a shadow on television. Then I remembered his heavy hand pushing my head down on his show, holding it down in his lap. How Mr Hopper got me seeing crosses after that.

This was Thomas Flood. The famous, the powerful Thomas Flood I'd promised to kill. He was watching me, wondering what I was going to do. I made him nervous.

"Maybe she forgives you, but I won't. You have my word on that," I told him. It was fun watching him try to guess what my role was in his punishment.

He was a big one, all right. Like a football player. I'd want to take him apart piece by piece. I knew that I didn't want to rush it.

"Robin, you said there'd just be the two of us."

"Well, father. Buddy is my husband."

I smiled at him like a good son-in-law and punched him in the stomach as hard as I could. He made a noise and puked over himself. It was satisfying to hear him try to catch his breath.

"Hello, father," I said.

Robin was watching me like I was somebody not real, somebody she'd made up in her own mind. But she liked what she saw. She had that turned-on look I recognised. She put her hand out and I grabbed it and pulled her close to kiss her. She was naked under the white dress and I reached down behind to squeeze the cheeks or her ass and pull her pussy against my crotch, grinding it into her. She pulled down my zipper and out popped Chester the Molester half-hard already.

"You're hot for it," I said, putting my finger in her crack from behind. Flood was still gasping for air behind us.

"I like your idea of foreplay."

I pulled her to the stool and bent her over it. Her ass was in Flood's line of sight, which was what I wanted. I knelt on the floor and started kissing and sucking her bare butt, using my tongue to lubricate her while I got three fingers into her cunt and stabbed them in and out till she got so excited she farted in my face. It was a chewy one I let sit on my palate to mix with the other flavours of her.

When I was stone stiff, I pulled the cheeks of her ass apart and slowly pushed it all the way in the tight wet heat that squeezed and tightened and clutched.

God, it was good. Moving in and out of her sent chills and sparks up my spine to explode in the top of my head, soft little pops of pure pleasure. But I didn't want to come. Not yet.

She must have felt it building in me, because she pulled away and stood up to face her father. We both stared. Poking up through his white underpants was the evidence of his arousal. It was just average, but Robin looked at it like she'd never seen a dick before.

I guess she was thinking that he'd raped her with it.

She went over to him in the white dress we'd messed up and stood looking at his erection.

"You're just like me, aren't you, father? Lust. There it is. You *lust*. You want a piece of what Buddy just got from me, don't you?"

She whacked his cock with her open hand, and he grunted. She spat on him, again and again. He was mumbling something but neither one of us was listening to him.

Robin picked up the knife she had used to cut him out of his suit and got up on the stool so she could cut off his underpants. She wasn't gentle, and she made careless superficial cuts on his thighs cutting then off.

"I'm going to drink your blood, father," she said to him. He shook his head and struggled with his wrist straps. His prick stuck out just like any other prick. Nothing special about it — cut meat, wide, not long. But she was fascinated.

She leaned close to lick the blood off his thighs and rubbed her breasts against his legs until the front of her white dress was stained with his blood.

"Asmodeus," he was saying. Just that one word over and over, rolling his head back and forth. He wasn't screaming yet and I was tired of him. I guess I don't have much imagination when it comes to torture. He wasn't worth my trouble. It was time to send the son-of-a-bitch down to Hell.

But Robin had a few ideas left in her spooky head.

She grabbed his cock and pulled on it. "This is what you used to rape me, father. Didn't you?"

He shook his head. "The serpent... the serpent, not me..."

"I'm going to forgive this part of you that hurt me, father. I'm going to put it in my mouth and taste your flesh."

She looked at me — just a quick, guilty, over the shoulder look so I could see she was crazy — and opened her mouth. The fat tip of her father's dick bulged in her cheek and she moved her head back and forth a few times. I knew this was sick, but it was too late to stop her. Then her jaw tightened and Flood screamed. She had the head of his cock in her mouth and his ruined penis was pumping blood in her face.

When she turned my way she had a look on her face I've seen dogs get after a fight when they're chewing on an enemy's ear.

Pure defiant savage satisfaction. She spat what she'd bitten off at him and shouted, "Father, I forgive you, now."

Flood was screaming and blood was spurting from him. Robin looked at me like now was the time.

But I was freaked. What she'd done had pushed an edge. It had lifted up a rock and there beneath it was something truly scary. I took out the K. Farouk .38 and held it in both hands, listening to him scream.

I felt like puking. Like crying. I didn't have any strength in my legs and I just sank to the floor on top of his cut-up clothes, looking up at him. And then I was crying for him, and for Robin, and for me. What had we done?

I put the pistol in my lap and started picking up pieces of his suit, like I might be able to piece them together for him. Piece him back together. There was something that was not clothes in the pile. It was smooth and leathery and had bristles on it. I looked down. The bristles were kinky black hair. Poor Dollar's pussy lay in my hand. The cooch he'd cut from her.

That put the starch in me. I stood up with the .38 already cocked, climbed on the stool and put the barrel in his still open, still screaming mouth, and pulled the trigger.

I did it. If the video camera got the pictures, they would show that I, Buddy Tate, shot the famous Reverend Thomas Flood in the mouth and blew out the back of his head.

They'd hear about me now. Daddy told me, be extravagant, and if blowing out a preacher's brains while he's hanging on a cross with a bitten-off dick spurting blood isn't extravagant, well then you can kiss me where the sun don't shine. Look out, Oswald, Bremer and Chapman, Buddy Tate is comin' up for glory.

Robin stood there looking at him, like she couldn't believe we'd done it. I thought about Anyguy's limousine waiting for us outside and knew we should get the hell out. Mr. Hopper would be looking for us, and behind him would be all the cops in the world, and after them a whole bunch of television Christians.

She was covered with blood, so I thought the place to start was to clean up. I put my arm around her and she was shaking. I didn't want to look at her face.

"I think we should get cleaned up. There's a car outside waiting for us."

"No, I can't. That's my father. I have to take care of him." She was crying.

"Robin, it's over."

She looked up at me, lips still bloody from biting him.

"You killed my father!"

This was bullshit I couldn't take.

"It was no different than cutting off a snake's head. You did the damage, Robin."

Then she was babbling something just like he had about Asmodeus, whoever that was. I didn't care. I just wanted to get the fuck out of there. I pulled her to a door that looked like it had a bathroom behind it and saw urinals with signs over each one and a sink. I cleaned her up and left her butt naked and shivering, still babbling about getting Asmodeus out of her, and went to find some clothes. In a closet I found enough leather to dress a herd of Black Angus and took a skirt and jacket back to her. She seemed to have calmed down when I brought the clothes in. She was even putting on lipstick and combing her hair.

I cleaned up and then we were ready to hit the getaway trail. In the big room I took the videotape from the camera and put it in my pocket. I needed it to send out to the media, otherwise I couldn't prove that I was now the Buddy Tate I knew I was.

No one to mess with. Someone to recognise and get back from. An American hero in his own crime.

It felt good, and it felt like shit. We left Thomas Flood hanging on the cross and walked slowly down the wooden steps, afraid of losing our balance, to the outside world.

It was the same world I'd come from: smoke, sirens, and a feeling in the air that the future had happened and it wasn't something a lot of people liked. I took a deep breath of it and helped Robin to Anyguy's limo. The chauffeur got out to open the door for us. I pushed Robin inside and got in after her, and the limo moved off.

Anyguy looked at Robin and read it on her face. It wasn't hard to see.

"So you did it. Now you have to run."

"Any ideas about where?" I asked him.

"We'll drive south. I know some places where even mountain lions don't go. Hiding places where some of my people went when they had to run from the Spanish soldiers, and the missions."

"I guess we're big time outlaws now."

"Hunted dogs," he snorted. "They'll come after you."

"The Goddess will protect us," Robin said, speaking up like a sleepwalker. I held her tight. Kissed her damp forehead.

"Maybe," Anyguy said. "Maybe she will."

"He needed killing," I told him, feeling defensive.

"Why didn't you bring me his dick?" he asked.

"It wasn't worth it, after she got through with it."

He got the picture right away, but he didn't say anything. He just stared at Robin for a long time. Then he reached out to touch the hollow of her throat.

"She's tired, but she's strong. I think she got it out of her — that thing that was in her."

We looked at each other, and then at Robin. Her head was on my shoulder, and her eyes were closed. The corners of her mouth were turned up a little, as if she might smile. She was innocent. She was clean. I'd done the deed, not her. What would I say when they caught us — my penis made me do it?

Available now from

EROS

The Best of the Journal of Erotica

Edited by
Maxim and Dolores Jakubowski

Launched in 1992, *The Journal of Erotica* has quickly established itself as the leading magazine in the field. Published every three months, it offers provocative short stories with fascinating, daring visuals from the best photographers and illustrators from all over the world.

In this collection Maxim and Dolores Jakubowski have selected the best short stories to have appeared in *The Journal of Erotica* during its first three years: a luxurious and sensual exploration of the world of erotic love.

EROS
MAIL ORDER

All Eros Plus titles are available from good bookshops or by mail order from Eros Plus Mail Order Department, 42-44 Dolben Street, London, SE1 0UP. For a free catalogue and regular updates on forthcoming titles, please enclose a large stamped SAE to the above address, quoting reference EP5-DM on both envelopes.